~*MELANCHOLY*~

All rights reserved. This eBook is licensed for your personal enjoyment only. This eBook is copyright material and must not be copied, reproduced, transferred, distributed, leased, licensed or publicly performed or used in any form without prior written permission of the publisher, as allowed under the terms and conditions under which it was purchased or as strictly permitted by applicable copyright law. Any unauthorized distribution, circulation or use of this text may be a direct infringement of the author's rights, and those responsible may be liable in law accordingly. Thank you for respecting the work of this author.

MELANCHOLY

D1523647

Copyright © 2014 Bella Jewel

Melancholy is a work of fiction. All names, characters, places and events portrayed in this book either are from the author's imagination or are used fictitiously. Any similarity to real persons, living or dead, establishments, events, or location is purely coincidental and not intended by the author. Please do not take offence to the content, as it is FICTION.

ACKNOWLEDGMENTS

A massive thanks to all the blogs on my tours. You're amazing for taking the time to share and review for me; you'll never know how much that means to me.

A special thanks to Love Between The Sheets for always having time to organize my Release Day Blitz and Cover Reveals. You ladies are super amazing and I'll always appreciate the effort you've given me.

Thanks to Lisa from Three Chicks and Their Books for always reading an ARC before releasing and helping me out. Thanks to Kylie from Give Me Books for always sharing and reading for me, too. You girls are amazing. I adore you.

A massive thanks to Ari from Cover it Designs for this gorgeous cover. You never disappoint.

To Lauren, my crazy, awesome editor. You do such a great job. I couldn't do it without you. I adore you, lovely.

To my girls, Belle Aurora and Sali. For always reading and helping me create the best work I can. For always talking to me and making me smile. I love you two, my besties.

And of course, to my admin MJ for ALWAYS keeping my page running beautifully. I couldn't do it without you, girly.

A massive thank you to Kris Scharr. For coming up with the amazing name of Jokers' Wrath MC. As well as picking the name of a character to show throughout the series. You're a gorgeous girl and an amazing fan. Thank you.

And, last but certainly not least. To my loyal readers. You make this real for me; never stop giving such love and passion. You make our journey so amazing.

DEDICATION

This book is dedicated to my very own biker, my husband. Thank you for the countless hours you have put in to helping me out with my work, or just keeping the kids busy while I write.

You know I'll love you forever, my big man.

PROLOGUE

To truly understand a story you need to start from the beginning, but to start from the beginning you have to go back, further than just *you*. After all, our stories don't start with us, do they? Our stories start with the person before us, and the person before them. We are created from the stories of those people—from their mistakes, from their achievements, from their love, and their hate.

No one's story is ever truly their own.

I tried to create my own story, my own path, and my own actions. I've seen things people only see in their worst nightmares, but I never let them beat me down. I never let that become who I *was*. I picked myself up, and I kept going. Everything was what it was. There was no point analyzing what it *could* be.

Could be didn't matter.

Until Maddox came into the picture. He saved my life. He changed my world, giving me the second chance some of us only dream about. There was only one thing missing in my second chance, and she was the reason I fought so hard to survive.

My sister.

My sister who is supposed to be dead—well, at least, that's what I thought.

That's what *he* told me.

Now is where my story changes, but to understand this story, you have to start at the beginning . . . where it all began . . . and *before*.

CHAPTER ONE

2007 – Santana

My breathing comes in short, hard bursts as I press my body against the cool wall. My skin is clammy, but I'm too afraid to lift my hand to wipe it away, desperate to remove the beading sweat from my forehead. I squeeze my sister's hand as I close my eyes; if I close my eyes, I won't be so afraid. I can take myself to a world he isn't in.

When I close my eyes, I remember a better time. A time when my parents were alive, a time when my sister's smile lit up my life—a time when nothing hurt. Now everything hurts, my sister never smiles, and my parents are dead. My world went from beautiful to hell in a matter of hours.

That's all it takes to change a life—a mere few hours.

My first memory as a child is one I'll hold with me for a long, long time. It's where I go when fear takes over. I smile when I think of my sister's happy face as my father led her outside, his brown eyes twinkling. I held onto his hand, and he squeezed mine tightly. My sister's eyes were firmly shut, but her body thrummed with excitement.

The moment she was able to open them, her squeals filled the silent air around us. Her face lit up as she saw the cubby house Dad and I had spent hours putting together for her birthday. Her blond ringlets bounced as she spun around, throwing her arms around Dad, then me. It was the best moment of my life.

Then an accident stole my parents from me. There was no family—well, none that wanted us anyway. We were sent into foster homes, constantly separated. Finally, when I was fourteen, we were put in together. That family was torture in its purest form, and our time there quickly became hell on earth.

Now I spend my days trying to protect my sister, putting myself first because I can't bear to see the pain in her face when he hurts her. Each day is a battle, and we'll fight that battle until I can get us out of here. I'd rather live on the streets than be at the hands of this monster any longer, so that leads me to the here and now, my sister and myself crushed against the wall, holding our breaths as he leaves the room.

Waiting. Praying. Hoping.

My fingers slide over hers, letting her know I'm still there, letting her know I won't let her go. Not ever. When I open my eyes and turn to her, she's in her happy place, too. Her eyes are tightly closed, her breathing steady. I taught her how to live in the beautiful space that lies in her mind—nothing can hurt her there.

"Girls!" Oscar barks, his heavy footfalls coming towards us.

I press myself further against the wall, praying with everything I have inside me that he won't open the closet. I pray he'll think we've gone to school. I squeeze Pippa's hand when I hear her breathing becoming deeper. She squeezes back, a silent answer to my question. She's okay. *We're* okay . . . for now.

"Girls? Where the fuck are you? If you're ignoring me, so help me God, I'll fuckin' make it hurt!"

He will, too. He doesn't abuse us sexually, which I'm thankful for every day. Instead, he has an obsession with control. He likes the feeling of power he gets when he holds us down, and brings his fists to our faces. He'll do anything he can to call us out on a lie so he can have the satisfaction of carrying out the punishment.

His footsteps get closer and we both stop breathing, our hands squeezed so tightly my fingers ache. He stops, grunts, and then stomps away down the hall. I let the breath I was holding out, and tears prick my eyelids with relief. That relief grows when the car starts up, and skids off down the road.

We open the door quickly, stepping out. We only have a tiny backpack that contains enough for us to survive and keep warm. We've stolen money during the past six months, gathering around five hundred dollars in that time. He suspected we were stealing, of course, and we dealt with the beatings he dished out because of it. He never found our stash, though.

Another small miracle, I'm sure.

"We have to hurry. He'll be back in less than ten minutes."

Pippa nods, tucking a strand of faded, ratty blond hair behind her ear. Her once chocolate-brown eyes are now dull and lifeless. Pippa and I are two completely different girls — she's just like our father and I'm more like our mom. She's fair, with blond hair, lighter skin and brown eyes, while I'm dark. My skin is olive, my hair is dark brown and there are days my eyes seem nearly black.

Our bond, however, is unbreakable.

"I don't want him to find us," Pippa whispers, staring at me with a frightened expression.

I cup her face in my battered hands, smiling down at her with everything I have. "I'll never let him hurt you again, Pippi. Never."

She smiles up at me. I've called her Pippi since the day she was born. I always thought it suited her more.

"Let's go," I encourage her, taking our bag and running towards the front door.

Stepping out onto the street today seems different. It feels like there's hope in the air, like we might actually have a chance to live and breathe again.

Taking my sister's hand, I take the first step to freedom. No more foster homes, no more evil men, and no more being apart.

This is our chance at freedom, and I'm not letting it go.

~*~*~*~

2014

Santana

Bright lights jerk me awake. The shrill sound of beeping monitors is the only noise that fills my aching ears. I try to blink, but my eyes feel like two heavy pieces of lead in my skull. My tongue is dry and it burns, like a scratchy piece of sandpaper in my mouth. I gasp out a breath, flicking it about to try and get some saliva to coat it.

"Santana?" A voice calls. "My name is Roberta, I'm a nurse here. Can you hear me?"

Of course I can hear you, you're yelling in my face. The words want to come out, but my stiff tongue won't move enough to let them. Tears burn under my heavy eyelids as I try hard to speak. *Where am I? What happened?*

"You're in the hospital. Squeeze my hand if you can hear me?"

A soft hand is in mine. How did I not notice that? I squeeze it, mulling over her words. *Hospital.* You're in the hospital. My hazy mind swims as I go over the memories lying dormant inside it. Why am I in the hospital? What happened? Did something go wrong? Where is Pippa?

"You were shot," the nurse goes on.

Shot? I shake my head from side to side, confused. I cry out, but it sounds like nothing more than a hoarse gasp. The sounds of creaking doors and beeping are too loud.

10

"Is she awake? Why the fuck wasn't I called?"

A barking voice fills the room, so familiar. My mind swims, trying to figure out whom that voice belongs to. God, why can't I remember anything? My mind aches.

"Santana? Hey, it's me. Maddox."

Maddox?

More tears run as fuzzy memories become clearer. Running from the compound. Ash, Krypt and Maddox. *Together.* Having sex. Bullets firing at me. I hiccup loudly, and begin to cry harder as my hand reaches out for the comfort I need the most. *Maddox.*

"I'm here," he says, and the bed dips as my body is pulled into solid arms. "No one can hurt you now."

The words he's told me so many times. *So many times.* I flutter my eyes open, and everything is blurry. The nurse comes into view first, her round face staring down at me. She blinks her green eyes and smiles. "Hi, would you like some water?"

I nod, and she passes me a small plastic cup with a straw poking out. I take it, and press it to my mouth. My hand shakes, and Maddox's goes up to curl around mine. He holds it steady as I take gulping sips, desperate to ease the ache in my throat. I shift, and a sharp pain radiates through my calf.

I got shot.

Someone *shot* at me.

I let the cup go, and Maddox thrusts it towards the nurse. "Leave," he demands.

"But I have only just finished checking her vitals. The doctor will want to see her, and . . ."

"I said," he barks, his voice a deadly hiss. "*Leave.*"

"I . . ."

"Now," he bellows.

She hurries out of the room, and the door closes quietly behind her. Maddox shifts, moving out from behind me and getting off the bed. He gets a chair and drags it over, sitting beside me and staring at me with blue eyes that have clearly had no sleep. He's got dark rings under them, and his jaw is tense, his muscles ticking.

I watch him, and my heart clenches. He slept with Ash. *He slept with Ash.* My heart burns, it burns like someone has shoved a match inside and lit it on fire. I have no reason for this kind of jealousy; Maddox and I have never been an item. But the way it hurt shocked me. It shocked me, because I didn't realize it would bother me.

"You slept with Ash . . ." I whisper, dropping my eyes.

"Look at me, Santana," he orders.

I shift my gaze, staring into his, hating that I love his eyes so much, but I do. I love his eyes. I love his entire, rugged, gorgeous face.

"You have never cared who I fucked before," his voice is a low rasp. "Why now?"

"I . . . she was my friend," I say, turning away again.

His voice comes out like a deadly whip. "Didn't say you could look away. Now turn your eyes back to me."

I grind my teeth, but I turn back to him. He leans in closer, his leather jacket squeaking with each movement.

"I didn't fuck her."

I blink at him. "Y-y-y-y-you didn't?"

"No."

"But you were still with her," I whisper.

His eyes scan over my face before his mouth pulls into a thin line. "Ain't goin' into details with you, but yeah, I was still with her. Didn't know it would matter to you."

"It doesn't, it's fine. I . . . I've just had a hard time. It's nothing."

"You lyin' to me?"

"No, Maddox."

"Santana."

"Don't," I growl. "I have enough to worry about. Do you hear me?"

"Who shot you?" he murmurs, dropping the subject.

I shake my head, my tears burning again. "I don't know. I left the compound and drove to your house. I got out and suddenly, out of the blue, someone was shooting at me. I had no idea where it was coming from, or who was doing it. I leapt back into my car, too scared to go inside. The bullet hit my calf as I was diving in. I drove as far as I could, but the pain was intense. I got out and went for help, but I don't remember what happened after that."

"Someone found you out cold." His voice is hard. "By the time I got notified, you were already in hospital."

"Someone shot at me, Maddox. Why?"

He shakes his head. "I'm goin' to find out."

I nod, turning away.

"Tana," he begins, but the door opens and a doctor and police officer come inside.

Maddox growls, low and throaty, and shoves out of the chair. "Why the fuck is a cop in here?"

The cop steps forward, and extends his hand. Maddox looks at it with pure disgust. "My name is Sergeant Rambo."

Maddox snorts. "That so? Your parents watch too many movies, Sergeant?"

Sergeant Rambo, clearly having lived with jokes about his name, stiffens and nods his head. "I've heard every joke about my name. Now, if you're finished, I'd like to talk to Santana while the doctor checks her over."

Maddox crosses his arms, unperturbed. "Anything you ask her, you ask her in front of me."

Rambo glares at him, but nods. He walks over towards me, and as he nears closer I see he's quite an attractive man. He's got messy brunette hair, with light grey eyes. He smiles as he sits down on the chair Maddox was on, and I give him a weak smile back.

"How are you feeling, Santana?"

"I'm fine," I croak.

"I just wanted to ask you a few questions about the shooting."

"It was a drive-by," Maddox snaps. "Are you done?"

Sergeant Rambo growls now, turning to Maddox. "I hear you've had a few problems with your club lately, Maddox. You'll appreciate that it seems strange that this young lady was shot only weeks after one of your members was locked away."

"That shit has been dealt with," Maddox snarls. "You got Howard in prison. Anything that was goin' down with the clubs, was on him. Now, are you finished?"

"I'm not," Rambo says, turning back to me. "What happened, Santana?"

"It was like he said," I say, meeting Rambo's gaze dead-on. "I was just driving, and I got out of my car. I heard shots and yelling, and I got back into my car quickly. A shot hit my calf."

"You see who did it?"

"No," I say.

"And you're sure it wasn't aimed at you?"

I keep my face expressionless. "Yes, I'm sure. I heard yelling over the road, lots of it. Cars were going past, it was hectic. The shot wasn't aimed at me."

"It seems strange a shot would come so close, if it wasn't aimed at you."

"There were shots being fired at a car, it missed, and came towards me. I don't see how that's so complicated."

He narrows his eyes. "Very well."

He asks me a few more questions, and then he leaves. The doctor watches him go, before turning to me. He's been checking my wound. I watched as he unraveled it. It's not as bad as I thought. It hurt like hell when it went in, like a hot poker through my flesh – but maybe that's the beauty of it. A neat wound.

"Your wound is looking good, Santana," the doctor says. "We were able to get the bullet out. There seems to be no nerve damage."

I nod. "Thank you."

"She ready to come home?" Maddox demands.

I turn to him. He's standing by the door, arms crossed. The doctor swallows. "I'd like to keep her another night. She's only just come out from being put under, and I want to make sure there are no side affects."

"Then I'm puttin' two guys on her door."

The doctor shakes his head. "No, I'm sorry. The patients need their rest."

"I said," Maddox snarls, "I'm puttin' a few boys on her door. She needs to feel safe, and she will."

"You said it was a drive-by," the doctor protests. "Why would she need protection if it was a drive-by?"

Maddox charges towards him, causing the doctor to take a few steps back. "Because I don't trust any fucker, and that girl on the bed, she's *my* fuckin' girl. Now, I'll be puttin' two of my guys on, and you'll fuckin' *like* it."

The doctor nods. "Very well, but they need to stay quiet . . ."

Maddox smirks. "Unless the nurses feel like gettin' a good fuckin', they'll stay quiet."

I slap my hand to my forehead. The doctor makes a disgusted sound and Maddox laughs. I peek through my fingers and watch the doctor leave.

"That was cruel," I say, dropping my hand.

"He deserved it. Who do you want on your door, darlin'?"

I shrug. "I don't care."

16

He narrows his eyes and walks over, lowering himself down. His fingers go up and around the back of my neck, and he pulls me forward so his mouth is only an inch or less from mine. "I said, who do you want on the door?"

"I said, I don't *care*," I snap.

"Santana."

"Maddox."

He makes a low hissing sound, and presses his forehead to mine. This has always been his way of showing me affection. It's strange, but it's his. He smells so good, and I want to wrap myself in him. The ache in my chest is getting bigger, and I feel so frightened.

"I'm sendin' Mack in, and maybe Tyke."

"Mack is back?" I whisper, pulling away.

Maddox grunts. "Yeah."

I smile; I can't help it. I adore Miakoda 'Mack' Williams. He's Maddox's adopted brother, and somewhat of a nomad. He travels around, joining in different chapters instead of sticking with one. He enjoys traveling, and being alone.

"Then yes, send him in."

"You got a thing for my brother?"

I snort. "Would it matter if I did? You have a thing for my friends."

"Santana," he warns.

"Maddox."

With a grunt, he stands. "I'm goin' to get some things for you. I'll send the guys in now."

I nod.

He walks to the door.

When he gets there, he turns back to me. "Santana?"

I stare up at him. "Yeah?"

"Don't you ever scare me like that again."

CHAPTER TWO

2008 – Santana

I'm cold, so cold my entire body has stopped hurting, and now I can't feel anything. I can't feel my sister's hand in mine, I can't feel my toes or my legs, or even the hard concrete beneath us. I could die like this, and I know I wouldn't feel it.

We're going to die if we don't get warm soon.

I sit up, crying out in pain as what feels like a thousand tiny needles stabbing into my skin radiates through my body. I need to find shelter, I need to find warmth, and I need to get us out of this weather. I rub my hands over the holes that have appeared in my old blue jeans.

I turn and stare down at Pippa who has grown frail and weak. Her eyes are sunken, her hair is dull, and her body is so tiny she's got nothing to fall back on. This is all my fault, I took her onto the streets, thinking we had a chance at freedom. Instead, we found ourselves trapped once more, only this time it was from hunger, desperation, cold, and dangerous people.

"Come on, Pippi," I whisper, reaching down to take her hands. "I'm going to find us somewhere warm."

She stares up at me, her lips cracked and a dark shade of blue. She's freezing. We need to get warm or she'll die. Or worse, I'll die, and she'll be left with no one. I can't allow that. I pull her up and she comes, slowly. Her knees wobble as she holds onto me. I wrap an arm around her, trying not to become fearful at how cold her skin is.

"We're going to get some help, you hear me?"

We've been out here for around six months now, and more often than not we've been able to get through. It's only been in the last month that we've started to struggle. People are heartless when it comes to the homeless. They don't want to help; they just want to keep walking and pretend they never met our desperate eyes.

After all, the people with homes have a warm bed to sleep in each night. What do they need to worry about, aside from what to eat for breakfast?

Breakfast.

My stomach rumbles as I pull Pippa down the pathway. My parents raised me never to trust strangers, but now I'm going to do the only thing I can think of. I'm going to beg. I'm going to knock on as many doors as I have to, and beg until someone gives in. Until someone gives us something warm, or some food.

I lead Pippa into the housing area closest to where we were sleeping. She's slowing, her body struggling to even take a step. I pull her up the first driveway, and lean her against a pole while I knock. An elderly man answers, his eyes narrowing in disgust as he takes us in.

"Not interested," he barks, slamming the door.

That's it?

I knock again, but he doesn't answer.

"It's okay." I smile weakly to Pippa. "There are so many more houses."

I lead her through a solid fifty houses before we reach one that gives us a chance. The man in this house is younger, only about thirty-five or so. He's got a light scattering of grey in his dark hair and eyes the color of champagne. He's quite attractive, and seems friendly enough as he looks us over.

"Can I help you?" he asks.

"My sister and I . . . we're homeless. We have nowhere to go, and she's freezing. Please, sir, if you could spare a blanket or some food, I would be forever grateful," I whisper.

He stares at us, his eyes scanning over me and then Pippa. A smile appears on his face as he shoves the door open. "Come in, let's get you warmed up."

My eyes widen. All I can think of is the old saying that states *if it's too good to be true, it probably is.* What if this man is going to murder us? Or rape us? It's clear he can see my hesitation, because he gives me a warm smile and steps forward. "I've lived a hard life before—I understand. I'm not going to hurt you. Come in, please."

I turn to Pippa, and one look at her frail body has me reaching for her.

"What's your names?" he asks as we step inside his warm house.

"I'm Santana," I whisper. "And this is Pippa."

"Welcome girls. I'm Kennedy."

~*~*~*~

2014 – Maddox

"Who do you think shot her, Prez?" Krypt asks, leaning against the desk, crossing his boots.

"I am guessin' someone from the Tinman's Soldiers. It has to be. Nothin' else makes sense. They know we sent her in to save Claire, and now they want revenge. Not to mention all the shit that went down with you and Ash. Wouldn't take much to figure out what she meant to me. Howard might be in prison, but his VP has stood up and taken his spot. We're still at war."

Krypt nods. "Yeah, we fuckin' are. She got anyone else who might wanna hurt her?"

I shrug. "I don't fuckin' know. There are some people from her past…but I don't know any of them or what they're about."

"You told her about her sister yet?"

My eyes shoot to his, and I glare so fuckin' hard he flinches.

"Calm down," he snaps, throwing his hands up. "I'm only askin'."

"I'm not tellin' her a damned word about her sister, until I know more."

"You got any more?"

"Nothin'."

"Nothin' at all?"

"I got a name."

Krypt nods, encouraging me on.

"Kennedy Bayne."

Krypt flinches. "Say again?"

"Kennedy Bayne."

"Motherfucker," Krypt barks.

"What?"

"Kennedy Bayne is in prison, Maddox. I know, I heard his name when I was in there."

My eyes wide and I step forward. "That so?"

"That's so. The fucker is in there for drug possession. He's a huge dealer, but he got fucked over."

I reach up, running a hand through my hair. Santana was high as a fuckin' kite when I found her, and she'd been that way for a while. She used to murmur the name Kennedy in her sleep, but she never told me what the man meant to her. I'm assuming it's the same man. After all, his name is linked to her sister.

"How does he fall into this shit with her sister?" Krypt asks.

I swing my eyes to him. "He's a name that keeps poppin' up."

"Santana know him?"

"Far as I know, yeah. She won't tell me what he means to her."

Krypt thinks about that, then mutters, "You thought of takin' her to him and findin' out?"

"No fuckin' way," I bark. "I don't know what that man means to her, or even if he's the same one, and until I do I'm not tellin' her where he is. She is in enough danger. Until I know he's no threat, she ain't goin' to know about any of this."

"She's goin' to hate you, Prez. She's goin' to fuckin' lose her shit when she finds out what you've been hidin'."

I lift a smoke, lighting it and pressing it to my lips. "I know that."

"Well, you got my silence. What're you gonna do about Kennedy?"

I smirk at Krypt as I take a long drag. "I'm goin' to pay him a visit."

CHAPTER THREE

2014 – Santana

I fall asleep as soon as Maddox leaves, and remain that way until a hand touches my shoulder. I flutter my eyes open and look up to see Mack, standing over me. A small croak leaves my throat as a big smile appears on my lips. He leans down, brushing his scratchy lips over my forehead. "How you doin', *chante?*"

I smile at his nickname for me, which means 'heart' and reach out, touching his cheek. "Chief," I whisper. "You haven't called me."

He grins. He hates being called Chief, and I'm the only one he allows to get away with it without a fight. Mack is Native American, and one of the most breathtaking men I've ever had the pleasure of laying my eyes on, aside from Maddox.

He's got these deep, dark brown eyes set in the most defined, chiseled face I've ever seen on a man. He has a square jaw, full lips, and dark olive skin that's so silky, it's hard not to reach out and touch it. His long, thick, dark brown hair flows halfway down his back.

He's tall, lean but beautifully muscled, and doesn't have one tattoo on his perfect skin. He's a bad boy, though. More temperamental and aggressive than half the bikers in the club. Mack had a hard life, and was adopted out to Maddox's family when he was only five. No one really knows his history.

Mack runs a hand over his jaw. "I've been busy."

I pout at him, and he grins again, leaning down to kiss my lips. Mack and I have always had a good relationship. He was the solid rock when I was coming out of my drug haze. Maddox stayed by my side, night and day, but it was Mack who kicked my ass when I didn't want to go on. He never showed me any sympathy; he just pulled me out and made me start again.

"Well," I say when he pulls away. "I should announce to the world that I've been kissed by the maddest biker around."

He snorts. "That wasn't a kiss, *chante*, it was a fuckin' peck."

"Am I not good enough to get a real kiss from you, Chief?"

He laughs throatily. "Course you are, but my brother would cut my cock off and feed it to me in pieces."

I laugh. "He would not."

"Oh, he *would.*"

I reach out and take his hand. His rough fingers are covered with a whole lot of scars. "How have you been?"

He sits down beside me, letting me hang on to his hand. This is a surprise, because Mack doesn't like to be touched a whole lot.

"Good. Decided to come back and hang around for a while. Sick of ridin', and it seems like my little bro needs me here."

"He's a big boy." I smirk. "He can take care of himself."

Mack laughs. "No doubt. I need a break, all the same."

"Are you staying with us?"

He nods. "For a while. Got my own place lined up."

He lets go of my hand and takes me by the back of my head, bringing me close. He kisses my head, lingering for a long moment before standing. "But enough of that. There's someone outside hangin' to see you. Goin' to be out there; you yell out if you need me."

25

"Okay," I say, watching him retreat.

A moment later, Ash enters. She stands at the door for a long time, her hands fumbling with each other, her eyes puffy and red. I watch her, knowing that it isn't entirely her fault what happened between her, Krypt and Maddox. She takes a hesitant step forward.

"You can come in," I say softly.

She walks over and sits on the seat beside my bed. We stare at each other for a long, *long* time.

"I'm so sorry, Santana" she says, breaking the silence. "I didn't . . . I thought . . ."

I shake my head. "I made it clear I wasn't interested in Maddox. I over-reacted, it hurt me, shocked me, and I've still got to come to terms with how I feel, but it wasn't your fault. I told you I was seeing someone else. I told you Maddox meant nothing to me."

She shakes her head. "Doesn't matter. I knew he cared about you, and I did it anyway."

I smile sadly. "If he cared about me, Ash, he wouldn't have done it in the first place. This . . . it isn't on you—it's on him. He's the one holding back, and he's the one dancing around whatever the hell is going on between us."

"He's dancing because he's scared," she says softly. "He's scared to hurt you."

I shrug. "Maybe, but he's making his own choices. So am I. Us being apart, it's for the best."

"Do you really believe that?"

I nod. "Yes."

26

She sighs and leans in, wrapping her fingers around mine. "You scared me, Santana. I thought . . ."

"I'm okay," I assure her. "It'll all be fine."

~*~*~*~

Later that night, my phone buzzes beside me just as my eyes flutter closed. With a groan, I roll, and flip it open. I see a message from Alec. He is so sweet, so kind and real. He's what most girls dream about, because of course, we don't dream of falling in love with a bad boy. No, we dream of white picket fences, big houses and three children.

I wish I were most girls.

I dream of two things. A tall, dark man who I know is bad for me, and a man who can give me a white picket fence. There is a true battle between good and evil, and evil is so tempting. Maddox is my evil—he's my dark place, yet I can't seem to push myself away from him. He makes me feel things I've never felt before.

Then there's Alec.

Sweet, charming, and so damned perfect. He's almost too perfect. I've tried to find flaws, but it would appear he has none. He's just a genuine good guy. His message has a big smile breaking out across my face, so much so that it begins to hurt. He always knows how to make me feel better, and that's something to hold onto.

A – Roses are red, violets are blue, but nothing is as beautiful or as sweet as you.

I want to roll my eyes, but I can't wipe the smile off my face long enough to do that. Instead, I respond.

S – Are you always this charming to the girls you date?

27

A – Only the pretty ones.

S – What else do the pretty girls get?

A – You'll just have to find out. How are you, sweetheart?

S – My leg is sore, but I'm fine. Just a few stitches.

A – Are you still getting out tomorrow? I am busting to see you.

S – Yep, tomorrow morning.

A – You up for lunch then?

I frown.

S – I don't think that's a good idea. Maddox won't like if I go out as soon as I get home.

He takes a moment to respond. Alec knows about Maddox, about my past, and even though he agrees that Maddox was a good man for saving me, he doesn't like him. He's never met him, of course; I just don't think he likes the idea that Maddox is the President of a massive MC club.

A – Dinner Saturday?

S – That sounds perfect. I need a break. Where shall we meet?

A – I think it's about time I came and picked you up, don't you?

I sigh, but he's right. I can't hide him from Maddox forever.

S – I think you're right.

A – I'll be at your house around 6.30.

S – See you then.

A – Goodnight, sweetheart.

I smile, and tuck my phone away. I think about how Maddox will react to Alec showing up. I can only pray he's at the clubhouse, so I don't have to put up with his wrath. Because there will be wrath. Maddox is protective of me in a way that comes across as obsessive to some. I'm used to it now.

I rub my eyes and decide to text Maddox, too.

S – Hey . . .

M – Really? Hey?

I sigh. God, I wish I could say all the things I want to say to Maddox. But I can't. I just can't. We're a time bomb, slowly ticking together.

S – I just wanted to see how you were.

M – I'm fine. Goin' to be there in ten.

S – You're coming to see me?

M – Don't act like that shocks you. Mack said you wanted to shower.

S – You might not be allowed in. It's getting late.

M – I'll get in.

I sigh, and put the phone on the table beside the bed. He'll get in, all right. I lie back against the pillows and close my eyes, waiting. I must drift off, because I feel a hand against my cheek what seems like only seconds later. I open my eyes, and Maddox is staring down at me.

"Just droppin' your clothes off."

"I . . . ah . . . thanks."

He tilts his head to the side. God, he's beautiful. So fucking beautiful. I hate that any man would look this good. His long, dark hair falls down over his shoulders, so thick and beautiful. He's built like a statue. His muscles are big and hard. His chest, which I've had the pleasure of seeing many times, is defined, and runs perfectly down to his eight-pack.

Yeah, the man has the full eight-pack of love bumps. Then there's that V . . . oh boy. He's got a chest full of tattoos, even some running down his belly. The one I hate is across his back. I hate it because it's my name, *Santana* in big, black, angry letters.

"Maddox," I whisper.

He leans in closer. "Mmmm."

"I'm safe . . . right?"

He nods. "Never let anything happen to you, Tana. You know that."

"So, I can . . . go out once I get home?"

He tilts his head to the side, studying me. "Depends."

"On?"

"You can go out, with the protection of the guys or me."

I close my eyes. "Maddox-" I begin, but he cuts me off.

"Ain't givin' you a choice. I can't keep you housebound, but I sure as shit ain't lettin' you out alone. You can argue, but it'll do you no fuckin' good."

"Fine," I mutter. "Fine."

"You wanna tell me why you're askin' that question?"

"I, ah, I want to go out with a friend Saturday night. That's all."

"You're a bad fuckin' liar. Now tell me the damn truth."

I sigh and turn to him, our eyes meeting. "I'm . . . I'm seeing someone, Maddox."

I've never seen a man change from relaxed to stiff so quickly in my life. His entire body jerks, and his shoulders straighten. His face hardens, and I watch in shock as his mouth forms a hard line. *Oh shit.*

"It's nothing serious," I say quickly. I don't know why I need to justify my actions, but his look . . . it's *hurting* me. "I just wanted you to know, considering all that's happened."

He proceeds to hurt me more when he turns without another word and disappears out of the room. I call out for him, but he doesn't come back in. I wait. I wait, and I wait. But I know he's gone.

Well shit.

CHAPTER FOUR

2008 – Santana

I stroke my sister's hair, singing softly to her as she falls into a deep slumber. I stare down at her, knowing all of this is for her. There is no other reason I fight the way I do. When her breathing evens out, I push to my feet and walk out of the room, closing the door softly behind me.

My feet feel heavy as I walk down the halls, knowing what I'm walking into, knowing how it's going to feel. The pain won't hold me back, though. Nothing will. Instead, the pain will be what drives me to let him hurt me. He knows I need him now. He knows he's all I've got, and if I'm honest, he's all I want.

There is no beautiful reason for the attachment I feel towards Kennedy. The reason I want him is because he gives me what I want, what I *need*. He knows how to take the pain away, to let me pretend for just a moment that I'm anywhere but here.

"Come here, Tanie," he murmurs, stroking his knee.

Kennedy isn't a cruel man; he doesn't hit me or hurt me. When I came to him six months ago, desperate and cold from the streets, he took Pippa and I in. One night only four months ago, four short months, he gave me something to help me feel better.

From that day on, he gives me what I need, when I need it.

I walk over to him, wishing I had the willpower to turn away. I've tried it, but nothing can make me turn from what he's offering. What he gives me makes me feel good inside, and I figure if I've got control over it, what can it hurt?

Oh, how stupid I am.

I slide onto his knee and his arm snakes around my waist. He smiles at me, showing me a dimple in his cheek as he ties a little yellow tube around my arm. I close my eyes, leaning into him, relishing in the feeling of the needle breaking my skin and the warm rush of liquid that fills my body as he injects me with pure heaven.

Everything leaves. Nothing hurts.

A smile plays lazily around my lips as I lean into him. He drops his ear to my lips, murmuring words I know I'll forget tomorrow. "I have big plans for you, Tanie. Big plans. This will help."

His words don't sink into the parts of my brain that they should. Instead, I'm drifting off into a happy place I've grown so accustomed to. A place where there is no pain, no heartache, and no lies. It's all beautiful, and amazing, and free.

"Good girl," he murmurs, kissing my temple. "My good, sweet little girl."

Hmmmm, being his good, sweet little girl feels good.

So good I never want to leave.

~*~*~*~

"Tana, wake up."

My mind is a foggy mess as I hear the voice, distant, in my mind. I groan, shoving the cold, clammy hand on my face away. I want to sleep. I'm tired. My body is tired. I'm cold.

"Tana, please."

Whimpering.

I blink my eyes open, but all I see is a blurred figure in front of me. I blink some more. My head is pounding, and my entire body hurts. Why do all things that feel good have to hurt so much after?

"Pippa?" I croak.

"I'm sick, Tana. I'm sick."

Sick.

I feel sick right now, too.

I push up onto my elbows, staring over at my little sister. She's pale, really pale, and she's got chunks of vomit covering her shirt. My eyes widen and I stand quickly, too quickly. My head spins, and I reach out to steady myself, using the wall as my strong hold.

"What . . . Why are you sick? Did you eat something bad?" I groan.

God, my head is pounding.

"I just feel sick, and then I started throwing up. I tried to wake you so many times."

Her voice hitches, and my entire body shakes with emotion as I realize I've let her down.

"I'm sorry, Pippi," I whisper. "Come on, let's get you cleaned up."

I lead her out of the room and down the halls. I reach the bathroom and gasp. There's vomit everywhere. "Oh, Pippi."

"I tried to keep it in the toilet, but I just . . . it was coming so hard, Tana."

"It's okay," I murmur. "I'll get it."

I slowly walk out and gather up a bucket and sponge. Then I head back in. Pippa is looking a little less pale, but she's still clutching her stomach. I lower my aching body to my hands and knees, and start to clean up the mess. My stomach turns violently, and before I know it, my own vomit rises and joins hers on the floor.

It's at that exact moment I know I've let my life spiral out of control.

I know because my sister is sick, and instead of taking care of her, I'm suffering in my own self-inflicted world of pain.

I've failed her.

CHAPTER FIVE

2014 – Santana

I get out of the hospital early the next morning. Maddox is there to collect me, and he doesn't say a word as I hobble out with my bag. He's angry at me—I know he is. He doesn't like the idea of Alec, and I don't like the idea that it hurts him. But he's not yet once told me he regrets being with Ash, or even that he wants anything from me. I can't play games.

"Get on my bike, throw your bag to Mack," he grunts.

"Maddox," I begin, but his hand shoots up in front of my face.

"Don't."

"You're angry at me, and I don't understand why. You were with Ash and Krypt, at the same damned time, and now you're angry because I'm going on a date?"

"I said, fuckin' don't," he warns, his voice a low, lethal hiss.

"Jesus," I snap. "Fine. You broody, arrogant—"

He cuts me off with a look so deadly, my mouth snaps closed. I say nothing more; I just get on his bike, tossing my pack at Mack who is watching the two of us argue. He catches it with one hand, throwing it in his side pannier.

I get on the back of Maddox's bike; my leg stretches and pulls, burning slightly. Maddox gets on in front of me, starting the bike without another word.

I hesitate, not wanting to put my arms around him. With a grunt, he reaches back and jerks my hands forward until they're curled around him. I grit my teeth as he pulls out onto the road, waving for the guys to follow. There are ten or so bikers with us, for protection purposes, no doubt. They surround him as he rides, ensuring that if shots are fired, they have to go through them first.

We arrive at his house, and another four bikers are already outside, watching to make sure no one came past while Maddox was gone. They'll trail me wherever I go now, and that's the sucky part of being protected by a club. When shit goes down, you can't get rid of them.

I get off Maddox's bike, but his hand lashes out, curling around my wrist and holding me still. He turns to Tyke and Rhyder, and barks, "The house good?"

"Good Prez, checked every inch, and there ain't no one come past."

Maddox gives a sharp nod and lets me go. I throw the pack Mack hands me over my shoulder, ignoring his smirk. I trudge past the bikers—well, I hobble past, and head inside. The house is clean, surprisingly. My guess is Ash and possibly some of the Old Ladies have come around and cleaned it.

Ignoring the voices below, I got straight to my room. I drop my bag onto the bed and sit down. I shove my jeans down over my hips and flick them off. I need a decent shower – I feel...*stale*. Staring down at the bandage on my calf, I frown. I already know it's going to leave a good scar, and God it hurts.

I stretch it out a little, and then finish undressing. I disappear into my bathroom, closing the door softly. The moment I step in and the warm water hits my skin, is like heaven. I've missed it. I wash my hair twice, exfoliate my skin, and then get out. I dry my hair, and pull a towel around myself.

When I step out, I see Maddox right away. He's at the door, staring at me. His big arms are across his chest. He narrows his eyes when he sees I've showered, and mutters, "Are you supposed to get that wet?" He nods his head in the direction of my leg.

I shrug. "It's fine, the dressing is waterproof."

He nods and lifts a package. "Pain killers."

"I don't want them."

He stares at me, shaking his head as if not understanding.

"I've had an addiction, a severe one. I don't want them."

"You're goin' to be fuckin' sore."

"So be it."

He tucks them into his jeans, and then he lifts his eyes to mine. I can see how tight his jaw is, and I know he's pissed off because I'm going out with Alec.

"Are you going to make me suffer all night?" I ask, pulling my towel tighter around myself.

"Nah."

"Is there a problem with me dating?"

"Nah."

"Fuck, Maddox. Come on."

He growls, and runs his fingers through his long hair. "Shit is goin' down, and all you're thinkin' about is seein' some pansy fuckin' *boy*."

I glare at him, my fingers growing tight on my towel. "Firstly, I *care* about the shit that's going down, and secondly, he is not a boy."

Maddox grunts and uncrosses his arms. "He's a God damned boy, but you wouldn't know, because you ain't ever had a fuckin' man."

Then he turns and walks towards the door.

"Seriously? That's it?"

He grunts.

"Maddox!"

Another grunt.

"Asshole," I mutter.

"Brat," he retorts, and then closes the door behind me.

Men.

~*~*~*~

2014 Santana

I wake up sobbing. The pain in my leg is intense—it burns and itches, and my head is pounding from lack of decent sleep. I move and it's clear the bruising has started to shine through, because it feels as if someone has hit me with a sledgehammer. I try to throw my legs out of the bed, but a ragged cry leaves my throat.

God, it hurts.

My door flies open, and I look up to see a sleep-ruffled Maddox, half naked, staring over at me. He runs his hand through his messy hair, his muscles flexing and pulling as he does. "What's goin' on?"

"Nothing."

He mutters a few choice words, and then growls, "What's fuckin' goin' on?"

"I'm in pain," I snap. "Can you leave?"

He walks over, dropping onto the bed beside me. "Got some good pain killers there."

"I can't take them," I mutter, crossing my arms.

"You can."

"No," I say, turning to him. "I have a problem with addiction."

"Santana . . .you had some in the hospital…"

"I know, but I can't take anymore. The more I take, the harder it'll get. Don't make me take those," I whisper, exhausted. "Please."

He sighs. "You're askin' me to sit here and watch you suffer in pain."

"I'll be okay, I swear. It'll ease."

"Let me get somethin' for the swelling then."

He stands and walks out. He returns five minutes later with a bag of peas wrapped in a towel. He sits back on the bed, and points to the pillows. "Lie down."

I do as he asks, crying out with each movement. He takes my leg, gently, and places the pack over it. Then he stuffs some pillows under it, raising it slightly. "This should help."

"Thanks."

He stares over at me, and a sing-song voice calls out from his room. "Maddox?"

Our eyes hold. I'm used to Maddox having women around, and I'm not in a position to argue—how can I? I am seeing someone else on the weekend, and I am asking him to be okay with that. He's challenging me, though. Staring at me, daring me to throw a fit.

I won't.

"You better go," I say, my voice weaker than I'd like.

He rubs his hand over his muscled belly. "Yeah."

He gets up and walks towards the door, looks back at me before leaving, but says nothing.

What is there to say? Really?

~*~*~*~

I stare at myself in the mirror, eyeing my short dress. It's one Ash gave me, and I'm not sure it's appropriate. It's hot, sure, but I think it's a little *too* hot. I frown and turn, checking out the back again. Well, the back it *doesn't* have. I sigh and spin around, instead focusing on fluffing up my hair.

Alec will be here in an hour, and I'm still not sure I look right. Is he expecting a pretty dress? A sexy dress? Something casual? Will this be too much for where we're going? I shake my head, and decide that it's just too hard to make a choice; I'm going with it. I apply some extra lipstick and turn, walking out of my room and down the stairs.

I skid to a halt when I see Maddox in the living area. He's not meant to be here. I know he has club business, so there's only one reason he's stuck around–to make sure Alec knows he's in my life, and isn't leaving. I glare at him as I hit the bottom step, but he's not noticing, instead, he's staring at my dress.

"Came home to meet this *man*," he practically spits the word at me, "and you come down in *that*."

"That," I growl, "is none of your business."

"There ain't no way in fuckin' hell I'm lettin' you out in that."

My mouth drops open, and my hands fly to my hips. "You don't get a choice."

His eyes meet mine, piercing and angry. "I do fuckin' get a choice. Go and change it, or I'll throw you over my shoulder, dump you on the bed and do it myself. You want your boyfriend to come in with me between your legs, baby?"

"Fuck you, Maddox."

He grins, the fucker. "Anytime, honey."

"I'm not changing, and you're not my father, so you can't fucking make me."

His grin widens. "Can't I?"

I take a step back. "This is sick—you know that, right? The control you think you have over me. I'm a grown woman, and I can do what I like."

"You want this man to respect you?"

"What?"

He crosses his big arms across his chest. "I said, you want this fuckin' man to respect you?"

"He already does."

"Not in that fuckin' dress he doesn't."

"You don't know him!"

"Alec Ramas. Twenty-eight. Works for a massive chain of clubs. Married once. No kids."

I gape, seriously gape. "You checked him out?"

"Of course I fuckin' did. There ain't no way I was lettin' you out with a fucker I hadn't checked out."

He gives me a "*ah derr*" look. I splutter, before storming forward and getting in his face. "What gives you the right to do that?"

"You in my house?"

"That is beside the point."

He leans in closer. "Are. You. In. My. House?"

"Yes!" I cry.

"Then it's my fuckin' rules. You want Alec to respect you? Then you don't wear slutty dresses. You wear something so fuckin' ugly he's forced to see you and only you."

"We don't live in the fifties, Maddox."

He smirks. "No, but men are still men."

"Not all men are pigs like you. Not all men are after a bit of cheap pussy."

"How will you know if you wear that dress? After all, he'll be seein' every part of you before you choose to show it to him. Just bend over and he'll get a good view of what you-"

I shove him. "Don't!"

He takes my hands and brings me close, so I'm flush against him. "Then go and get fuckin' changed, *now*."

We have a staring contest. He wins. I growl and shove back. "Fine, but I'm only doing it to prove to you that Alec is twenty times the man you are."

He winks at me. "We'll see, baby."

"Fuck you."

"Again, anytime."

With another exasperated sound, I storm up the stairs.

Fucking bikers.

CHAPTER SIX

2014 – Santana

A knock sounds out, and my heart clenches. I've changed into a nicer halter dress that flows around my knees, and binds up a little tighter around my breasts. It's dark blue with small white spots. It seems ugly on the rack, but when I'm wearing it, it's lovely. I've left my hair down and kept the makeup.

I hurry as quickly as I can out of the room when I hear another knock. I already know Maddox will get it before me no matter what, but I can save poor Alec. I skid to a stop at the bottom of the stairs when I see Maddox standing, his large body filling the doorframe as he stares at Alec. God, he's huge; he makes Alec look like a toy doll next to him.

Alec's face is pale as Maddox squeezes his hand so hard his fingers are bunched together. *Great, he's going to break my date's fingers before we even get two steps out the front door.* "Alec," I say quickly, shoving Maddox out of the way and forcing them to part. "I see you've met Maddox."

Alec is rubbing his hand, his face twisted in pain. Maddox is grinning. I ignore him as I lean in and kiss Alec on the cheek. Maddox growls and I turn, giving him a sardonic smile. "I'll see you later. Don't wait up."

"One thing before you go," Maddox rumbles, his eyes pinning Alec. "You so much as lay a harmful hand on her, I'll cut your balls off and shove them—"

"Maddox!" I protest.

"It's okay," Alec says, taking my hand and squeezing it. "Let him speak."

"Smart man," Maddox grunts. "As I was sayin', you hurt her, I'll make it hurt for you. She's a big girl, she can take care of herself real good, but it don't mean I won't be there to back her up if I need to. And let me tell you somethin', fucker—you don't wanna see what I'll do if that girl so much as comes home with a scratch."

I stare at Maddox, surprised he's actually admitted that I can take care of myself. I give him a half smile, and he throws one back at me. The way it changes his face from gorgeous to stunning slams into me. I turn away, cheeks pink. "Are you ready?" I ask Alec.

"I'm ready."

I give Maddox one last stare and turn, following Alec to his car. He opens the door for me and I slide onto the brown leather seats. When he gets in, I turn and give him a smile. Alec is a good looking man—not the same kind of good looking that Maddox is, but very appealing. He's got messy blond hair and big hazel eyes. His body is well-built but lean, and he's always impeccably dressed.

"You look beautiful tonight, Santana," he murmurs, leaning over and kissing me softly.

"You look pretty good yourself," I say back.

"Are you ready?"

I nod, beaming. "I'm ready."

Neither of us says anything about the rumble of Harley Davidsons that roar to life behind us. He knows they're following me, I know they're following me, and we both know there's nothing that can be done about it. He pulls out and drives away from the house. I turn to him as we're heading off down the road. "I'm sorry about Maddox."

He shrugs. "He cares about you. It's fine."

"Things are strained between us right now, but we're getting there."

He smiles, but it seems slightly tight. He quickly changes the subject. "How are you going finding a job?"

I frown. "I haven't found one, but I'm still actively looking."

That was mostly a lie. I've been shot at and shuffled around too much for me to have a good chance at getting a job.

"I think I might have something for you," he says.

My eyes widen. "You have?"

He nods. "My sister owns a café just a few blocks down. You've probably heard of it—Moxie's."

"Oh yeah." I smile. "They make great coffee."

"Well, she has an opening. It's only casual for now, but it's something."

"I'm all for it. Can I go and speak to her?"

He smiles. "I'll set it up for tomorrow."

"Okay." I grin.

Alec takes me down to the wharf and my smile widens when I see the yacht that's docked, waiting for us. "Is that . . ."

"For us." He winks, stopping the car and getting out. He comes around to my door and opens it. "My Lady."

I giggle stupidly and climb out, taking his hand. He leads me down to the gorgeous yacht and we climb on board. I hear the bikes come to a stop; they won't leave from that spot. I turn my focus back to the yacht. It isn't a big yacht, but it's got a big enough deck space that we can move around freely. Enough that a gorgeous table is set in the middle of the space, lit with candles and roses.

"Oh Alec, it's beautiful."

He smiles and leads me over, pulling my chair out. "Wine?"

"Please."

He sits down and a man in a tux comes out, bottle of wine in hand. I laugh softly as he leans over and pours us a glass. Then he announces, "First course will be served momentarily."

I take my glass, smiling as the man disappears. I've had a hell of a time lately, and this is exactly what I need.

Alec sips his wine, studying me with appreciation. I can see it in his eyes, the way they sparkle as they run over me.

"How is your leg healing?"

I've been home three days, and while my leg is starting to itch as it heals, it's mostly feeling okay.

"It's doing great, thanks."

He beams. "I'm glad. Tell me something about yourself, Santana."

I pout and say, "What do you want to know?"

"Where did you grow up?"

I frown. I've told Alec basics about my life, but I'm not ready to get into great detail so I give him a basic answer.

"My parents died in an accident when I was young. I spent my life in foster homes until Maddox took me in – which you already know most of."

His face softens. "It must have been awful."

I shrug. "There are worse things."

I don't tell him the rest; that's a conversation for another day.

"What about you?" I ask, sipping the cool wine.

"I grew up here with my family. Just your normal life, you know? I don't really have anything to tell."

"We're terribly boring," I point out and he laughs.

"Okay how about ten questions?" He winks.

"I'm all up for that."

"What's your favorite color?" he asks.

"White."

He chuckles. "White isn't a color."

I grin. "Exactly."

The waiter brings out our first course of seafood. I stare down at the display, and my stomach grumbles.

"I hope you eat seafood?"

"I eat everything," I say, "It looks amazing."

We talk through dinner, asking random questions and laughing a lot. By the time we're finished dessert, I feel amazing, and my entire body is thrumming with happiness. Alec even gets me up to dance, holding me close as we move around the deck to a soft song. He leans down to kiss me midway through, and it's a nice kiss.

Soft. Sweet. *Perfect.*

By the time he pulls back, I'm panting and staring up at him. He strokes my cheek, staring down at me. "I'm glad I met you, Santana, and I hope I get to see more of you."

He kisses me again, his hands slowly going down to graze over my backside. I let him do this for a while, but quickly stop it. I like Alec, a lot, but I'm not ready for things to move so quickly. He stiffens when I shift the direction of his hand, but he says nothing. We keep dancing, our bodies moving together.

A hand grazes my ass.

Okay, it's a romantic situation, but seriously?

"Hands off," I say lightly.

"You're no fun," he complains.

"It's our first official date. You're not seriously expecting anything, are you?"

He pulls back and stares down at me. "Of course not."

But I can see something else behind his eyes—disappointment, frustration? Is that what he wanted?

I hope not.

~*~*~*~

Alec takes me home as the night gets on, and waits until the bikes trailing us pull up before leaving me—he doesn't kiss me again, and I try not to think too much about it. I watch him go, walking straight past the angry glares being shot his way. I roll my eyes and walk down to the three members, Mack being one of them.

"Chief, since when did you become a babysitter?"

He grins. "Since you decided to date that douchebag."

"He's not a douchebag," I say, poking his chest with my finger.

"He *is* a douchebag." He smirks. "The man probably has never done anything but stroke his own—"

"Mack," I warn.

He flashes a sexy grin at me.

"Take me to the club. I want to see Maddox."

His eyes grow serious. "Why? Did that fucker hurt you?"

I roll my eyes again, and climb onto the back of his bike.

"Get moving, oh mighty one."

He laughs and pulls out, patting my hand with amusement. We arrive at the clubhouse and the moment the bike stops, I leap off. "Save me a drink," I yell as I hurry into the space.

The moment I step inside, a party is in full swing. Bikers are lazed about drinking beer, girls are walking around, slinking all over them, and old ladies are laughing and chatting in the corner. I wave to them as I pass and walk off down the hall.

I reach Maddox's room, and swing the door open, I don't care if he's occupied or not. He is. He's got the club whore, Cacey, dancing for him. Her naked body slinks about seductively. He swings his eyes to me, and a smirk appears on his face. God he looks good, damn him. Damn him to hell.

"You and I are going to talk," I say, stepping in. I turn to Cacey. "Shoo."

She glares at me. "Fuck off, Santana."

I laugh. "Out."

"Get out," Maddox grumbles.

Cacey takes her clothes, and glares at me once more before leaving. *Aw, I took her cock for the night.* I turn back to Maddox and he reaches over, taking a cigarette and lighting it.

"Have a good time?" He smirks, taking a drag.

"It was great, except for the trail of bikes. How long do I have to let them follow me, Maddox?"

He snorts. "For as long as I say."

"Really? Alec can take care of me. He wouldn't let anyone hurt me. Besides, he couldn't even kiss me comfortably without those guys glaring at him."

Maddox snorts, taking another long drag. "Alec . . . what sort of name is that anyway?"

"What sort of name is Maddox?" I throw back.

He grins, unperturbed by my comment. "A very sexy one."

"Oh, dream on."

"I'm surprised Alec even knows how to kiss." He snorts.

"He kisses very well, thank you," I argue, throwing my hands on my hips.

"Does he now? And what have you got to compare it to?"

I flush, and shift from one foot to the other. I am a virgin. Which is a small miracle, considering the life I lived. I was lucky, truly blessed, that no one took what was mine before I wanted to give it. That also means kissing men is a big thing for me, I've only kissed two in my life: Kennedy and Alec. Kennedy is one that has lodged itself into a part of my brain I try not to access.

"He's the first one, ain't he, baby?"

"Stop calling me that," I snap. "And he isn't the first. Even if he were, it wouldn't matter. It felt amazing."

"Make your panties wet?"

"Maddox!" I snap.

He grins. "Did it, honey?"

"Fuck you."

"Answer the question."

"No it did not. It was a kiss, not a fondle."

His grin widens. "When a man kisses you, and he really means it, and you really feel it, then you will ache for him. *Everywhere*."

My cheeks flame, and I turn away. "We are not having this conversation."

"Alec is too good for you, Tana. He's a perfect man who will bore the shit out of you in a month."

"You're wrong, Maddox. He's much more than boring—he's sweet and kind, and he treats me how I want to be treated."

"You sure about that?"

I don't look at him as I walk towards the door. "Yes."

At least, I think I am.

CHAPTER SEVEN

2009 – Santana

My body aches. It hurts so badly I want to scream. I can't get the drugs I need, the drugs I so desperately want. Kennedy has been away for three days and without him, I can't get them. I rock in the corner, backwards and forwards, trying to keep calm. Pippa has come in a few times, offering water, but at my third refusal she left me alone.

Now I'm by myself, cold and terrified, desperate for something to take away this knowing pain in my soul. I scratch at my arms, my nails biting into the skin as it peels back, revealing crimson blood. I yell, but I can't stop. It's the only relief I can find. I wish he would come back. I wish he would hurry.

"Tanie, oh, sweet Tanie."

I look up through my haze and see Kennedy at the door. I lunge at him, my fingers scratching at his pants. "Please," I beg. "Make it go away."

"I'm going to make it go away, sweetheart."

He drops to his knees, tightening that yellow cord around my arm before plunging the needle in. Warmth floods me, and I whimper in relief as the drugs take over. "It's okay now, I'm sorry. I had to go away. I'm sorry, Tanie."

It doesn't matter now. He's here, that's all that matters.

~*~*~*~

"Get out!" Alyce screams, throwing a large saucepan at my head.

My legs tremble as I take Pippa's hand, pulling her towards the door. Kennedy convulses on the ground, vomit rising up and dribbling out of his mouth. I stare at him, wanting to help but this woman . . . his mother . . . won't let us near him. She doesn't understand what he's taken.

Why did he take so much?

"This is all your fault, you little sluts!" she bellows, sending a knife soaring across the room. Pippa screams, and clutches me tighter.

Kennedy brought us over for dinner tonight, telling us it was time to meet his family. He was acting strangely on the way here, slurring his words, and groaning about a pain in his stomach. I didn't know he'd taken anything; he seemed fine before we left. Midway through dinner he excused himself, and fell to the ground in a fit.

His mother blamed us. Her precious son would have never taken drugs if it weren't for us.

"What did you give him?" she screams. "What did you poison my baby with?"

"I . . . I . . . I didn't give him anything. He took them himself."

"Liar," she roars, charging towards me. I throw Pippa out of the way just as she reaches me, and her fingers curl into my hair. She drags me towards Kennedy, shoving my face down until I'm so close to him I can smell his vomit. "Tell me, *Puta*, what did you give my son?"

"I didn't, I swear. He gives it to me, he—"

She shoves my face into the tiles so hard my nose splits. My entire mind fogs over as pain radiates through my face, like a thousand pins being punched into my head. I can faintly hear Pippa screaming. Alyce spits words at me in a language I don't understand.

She lifts my head, my face covered in my own blood and Kennedy's vomit. "Tell me," she screams. "What did you give him?"

Denying this is clearly not working, and I'm scared for my life, and my sisters. So, I do the only thing I can. "H-h-h-heroine."

"You stupid, filthy, dirty little . . ."

Sirens blare in the distance. She pulls me to my feet, with incredible strength for a woman her age. She shoves me towards the door, blood still flowing down my face. "Get out of here, and never, *never* come back, or I'll make good on my threats."

I turn, rushing towards my sobbing sister. "Come on."

I take her hand and we run from the chaos, terrified and not knowing if Kennedy will ever come back.

Where will that leave us?

CHAPTER EIGHT

2014 – Santana

I sway my hips to the song. My mind is a haze of alcohol and happy thoughts from the amount of it I've had. The party is in full swing—bikers are drinking, whores are doing what they do best, and Ash and I are swinging our butts on top of the table. My leg is numb, which I'm not entirely sure is a good thing because I could be doing serious damage, though I am only swinging my hips, not parading around flicking my legs out.

Krypt and Maddox are watching us, smirks on their handsome faces. No one tries to interfere. We sway and sing, our drinks sloshing about in our glasses as the music carries us away. "Play it again!" Ash squeals when her favorite song ends.

"Noooo," I groan. "Another one."

I take a step back, a little too far, and with flailing arms I make my rapid descent towards the floor. I never make it, of course—my knight in shining . . . errr . . . *leather* . . . catches me. His arms wrap around me and he scoops me up, holding me close to his chest.

"Time to get you home," he murmurs.

"Aw, Maddox," I complain. "I was having fun."

"A little too much, it would seem. Time to go."

"Fun spoiler," I murmur as he carries me out the door. "Bye Ash!" I call before we exit.

"I'm coming to see you tomorrow, Tana!" she squeals. "I need to know more about that kiss."

I flush and giggle as Maddox carries me outside to his truck. He opens the door and shoves me inside. I land awkwardly, my legs sprawled, my dress sliding up way too high.

"Jesus, Tana, I can see your fuckin' ass."

"It's a nice ass." I laugh.

He yanks my dress down, muttering a curse before slamming the door. By the time he gets into the driver's side, I'm up and already fiddling with the radio.

"Stop it," he growls, smacking my hand away.

"No," I protest. "I want to listen to this song."

"Santana so help me God, I'll tie your fuckin' hands together."

"Bite me, Maddox."

"With fuckin' pleasure."

I laugh again, and start singing loudly to the song as he pulls out of the compound. We cruise down the highway, headed for home, when the shots come. Out of the blue. Right into the tires of the truck. They come so suddenly, it takes me a moment to realize what the loud cracking sound is.

Then it clicks.

"Maddox?" I cry, holding onto the door as the car lurches to the side.

"Fuck, fuck, fuck. Find my phone, Santana."

"What's happening?" I cry.

"Find my phone," he barks.

"W-w-w-where is it?"

"My pocket, right."

58

I reach over to his pocket, shoving my hand inside his jeans to bring out his phone just as another shot fires, smashing the windscreen. The car swerves again, and I scream as bits of glass explode into my face.

"Fuck," Maddox roars. "Tana, are you hurt?"

My face stings, and my arms burn, but I'm okay. "I think . . . I'm okay."

"Call Krypt or Mack."

I open his phone with shaky fingers as he speeds up. The car is bumping and grinding against the road, but it doesn't stop him. He swerves to the right, down a busier street. We're closer to town, and the closer we can get, the safer we are.

"Mack."

Mack answers his phone on the first ring.

"Mack, it's Santana. We're being shot at."

"What?" he says, his voice hardening. "Where are you?"

"Maddox," I say quickly. "Where are we?"

Maddox glances at me and his eyes widen. "Motherfucker, you're hurt."

I don't have time to process that before he barks, "Main Street."

"We're nearly at Main Street."

"You got a visual?"

"Visual?" I ask Maddox.

"Nothin'. It's too dark."

"No."

"We're on our way."

I can see the lights as we near Main Street, but not before another shot rings out, hitting another tire. The car swerves again, but Maddox refuses to let it stop. It grinds against the pavement, the blown tires no doubt destroyed, and the metal carving a path as we move. We skid onto Main Street and whizz past cars, causing horns to honk.

Maddox doesn't stop until he reaches the back road to Krypt's house. He skids down it, pulling over on a large grassy patch. He is out of the car in a split second, swinging my door open. "Get out and run."

"Where?" I gasp.

"Over Krypt's fence. He's got thick bushes running alongside of it. Get in them, and don't fuckin' breathe until I come to you."

I nod and turn, running with everything I have towards the fence. My heart is pounding, and my legs feel numb as I near my destination. I trip three times because of the alcohol consumption and my aching calf. When I reach the fence, I hear another gun shot. I make a strangled, gasping sound as I throw myself over. I land on the other side with a thump. I don't hesitate, diving into the trees.

Branches scrape up my arms, and I grit my teeth to stop from shouting in pain. Tears leak out of the corners of my eyes as I wait, the eerie silence making me feel ill. I wrap my arms around myself and I sit, waiting. The rumbling sounds of Harley Davidson's in the distance have me crying with relief.

Voices, the sounds of the bikes starting again, and then the sounds of doors slamming in Krypt's house drift out to me. The back door swings open and Maddox barks, "Tana? Are you there? Shit." His voice is frantic, so I push to my feet quickly, shoving out of the bushes. The moment he notices me, I see him visibly relax.

"Thank fuckin' God," he murmurs. "Come inside, darlin'."

I follow him inside and the moment we're in the light, he turns to me, his face scrunching in pain. "Shit, your face is bleeding. Come and sit down."

I don't argue, still too shaken up. I sit at the table as Krypt, Ash, Mack and Tyke come inside. Ash sees me and rushes over, sliding into the seat beside me. "Are you okay?"

I nod weakly. "I'm okay, just shaken."

Maddox returns with a first-aid kit. I catch a glimpse of his face and see he's got a few cuts of his own. I point to his cheek. "You're bleeding, too."

"I don't care, honey," he murmurs. "I'm goin' to fix you first."

"Are we safe?" I whisper.

He looks to Mack, who walks over and puts his hand out. "Let me fix her. Make some calls, Maddox."

Maddox hesitates, but he hands Mack the wipe and disappears down the hall with Krypt close behind. Mack sits in front of me, his eyes studying my face as he wipes the drying blood off. "You know how to get them all wound up, don't you?"

"This is my fault?" I gasp.

He stops. "No, God, fuck no."

I sigh, and close my eyes. Ash takes my hand "We'll be okay," she assures me.

"They shot at us, with no hesitation at all," I point out. "This is the second time. Someone wants to hurt me."

"Maddox has got this," Mack says.

He finishes cleaning my face, and Maddox returns. He's angry, I can tell, so I don't push. He'll tell me what happened when he's ready. I'm suddenly tired, having sobered up too quickly. Maddox takes Krypt's keys and turns to me. "We're goin' home. Come on."

I stand, not arguing. My leg aches, but I ignore it. There more pressing issues right now.

We live around the corner from Krypt, so it's not too far to have to drive.

"Mack will follow, make sure we aren't bein' trailed."

I nod, not bothering to speak. I hug Ash, and then follow Maddox out to Tyke's car. We pass the truck on the way, and seeing it bullet filled has my chest clenching. Maddox stops, too. He stares at it, and then over to me, and his hand comes out in silent comfort, squeezing mine. So close...it was *so close.*

"Come on," he says, his voice low. "Let's get you home."

The entire ride home is silent, and my face is starting to ache. I wait in the car while Maddox and Mack check out the house, and then I'm allowed in.

I go right to my room, holding my emotions in the best I can. Maddox is talking to Mack downstairs, so I figure I have the chance to change and have a shower. It's an awkward shower, too. I have to lean forward so my face doesn't get wet. My leg surprisingly didn't bust open with my running, but it's pounding now. When I'm clean, I change and slide into bed.

Tears come spilling out the moment that my head hits the pillow, and I sob, loudly and freely. I vaguely hear the sounds of my door opening and then my bed dips. I don't bother to fight as Maddox curls his arms around my weak body and pulls me into him. His skin is warm, hot even, and completely bare. My face presses against his chest and I breathe him in, just needing someone.

We say nothing--there's really nothing to say. I think he needs my comfort as much as I need his. Maddox and I have always had a strange, quiet connection. We fight a whole lot, but when it comes down to being there, we've always had each other's backs. I nestle in closer, his heart steadily pounding against my ear.

"I'm scared, Maddox," I finally whisper.

"Ain't no fucker touchin' you, do you hear me? Tomorrow you'll move to the club; you're safer there. Tonight, I've got a watch on the house."

I nod, pulling back so I can nestle up into his neck. He makes a throaty sound, and his arms tighten around me. Desperate for comfort, I lift my lips and kiss his cheek. It's innocent, it truly is, and yet it quickly changes. Like a flash, Maddox turns his head and his lips capture mine.

I'm frozen in shock for longer than a minute, our lips locked, our bodies still, the air around us crackling.

Then he moves, and he changes everything.

His lips don't force, *no*, they coax mine apart in a gentle caress that has all the breath leaving my body. His mouth is rough, yet soft, a perfect combination of dark and light. His tongue slips in and fireworks explode in my body, from my head to my feet.

And I finally understand his words.

When you get kissed for real, in the way that involves passion, you feel it right to your toes. My sex clenches, and a moan is wrenched from my lips as his mouth continues it's slow, agonizing torture, exploring me until my fingers are clawing at his naked back.

He pulls away on a pant, and in the darkness I can hear nothing but our breathing.

"That," he growls, his voice low and husky, "is how it should feel when a man kisses you."

I have nothing to say. He just blew my mind with one simple connection of our lips. Maddox and I have always had some sort of sexual attraction, but for me he's always driven me too crazy to ever act on it. I thought I could get through my life and never need him the way I need him right now.

"Stay with me," I whisper. "Please, Maddox."

"Wasn't goin' to go anywhere, babe. Go to sleep before I change my mind and kiss you again."

He curls his arms around me once more and we fall into a relaxed position that feels just too perfect. I close my eyes, trying to push that kiss from my mind but failing miserably. Eventually, though, exhaustion takes over, and I slip off into oblivion.

CHAPTER NINE

2014 – Santana

I wake from a nightmare I can't remember; sweating and grabbing anything I can curl my fingers around. That happens to be Maddox. His hands go over the top of mine, prying my fingers from his arms. Shit, I didn't realize I had latched onto him so hard. I pull back suddenly, nearly falling from the bed. It's only his hand shooting out and catching me that prevents that.

"You're okay," he murmurs. "I got you."

I don't say anything as he rolls me back towards him. My face presses against his chest, and I take a moment to breathe him in. God, his skin is hot, *so hot.* My heart begins to slow and I part my lips, pressing my open mouth to his hot flesh. My mind spins as my tongue slides out and across his hard, muscled chest.

"Fuck," he hisses. "Santana, stop lickin' me."

I stop what I'm doing, but not before I feel the little bumps break out across his flesh from my tongue. I just need to feel okay. I know I'll wake in the morning, and I'll regret this, but lying next to him like this . . . it feels *so* good.

"Santana, honey," he rasps. "You either stop, or I'll flip you over and fuck you so hard you'll never forget me."

I flush and swallow, moving my mouth from his flesh. Maddox doesn't know I'm a virgin—no one does. It's something I hold close, not ashamed for a second that I haven't given it away, even though I'm twenty-one now.

"Sorry," I whisper. "I just . . ."

"I know," he rasps, rolling and using my hips to pin me to the bed.

I'm half on my side, half on my back. His body presses against mine every inch of him. Every. Inch. It's when his . . . *cock* . . . presses against me that I realize the position we're in. I'm reminded of Alec, and my heart begins to pound. I stiffen.

"Don't," Maddox warns. "Push me away. Tell me that Pretty Boy is what you want. But don't, I swear to fucking God, *don't* tell me that you regret my mouth on yours, Santana."

My heart pounds. He knows me so well.

"I'd never regret you, Maddox," I whisper. "No matter how angry you make me, I'd never . . . not for a second . . . regret you."

"Then go back to sleep and let me lay here, feelin' somethin' I've been waitin' so fuckin' long to feel."

So long? He's waited to feel me like this? I try to push that from my mind as he moves me over him, resting my cheek against his chest. I try not to think about his words, but I know, I just *know* they're going to consume me.

~*~*~*~

When I wake in the morning, I'm alone.

I slide out of bed, my face burning. I haven't got any cuts big enough for stitches, thank God, but there are a few achy gashes on my cheeks and forehead that hurt when I move my jaw. I also have a few on my arms. I pull on a pair of shorts and walk out of the room, towards the stairs.

I hear voices as I near and I stop, listening.

It's Mack and Maddox. I shouldn't be listening in, but I can't help it. They're talking about last night, and I'm curious to know what went down. I press myself against the wall and tilt my head to the side so I can hear them more clearly.

66

"Howard's in prison, but the fucker still has a solid club. He's pissed, and he's going to make me pay by hurtin' her."

Mack grunts. "You sure they knew Tan was in that car with you?"

My heart stutters.

"The shot came through her side, Mack," Maddox mutters.

"Fuck. As I suspected."

My stomach turns. I feel a little ill.

"Gotta be revenge?"

"You sent her into his club, and fucked his plan. It's absolutely revenge," Mack grinds out.

"I gotta figure out how to keep her safe. Right now, I'm not sure how I'm gonna do that."

"Bring her to my new house. It's unknown, because most people don't know about me," Mack suggests.

No. No way.

"It's not a bad idea," Maddox says, though his voice sounds grumbly and not entirely convinced. "They'll be watchin' the club and this place. You've only just leased a joint – it'll work."

"I've yet to move in—I have the keys, no furniture, but I can make that happen. We'll make sure I'm not bein' followed at any time, and we'll get her over there and keep low."

"You know I'm not overjoyed with the idea of you bein' alone with her, Mack," Maddox grunts.

I hear a snort. "Not goin' to do anything, boss man. Wouldn't wanna piss on your shoes."

Maddox laughs. "No, you better fuckin' not. Right, it's done, then."

I push off and continue down the stairs. Both men turn when a creak fills the room. Maddox lets his gaze travel over me instantly, checking if I'm well. Mack simply smirks at me, as if he knows. My cheeks heat as I hurry past them towards the kitchen.

"You hear that, babe?" Maddox calls out.

"Yes."

"You goin' to fight me on it?"

I hesitate, but say, "That depends."

He makes a displeased sound in his throat. "It ain't negotiable. I was only hopin' you wouldn't fight because it makes it easier for both of us."

I pour a coffee and turn to him. "Can Alec still visit?"

He looks as if I've just slapped him. His face turns hard as stone in seconds, his mouth tight, his eyes flashing with rage and pain. I didn't mean that to sound so cold, but Alec is in the picture, even if Maddox and I did spend a night kissing. I can't just forget about him.

"Is Alec the pretty boy from the other night?" Mack asks.

I'm almost certain I can hear Maddox's jaw grinding with rage. *Jesus.* I look away; I can't stand to see that expression for a moment longer. I don't understand why he's so angry. Yes, we kissed, but in the end he's going to find a piece of club pussy soon, and fuck the shit out of it. I don't see why I can't have what he has.

"He's not a pretty boy," I snap.

Mack laughs. "He is a pretty boy, but if you're seein' him and he's a good man, then I've got no problem with him comin' around."

Maddox shoots Mack a scathing look that has even me flinching. "She ain't riskin' bringin' that piece of shit around when she's in danger."

"Maddox," I protest. "I'm not going to stop seeing him because I'm in danger. I'll be careful, sure, but I'm not going to stop."

Maddox turns back towards me and stalks over. The moment he reaches me his hand lashes out and curls around my shoulder. He pulls me in close, bringing his mouth down to my ear. "Did I have my tongue in your mouth last night?" he growls.

I swallow. "That doesn't matter . . . it doesn't because . . ."

"Because why?" he snarls, his breath hot against my skin.

"You fuck other women all the time, Maddox. I kissed you, it was amazing, but you and I . . . we're not exactly . . . we'll never . . ."

"Don't fuckin' bother. Do what you want."

He shoves me back and turns to Mack. "Take her now."

"Maddox," I say, my voice shaky.

He doesn't look at me; he just walks with slow purpose towards the back door. "I'm goin' for a ride. Don't be here when I get back."

My heart thumps in rapid bursts as I listen to him go. God dammit, I need to stop shoving my foot in my mouth so often. I turn to Mack, and he's studying me. He lifts a hand and runs it over the two days' growth on his chin, his brown eyes traveling over my face.

"You fuckin' Maddox, *chante?*"

"What?" I gasp. "No."

"What about this other man?"

"No."

"Then what the fuck is goin' on?"

I sigh. "I . . . ah . . . we . . . *shit*."

"That wasn't a coherent sentence. You wanna try again?"

"We kissed."

His brows shoot up. "He's got his knickers in a twist over a fuckin' kiss?"

"He slept in my bed last night."

"He's slept in your bed plenty of times."

"Yeah, but . . . it was different, Chief. We . . . there was something there."

He crosses his big arms. "You care about him?"

My stomach twists. "I don't know, and that's the honest truth. I'm confused."

"You reacted badly when you found out he was with Ash."

At the very sound of that, my body jerks with pain.

"I know."

"Care to tell me why?" he asks, taking a step towards me, still studying my face.

"I can't tell you why. It made no sense to me, either. It came as such a shock, it confused me. I was hurt, inexplicably hurt. Since then things have changed between us--it's like we've gone from being close to having sexual tension and it seems . . . wrong."

"Why?" he asks, pulling out a cigarette and lighting it.

"He saved me; he's taken care of me for five years now. He's never tried anything; he's never made any moves towards me. Now suddenly we're staring at each other like we want to rip each other's clothes off. I feel as though it's not right, I mean . . . he's been taking care of me like . . . like a father . . . for so long."

Mack snorts. "Honey, Maddox was never, *ever* pretending to be your father. That man has had eyes for you from the moment you turned eighteen."

"He has not," I protest.

"You fuckin' blind? He's controlling because he fuckin' wants you."

"If he wants me, why doesn't he say so?" I ask, throwing my hands on my hips.

"Because he thinks you deserve better."

That slams into my chest like a sledgehammer. I've always been a brat to Maddox, sure, but I never knew he cared about me in a sexual kind of way. Until recently, he'd never made any kind of move towards me. He's always kept his distance and been hard, a little too hard, actually.

"He's wrong about that. It's him who deserves better."

Mack narrows his eyes, and his expression hardens. "You really think that?"

I nod, not even hesitating. "Maddox is a good man. He saved my life, and gave me a second chance. I'd be nothing without him, but he deserves a loyal old lady who is going to adore him, not some washed up junkie brat who is a thorn in his side."

Mack studies me for so long I squirm. "Do you really see yourself like that?"

"Not entirely," I admit. "But I still think I'm not right for him, and that won't change."

"But you're right for that uppity girl-boy who is takin' you out."

"Alec is a good, caring man. He can make me a good woman, a real woman. If I stay with Maddox forever, I'm always going to be his burden."

"You ain't his burden, *chante*," Mack says, his voice going softer.

"Aren't I?" I say, my voice shaking. "I'm the one who causes all his heartache. He's always put everything towards taking care of me, and he still fucks club whores when we know there are plenty of good girls out there to be his old lady. If I move on, and find my own life, maybe he'll find his."

"You really want that?" Mack asks. "You really think it's going to be easy to see him fallin' for another woman?"

At that very thought, my entire stomach twists angrily, but I don't admit it. The truth is, Maddox deserves a good woman who isn't always fighting him, and I deserve to get away from a complicated life and just live normally.

"Yes," I answer, but my voice is still shaky. "If she was good for him, yes."

He shakes his head, almost sadly. "You're foolin' yourself if you think you two don't belong together."

Then he turns and walks towards the front door. "Pack your shit. I'll wait out front."

Great. Now I've pissed two men off in one morning.

CHAPTER TEN

2008 – Santana

Pippa trembles in my arms. I rub her shoulders, trying to keep her warm. It's been twenty-four hours since Kennedy's mom kicked us out, and we've been too frightened to go home. If she's there, or the police, it could end badly. Instead, we're huddled behind the bus stop over the road, just watching.

Pippa is freezing. She really has nothing to fall back on, she's so skinny, and that's scary. If she gets too cold, she could die. That's just how simple this is.

A flash of headlights causes my head to jerk up. A car arrives at Kennedy's house, then another, then another. My eyes widen as I peer through the small gap in the middle.

That's a whole lot of cars. I pull Pippa closer, staring as a heap of men in black clothes get out. One of them yells in the general direction of the house, "Get out here, Kennedy."

They want Kennedy? But he isn't here.

"You got three seconds, Kennedy. You owe us, and we're tired of waiting."

My heartbeat races as I stare through the gaps. A man, a really big man, walks up to the windows and raises a gun, shooting. The window smashes and Pippa makes a squealing sound. I press a hand over her mouth. "Shhh, if they hear you . . ."

"One," the man yells.

Kennedy isn't there, I want to scream it at them, but of course I'm not going to do that.

"Two," he yells again.

73

Another gunshot is sent through the window.

"Three!"

At least eight men charge the front door, kicking it down. I watch in horror as lights come on in all of the rooms. About ten minutes later, they come out and huddle about, chatting amongst themselves. Then they get in their cars and leave.

That wasn't good. I know it.

I tuck Pippa closer, and pull a jacket around us. I watch the house for hours and hours, even when the early light of the morning comes shining through my little gap. That's when another car arrives. I squint and see Kennedy get out. He looks terrible, but it's him, and he's alone. I wait for a minute before shaking Pippa awake.

"Pippa," I whisper. "Wake up."

She blinks her eyes open, staring up at me. "A-a-a-are they gone?"

"Kennedy is back."

We pack up our things, and rush across the road. Kennedy sees us and his face floods with relief. He looks terrible, with black under his eyes and sunken cheekbones, but he opens his arms to us. "I was worried, my girls. Where have you been?"

"We were over the road," I croak. "Someone came here when you were gone, and shot the windows in."

Kennedy jerks. "Who? Did you see them?"

"No, but they said they were sick of waiting."

His eyes dart around, and he fumbles about for his keys. "We have to go, let's go."

"Where are we going?" Pippa squeaks.

"Be calm, sweetheart," he murmurs to her. "It'll be okay."

He shoves us into his car, and speeds off down the road without any more words spoken. He drives for thirty or forty minutes and pulls up at a secluded hotel. Frantic, he gets out and rushes into the reception. A few minutes later he returns. He throws himself into the car without another word, and drives the car around to an old, crappy room.

We get out in silence, scared. He ushers us into the room and slams the door, locking it. He points to the bed, and mutters, "I'm making some calls. Order some food, have a shower, and get some sleep."

He takes his phone and hurries outside, shutting the door behind him. I turn to Pippa, who is watching him with wide eyes. "Are we in danger, Santana?"

"No, honey," I soothe. "Go and have a shower. It'll be nice, and it'll warm you up."

She nods, and hurries off without another word. She loves to shower—it's like her little piece of heaven. When she's gone, I walk over to the window and peer out. Kennedy is pacing up and down the footpath, yelling into his cell. I sigh and walk back to the bed, ordering some food for Pippa and I.

By the time our food arrives, Kennedy is back, and still frantic. His eyes are darting around the room, not really focusing on anything. His lips are a fine line, his skin pale. Pippa and I eat in silence as he sits, tapping his foot over and over. Then he turns to us, staring at me. "You trust me, don't you, Tanie?" he asks.

I nod. "Yes," I whisper.

"Then you know I'll try and keep you safe?"

Try.

"Yes."

He nods sharply, and points to the bed. "Get some sleep. There's no point worrying over this."

Pippa and I crawl into the bed.

This feels bad. Really. *Really*. Bad.

~*~*~*~

2014 – Santana

I pack as many things as I can, without taking too much. I have all the essentials—clothes, shoes, toiletries, and all my creams and makeup. I stuff it all into one big suitcase and drag it down the stairs. My heart hurts, even though I know it's not forever. The idea of being without this house frightens me.

The idea of being without Maddox frightens me more.

"You ready?" Mack asks, dropping a smoke and crushing it out with his boot.

I stare at him, then his SUV, and nod. He takes my suitcase, and tells me to stay at the door until he's got it in, and he's sure we're not being watched. Then he shrugs his jacket off and then his bandana and puts both on me. He tucks my hair down behind the jacket and tightens the bandana over my head. Then he slinks his arm over me and walks out.

It's not really a disguise as such, more a precaution. When I'm in the car, with its dark tinting, I hand the items back. He checks around, and then points to the floor. "Down you go."

"Seriously?" I gape.

"Seriously, *now*."

I growl, and drop onto the space on the floor. I tuck my knees up to my chest and glare at nothing in particular. Mack pulls out, and the rumble of the car radiates through my bottom. "How will you know if someone is following you?"

"There ain't a single person behind me now. If someone comes in the next twenty miles, I'll drive around in random places to see if they follow, but the fact that no one has popped up already tells me they're probably not there."

"Maddox has had watches all night; they probably know that."

"Won't stop them. I'd say they're regrouping."

Great.

"How far is your new place?"

"About half an hour."

"And you haven't moved in yet?"

"Nope."

"Where will we sleep?"

He smirks. "Side by side in the cubby house out the back."

"Ha ha. Maybe you can build us a fire, too. Eh, Chief?"

"Smart ass," he grunts.

"You started it."

He snorts. "I've ordered some new stuff that will come in this afternoon."

"I'm sorry you have to do this for me."

He shrugs. "I was doin' all this anyway, *chante*. You're just makin' it more fun."

I know he's just saying that, and it makes me feel worse. My phone buzzes in my pocket and I pull it out, staring down at the screen.

"You'll need a new one of those. I've got one coming."

I frown, but don't answer. Instead I stare at the message. It's from Alec.

A – Hi beautiful, how are you?

I hesitate, just staring at the screen. He's good for me, he really is. I shouldn't push him away because I'm confused about Maddox. Right? I reply.

S – I'm okay. How are you?

A – I'll be good when I can see you again. When will that be?

S – It might not b for a few days, but hopefully soon.

A – Thursday night? Did you still want to talk to my sister about that job?

I sigh, knowing that's not going to happen right now. Damned biker life.

S – I can't, sorry. I'll explain in person. I have to get a new number, I'll call you tonight.

A – So I can't see you before then?

Wow, he's being kind of pushy.

S – Sorry, things are bad.

A – Right. I'll talk to u later then.

I sigh and go to shove the phone into my pocket, but stop and decide to text Maddox. It's probably not the best decision, but I feel bad about how he left.

S – I just wanted you 2 know I'm safe.

M – Wonderful.

Really? I can almost hear the sarcasm in that message. *Men*. I put the phone away. I don't want to respond when it'll only be nasty. Besides, Maddox hates texting, and he only does it when he's too lazy to make a phone call. He's clearly angry at me, which is fine. I'll leave it for now.

I sit in silence until Mack pulls up. I look over to him, and he's glancing around, double checking we're not being followed. Then he opens the garage and drives in. He shuts the car off and turns to me. "Stay here."

He gets out and I hear him shuffling about, a door slamming, and then a moment later he's back. "We're good, you can get out."

I shove the door open and leave the car, stretching my legs with a groan. We're in a dark garage, but I can see light through the open door at the front right of the room. I walk towards it after Mack, and we step straight into a really nice place. It's super gorgeous and modern.

It's got grey tiles and white walls. The kitchen is the first thing I see, and it's massive, with granite countertops and shiny white laminate. The rest of the apartment is all walls and floors, because it has no furniture. The living area seems to have loads of space, and then it narrows off to a hallway that holds all the bedrooms, bathrooms and a laundry. I walk down the halls, checking it all out.

"This is really nice," I say to Mack, staring around.

He nods. "Yeah, it'll do. You can have the room on the right."

He points to a closed door, and I rush over, opening it. The room is large, and it faces the backyard where no one can sneak in because there are blocks of apartments restricting access. Smart man. I can see quite well out of the large, double windows. I smile, and turn back to Mack. "Thank you, it's lovely."

He nods. "The furniture will be here soon, so until then we'll just wait."

I follow him out, checking out the new bathroom and laundry as we walk. We both stop in the empty kitchen and stare at each other. Well, this isn't awkward at all. I walk over to the window that faces the front yard, but Mack grunts at me to get away from it. With a sigh, I find a spot on the cool floor, and pull out my phone to read while I wait.

The furniture arrives two hours later, and I stand back while Mack lets them through, ordering them about. He's gotten some really nice stuff. There is everything from lounge chairs to full kitchen appliances. This must have cost him a lot. I begin pulling plastic off and unpacking appliances while Maddox sets the beds up in the rooms.

We work well into the night, until we finally have the lounge and dining room set up, the kitchen appliances and necessities out, and the bedrooms all ready to sleep in. I make us both some coffee after the groceries are delivered, while Mack showers. He comes out in only a pair of jeans, and I have to keep my eyes trained on the coffee cups to keep myself from looking.

Mack is a stunning man, in clothes and out. I wouldn't be a red-blooded woman if I didn't think that he was extremely gorgeous. I turn, keeping my eyes on his face, trying to avoid staring at his well-built body, with his smooth clean skin. I'm a fan of tattoos, but there's something so beautiful about Mack's bare, muscled body that's completely ink free.

"You hungry?" he asks, taking the cup out of my hand.

"Sure. Did you want me to make something?"

He shakes his head. "Nah, tonight we'll order in."

"I don't mind."

He grins. "I know. I've got it."

He dials for a pizza and we both flop down onto the couch with a sigh while we wait. It's a nice, leather couch. Super comfortable and squishy.

"This is a good couch," I say.

He snorts. "You uncomfortable bein' here?"

I sigh. "Yes."

"Don't be. It ain't forever, and I'll hardly ever be here. Don't be scared to make yourself at home."

I nod, sipping my coffee. "So, Chief, tell me what's been happening on all your travels as a nomad?"

He snorts. "Nothin' much. Same old shit that happens here. Club life, pussy and a whole lot of drinkin'."

I roll my eyes. "Any pussy worth talking about?"

I expect him to laugh, but his face hardens and he barks, "no," before standing and stalking into the kitchen.

Okay, then.

This will be fun.

CHAPTER ELEVEN

2008 – Santana

Kennedy strokes my hair, his fingers moving softly yet constantly. I close my eyes, pressing myself closer to him, needing his comfort. I'm high, so high my mind is spinning, but he's got me. He's always got me. I curl my fingers around his leg, and my face is pressed against his firm belly.

"Don't leave me, Tanie. I will never be the same without you."

"I won't leave you. I love you," I murmur, closing my eyes and letting the drug-induced haze take over my mind and body.

"And I love you. One day, when you're old enough, I'll show you how much."

"Will you make love to me, Kennedy?"

He chuckles softly. "Yes, sweetheart. And I'll make it amazing."

Hmmmm. I know he will. He loves me. He tells me every day. He looks after me and Pippa, keeping us safe when no one else will. I don't know what my life would be like without him. I let my eyes open and I stare up at him.

"Can you kiss me? I'm not too young for that."

His eyes flicker. "You want me to kiss you, Tanie?"

I nod eagerly, pushing myself up until our mouths are close. "Yes."

"If I kiss you, I may not be able to stop."

"I trust you, Kennedy," I say, tangling my fingers into his shirt and pulling him forward.

He kisses me, softly. His lips move over mine, but he doesn't press to slide his tongue into my mouth like I've seen in the movies. He just moves his lips over mine, sending little tingles throughout my body. I whimper, clinging to him, my mind spinning.

"That's enough, sweetheart," he says, his voice husky and low. "I won't stop."

He tucks me back against his chest and I close my eyes again, feeling content, feeling safe, and feeling loved.

"Are those men in the black going to come back and take you from me?" I ask as sleep creeps up to take over.

"No, I won't let anyone take you from me, Tanie. No one."

I hope he's right.

~*~*~*~

2014 – Santana

I'm curled up on the couch; Alec is sitting by my side. I've been at Mack's house now for three nights, and not once has Maddox come by. He's still angry at me, and he won't take my calls or answer my texts. I know he's checking in with Mack, but he's refusing to speak to me.

Alec called yesterday, asking if we could hang out. I asked Mack and he was fine with it; he was heading in to the club to see Maddox and said he wouldn't be here. Of course Rhyder, Zaid and the new prospect Austin are outside watching. I couldn't be left alone.

Alec brought movies and popcorn, so we've spent the last few hours watching them. I'm enjoying being tucked into Alec's arm, but for some, strange reason, being tucked into him like this brings back old memories of Kennedy. I don't think about Kennedy much these days, figuring he's probably dead.

83

He was the first man I loved, but I know it was for all the wrong reasons. He was light in a dark time; only he was somewhat of a mirage. He wasn't what I thought he was, but he still meant something to me. He took care of Pippa and I, always making sure we were safe.

At least until that horrible night that changed my life, and took my sister with it.

I shudder thinking about it, and tuck myself further into Alec's arms. He squeezes my shoulder, clearly having felt my trembling. "Are you okay?" he asks, shifting so he can stare down at me. I look up and smile. "Sure."

He leans down then, capturing my mouth in a soft, gentle kiss. His mouth isn't rough like Maddox's—instead it caresses mine as if I'm made of silk. Maddox took me like we were the last two people on earth, and he needed me to breathe. I shake thoughts of Maddox from my mind and kiss Alec back, equally as gentle, running my hands over his chest and squeezing.

That's when the front door swings open. I leap backwards, stumbling and falling off the couch. I look up to see Mack, Maddox, Krypt and Ash standing at the door, staring at me. Then their eyes all turn to Alec. My cheeks burn as I look over to Alec, who has a pillow pressed to his . . . oh my God. He's got a boner.

With a squeak, I get to my feet. Maddox is glaring at Alec so hard I'm surprised the man hasn't lit on fire and burned to the ground. Mack is smothering a laugh alongside Krypt, who is doing the same. Ash is grinning at me, clearly proud.

"I . . . ah . . ." I begin, but there's nothing to say. They came in and busted us right in the middle of a make-out session. It wasn't hot and heavy, sure, but it was a make-out session all the same.

I reach for Alec. "Let's go to my room."

"I don't fuckin' think so," Maddox growls.

God help me.

I turn to him, my face tight. "It's not up to you."

"It is up to me, considerin' I was in your bed only a week ago with my mouth on your—"

"Fuck you!" I bellow, charging towards him, and shoving at his chest. "How dare you!"

"Whoa," Ash says, pulling me back. "Let's calm this down. Poor Alec looks super angry."

I turn back to Alec, who is now standing and gathering his things. He gives me a look, and it burns right through me. "Alec . . ."

"It's fine," he grates out. "I'll call."

No he won't; not if I don't stop him.

"Please . . ."

He gives me a hard stare. "It's clear you've made a joke of me."

"No!" I cry. "That's not true."

Maddox snorts. Alec glares at him, and then walks out the front door. I go to chase after him, but all the bikers stand in front of the opening, not letting me through. Tears burn in my eyes and I turn to Maddox. "How could you do something like that to him?"

"I don't fuckin' care about him," Maddox barks.

"No," I say, letting the tears fall. "But you're supposed to care about me."

I turn and rush off down the hall, slipping into my room. I try to ring Alec, but he doesn't answer. I can't let him go thinking that I was using him. I wasn't; I like him a lot. I don't want to stop dating him, because I know we could be good together. He could be what gets me out of here. He could be *real* for me.

After tonight, it's clear Maddox and I will never change.

I stuff my phone in my pocket and stare out my window. I've climbed out of Maddox's window many times, but this one is different. I stare at the apartments across from us. There would be a way out, but it certainly won't be easy. It's worth the risk. I shove the window up, staring down.

It's only a one-story home, so it's not far to go. I throw my leg over the side and slip out unnoticed. I run through the backyard, not looking back at the lights coming from the house. I find a large fence, blocking our house from the apartments next door. I could get over it, not easily…but I could. After five failed attempts, one harsh drop to my ass and a sore wrist, I get over. I rush out to the street.

I stop a cab and slip in.

"Where to, miss?"

I give him Alec's address and sit back in the seat, fumbling around with my fingers as I nervously pray I haven't been followed. Halfway there, my phone rings. I glance down to see Maddox's number. He's figured out I've gone. My heart hammers.

Another moment later, it rings again. Ash this time. This goes on until I've got more than eight missed calls. Finally, a text message flicks through. I stare at the words and my heart clenches. I know Maddox will be filled with rage over this, but I had to do it. He was cruel to Alec, and Alec didn't deserve that.

M – Get the fuck back here, right now. So help me God, Santana, if you don't do as I'm tellin' you, you'll regret it.

Anger swells inside my chest and I angrily type out my response.

S – Here's something for you. Go fuck yourself.

I turn the phone off before he can reply. I stare out the window in silence as we drive, and when we arrive at Alec's I pay the driver before slipping out. I stand in the front yard, checking to see if I've been followed before walking up to the front door. Hesitantly, I knock.

Alec answers nearly immediately, and when he sees me, his eyes widen and then harden. "Why are you here?"

"Can I come in, please?" I whisper. "Please, Alec."

With a grunt, he shoves the door open and lets me in. His house is huge, and perfectly arranged. It has polished wooden floors, stark white walls and expensive furniture. He points to the couch and I sit down, staring over at him when he sits over from me.

"What Maddox said . . ."

"Was he lying?"

I bite my bottom lip, shaking my head. "No, but you need to understand something about Maddox and I . . . We . . . we have a bond. He saved my life. What he did back there was wrong, and I'm so sorry I hurt you. I don't want to do that."

"I don't have time for games, Santana."

I jerk my head up. "I'd never do that."

"Do you love him?"

I hesitate, and it scares the shit out of me. I shake my head quickly, hoping he didn't notice my pause. "No, but I do care about him. I kissed him, yes, I won't lie. It meant nothing."

God, I'm lying. I can feel it with everything I am. But I care about Alec; I have to give this a chance. I have to. Maddox and I can never be.

"How do I know that's the truth?"

I look at him. "I care about you, Alec, and I want to get to know you better. That's the truth."

"Prove it."

"P-p-prove it?" I whisper.

"You push me away every time we get to more than a kiss. You tell me he means nothing, so prove it."

I want to show him I want to try. I *need* to try, for my sake and Maddox's. We can't keep hanging onto this nonsense and treating each other the way we do. He needs to move on and so do I, because there is no future for us. There never has been.

I lean forward and press my lips to Alec's mouth, knowing what to do, knowing what I want. It's time. He kisses me back, moving his mouth over mine. His hands slide up and down my back, almost soothingly. I kiss him harder, closing my eyes, shoving everything else from my mind.

Just here and now, Santana. Here and now.

Alec groans throatily when my fingers slide up his shirt, feeling his firm muscle. He doesn't even hesitate. His hands move over my body, fondling my breasts and clutching my ass. It's slightly rough, but I'm trying to go along with it. I've never done this before; I don't know how it's meant to feel. I'm letting him take the lead.

He makes light work of my clothes and lays me down over the couch. He throws his shirt off until he's in only his jeans. He looks good, really well-built and handsome. I smile up at him, and he strokes a thumb over my chin before leaning down and kissing me again.

His fingers trail down between my legs and I flinch upon first contact. I whimper as he slides his finger over my clit, stroking it softly. It feels nice, really good. He slips down further, pushing a finger inside my depths. My mouth opens and a ragged cry comes out, because God, it burns.

He doesn't notice. His mouth is now on my breasts, and his fingers are sliding in and out of my unprepared body. Oh God. Oh God, it hurts so badly. I didn't expect the first time to be pleasurable, but I didn't expect it to hurt so bad, either. I close my eyes, trying to relax my body, trying to feel his mouth on me.

He finally pulls his fingers away and pushes back, reaching into his jeans to pull out a condom. This bothers me, because I don't understand why he would have it in there to begin with. Did Alec plan on taking this tonight? I swallow it down, knowing I'm over-reacting. I need to be calm, I need to enjoy this.

Stop thinking, start feeling.

I watch as Alec rolls the condom over his cock. I've never seen a man like this, and finally laying my eyes on what makes them male has my cheeks growing pink. It's sexy, in its own special way. Alec strokes his hand over it as he leans over me with a sultry look.

"Are you ready?" he murmurs.

"Yes."

I close my eyes when his mouth finds my neck, and he presses his length to my entrance. I bite my bottom lip; waiting for him to just ease in and . . . he shoves in without hesitation. A burning fire courses through my body, causing a strangled cry to leave my lips. He doesn't even notice—he just grunts out a few words about how good it feels, and begins thrusting.

Tears roll down my cheeks as pain rips through my body. Oh God, it hurts, it hurts so bad. I whimper, but he doesn't even realize it's out of pain. He keeps his head in my shoulder as he thrusts, hard and fast. My sex is dry, and it feels like someone has put a piece of sandpaper inside me.

"God, you feel so fucking good," he groans. "So tight."

Make it stop, please.

It'll get better. It will. They all say it will. It's just the first time. That's all.

I tell myself this over and over as tears stream down my face, but when the burning gets too intense, I know I can't take it any longer. I shove at his chest, rapidly, over and over. "Stop," I croak. "Alec, stop. It hurts."

"I can't," he grinds out. "I'm so close."

"Please," I whimper. "Stop."

He thrusts quicker. "Nearly . . . there . . . oh God."

"Stop!" I wail, shoving harder. "I said stop, stop, stop!"

"Oh fuck," he bellows, and I can feel every pulse as he releases into the condom.

I hiccup angrily, hurt and used. He pulls out of me and stares down, a lazy smirk on his face. He notices my tears and narrows his eyes. "Why are you crying?"

"Why?" I screech, shoving his chest.

He moves off me quickly, and watches as I pull on my clothes. I hiccup, stumble and sob, horrified that I gave something I protected for so long to an asshole who was more concerned about getting his rocks off.

"So this is how it feels." I laugh bitterly. "This is what it's like to be played."

He stares at me. "You asked for that. Don't turn around and act like it's on me now."

Seriously?

"I thought you were a good guy," I sob. "When a girl asks you to stop, you fucking *stop.*"

He shakes his head. "I should have known you were one of them, one of those girls that tease and then cry when it happens."

I gape at him. "Excuse me?"

"You wanted that, Santana. And if you didn't want it, why come here? Don't you blame this on me. You've been playing around like a two-dollar hooker with both Maddox and me . . ."

I shake my head, turning sharply, and fetching my purse and phone. My sex aches and burns as I move, and my tears well and fall even heavier with each step towards the door.

"Where are you going?" he yells behind me.

"I'm calling Maddox and . . ."

"Hell no," he barks, charging towards me. Fear courses through my veins as I take two steps back. "You're not callin' him making up stories about what I did . . . I did fucking nothing."

My hands tremble as I turn, shoving his front door open. He curses, but has to pull his clothes on before he can follow me. It gives me a minute, if I'm lucky. I dial Maddox quickly.

"Where the fuck are—"

"Maddox," I croak, my voice weak.

"What's happened?" he barks.

"I . . . I need you to come and get me, please."

He must hear something in my voice, because his softens. "Where are you? Are you hurt?"

"Don't call that bastard!" Alec barks. "Don't you lie to him, Santana."

"What the fuck is goin' on?" Maddox demands.

"Please," I croak. "Come and get me."

I rattle off the address and hang up. I turn to Alec, who has just reached the door. "Don't come near me," I warn, my voice weak. "You touch me, you're dead."

"I knew it." He laughs bitterly. "I knew you were just looking for a good time, using me and playing with my head."

"Me?" I snap. "You had a condom in your pocket when you came over with your fake 'let's watch movies' bullshit tonight. You just wanted to fuck me; you're the true definition of a player, Alec, and here I was thinking you were a nice guy."

He snorts. "I am a nice guy, when the girl isn't a cheap whore. You dare tell Maddox I hurt you, there'll be problems."

"What are you going to do?" I laugh hoarsely. "Huh?"

He steps into the house, slamming the door in my face. I turn and go to sit down, but the moment I do, pain shoots up through my body. I stand again, my eyes filling with more hopeless tears. The rumble of a Harley Davidson fills my ears only twenty minutes later. Thank God Maddox is alone.

He stops the bike and gets off, striding towards me with a ferocity that's frightening. His black hair swishes around his face, and his blue eyes are fierce. He stops in front of me, his fists clenched. His eyes rake over me, stopping on my tousled hair.

"Where the fuck is that dirty, stinkin' cunt. I'll fuckin'—"

"It's not like that," I croak. "He didn't . . . I . . ."

He flicks his eyes to me, and grates out, "Tell. Me. What. Happened?"

I swallow. "I . . . We . . . were . . ." I drop my head.

Maddox takes my chin, forcing me to look at him. "Now, Santana."

"I slept with him!" I screech. "I told him to stop, and . . ."

Maddox has let me go before I've even finished my sentence. He goes to the door and he pounds on it, roaring Alec's name. Alec doesn't answer. I stare in horror as Maddox turns and charges towards the window, lifting his boot and kicking it so hard it shatters. Glass bursts out and goes everywhere.

"Maddox!" I scream.

He kicks the remaining glass in, and then he's gone. I hear the roaring sound of his voice in the house, and then the clear sounds of fists hitting skin, and bones crunching. Alec's pained bellows trail out the broken window. I rush towards the front door, shaking and rattling it. "Maddox!"

It swings open and he steps out, holding a bleeding, battered Alec by the back of the shirt. "You fuckin' apologize," he roars.

"I'm sorry, Santana," Alec croaks, blood dribbling from his mouth.

Maddox turns and throws Alec into the house. "You ever fuckin' come near her again, I'll blow your fuckin' brains right out your skull."

I press my hand to my mouth. In a matter of minutes, Maddox pummeled Alec to that bloody, pathetic mess lying on the ground.

Spinning, Maddox takes my arm and drags me down the footpath. He's bleeding, his knuckles and his face. There doesn't seem to be any deep lacerations. He's cut himself on the glass. He doesn't say another word to me; he just throws me on the back of the bike and gets on himself.

Then we're gone, into the darkness.

I let the tears go freely now; there's no point holding back.

CHAPTER TWELVE

2014 – Santana

The minute we arrive back at Mack's, Maddox gets off the bike and storms inside. He doesn't stop; he doesn't even check if anyone is around. I follow quickly, keeping my head down, ashamed of myself. When we step inside, Mack looks up and his eyes widen. "What the fuck happened?"

Maddox says nothing, he just disappears down the hall. I watch him go, and swing my eyes to Mack. He gives me a *well?* expression and I begin to sob again.

"Hey," he growls, standing. "Pull your shit together, stop that fuckin' crying, and tell me what went down."

I suck in my crying and nod, swiping my tears. "I went to Alec's and . . . I . . . we . . . had sex. I said stop, and he didn't . . ."

"Fuck."

"Maddox beat the shit out of him, Mack. He is lucky he didn't kill him."

Mack runs his hands through his hair, his jaw tight. "Had about enough of this shit."

I shake my head, confused.

Cold brown eyes turn to me. "You care about him, Santana?"

I nod.

"Then get your selfish ass in there and fuckin' make him see that. Grow the fuck up."

He turns and storms off, not giving me a chance to respond. My pride is wounded, but his words are true. I'm a selfish cow. I've been dancing around this for so long. I've been a horrible, crazy brat, and I could have gotten myself killed.

I turn on shaky legs and I walk down the hall. I see the bathroom door slightly opened, so I push it open and step in. Maddox is leaning over the sink, his head dropped, blood running down the sides of the sink. My heart breaks. What sort of girl am I? What have I done?

I take a step forward. My hands tremble as I near the shaking man leaning over the sink. He's shaking with rage—I know he is. I've upset him, hurt him, used him, and thrown it all in his face. I stop beside the sink, reaching out and placing my fingers on his hand. He flinches, but he doesn't look up.

"Get out," he rasps.

"No," I say, my voice not coming out as strong as I'd like.

He jerks his head up, and his eyes burn into mine. His jaw flexes as he grinds his teeth.

"I have had enough of your fuckin' bullshit for one fuckin'—"

"I know," I croak.

His eyes flicker over my face quickly.

"You know fuckin' nothin', Santana. Nothin'."

"I know you care about me, I know I've been a horrible little brat, and I know I've hurt you."

He glares at me. "You. Know. Nothin'."

"Then tell me!" I cry. "You dance around this as much as I do. We've both been playing games for more than a year now, Maddox. I'm done; I'm fucking done."

"You wanna play with the truth?" he bellows, swiping all the items off the sink. They crash onto the floor. "Then tell me why the fuck you ran off when you found out I got my cock sucked by Ash?"

His words cause me to jerk back. I stare at him, letting the hurt show on my face.

"I don't know why I ran," I say.

"Get out."

"It's the truth!" I cry. "I don't know what snapped."

"If you would open your fuckin' eyes instead of lookin' at me like I'm the worst fuckin' thing you could have in your life, you would see what's right in front of you. Now get the fuck out!"

He roars this so loudly, I flinch.

I turn and rush out of the bathroom, my chest aching like it's never ached before. I stumble into my room, and God, it hurts. It hurts so badly. I thought Alec was what I wanted—I thought he could give me the life I so desperately sought, only to find out he was fake. The only real thing in my world is Maddox, and yet I've fought so hard against him.

I always thought I knew, deep down inside, that this life wasn't for me.

Maybe I was wrong.

I don't know anything anymore.

~*~*~*~

I'm curled up on the floor of the shower, sobbing so loudly my entire body aches. My sex burns, and there was a lot of blood in my panties when I stripped to get in. I've been sitting down here for twenty minutes now, letting emotion and rage burn inside my belly.

97

I'm angry at myself.

I'm angry at Alec.

I'm angry at Maddox.

Everything is just a jumbled mess of emotions, and my heart hurts every time I think about what Maddox said to me. I slowly shove to my feet. I've already heard his bike disappear, and the very sound made my heart shatter into a thousand pieces.

I step out of the shower, pulling a towel around myself. I dry quickly, and lift a brush, dragging it through my hair, and then I slip into a nightie. I walk over to my bed, throwing the covers back and sliding in. More tears make an appearance as I stuff my face into the pillow, feeling like a fool. I hurt Maddox, he hurt me, and together we've made a royal mess of things.

The door creaks but I don't bother to turn. The bed sinks beside me and the covers are flicked back. I already know it's Mack; I know because he used to do this when I had nightmares. If Maddox wasn't around, Mack was my rock. A strong body wraps around mine, and he pulls me into his arms.

"I was a cunt," he murmurs. "Sorry, *chante*."

I shake my head. "You weren't. It was my fault you were put in this situation."

"He's hurtin'."

"I know," I croak.

"And so are you."

I don't answer.

"You okay?"

I swallow, and my eyes burn from all the crying I've done in the last few hours.

"He hurt me, Mack," I whimper.

"Maddox?"

"No. Alec."

He strokes a hand over my hair. Not many people see Mack like this. He's usually hard and broody.

"I was a virgin," I whisper. "And he was so rough."

"Fuck," Mack grunts. "That fuckin' piece of shit."

"Will you stay with me?"

"Yeah," he murmurs, pulling me closer.

We lay like that until sleep takes both of us, and in that moment I'm so grateful to Mack for being my friend.

God knows I need him.

CHAPTER THIRTEEN

2008 – Santana

Kennedy strokes his hands over my hair as the warm rush floods my body. He makes a soothing sound, filling my veins with his disease. That's what these drugs are like, a disease that sinks into your soul. He is preparing me. He told me I have to do something very special for him tonight.

I couldn't go without the drugs. I needed them.

Kennedy gave them to me, but not enough. By the time he lets me go and I'm on my feet, I already know I need more. He refuses, telling me I need to focus. "There is going to be a man that will meet you. All you have to do is give him this package, and then leave. Can you do that?"

I moan, but nod.

Kennedy hands me the package, and goes over and over what I have to do as he drives me to the location where I'm supposed to give it over. He drops me off five blocks away. "Go and wait. I'll be at home with Pippa, keeping her safe. You trust me, don't you, Tanie?"

"Will you take care of her? Promise me she'll be safe," I slur.

He nods. "I promise."

I nod, shoving myself out of the car.

"Tanie?"

I turn to him, staring through blurred vision. "You know I love you?"

I nod again.

He smiles and drives off. It's the last time I see Kennedy.

~*~*~*~

I shouldn't have opened the package, but I'm desperate. I need a hit, and I already know what's in here. One pill, one pill is all I'll take.

I take one, then another, then another. It's not working. Why isn't it working? My mind is already spinning, so I don't notice it progress to the next stage. Suddenly, I've gone from feeling it mildly to wishing I'd never taken them in the first place.

I drop to my knees, clutching the package to my chest, my head spinning. Vomit rises in my throat, and I struggle to keep it down. My entire body feels as if it's going to explode. God, what is this stuff? I gasp, trying to breathe as vomit blocks my throat. I fall flat on my back, still clutching the package. Oh God. Oh God. I'm going to die right here, and Pippa will be left alone.

Pippi . . .

I jump in and out of consciousness, vaguely hearing the sounds of cars on the street, the sounds of bars and the music blaring from them, and then the sound of a chuckling male voice. I try to roll further into the alley, but I can't move my body. Everything is heavy. Everything hurts.

"Fuck."

Warm hands press against my cheeks. I want to open my eyes, but I can't. They won't work.

"Hey, wake up."

I can't wake up. Vomit rises higher and higher, until I feel it choking me. Gasps and splutters leave my throat, but it's not enough. I'm going to die.

"Hang on, I'm goin' to get you help."

That's when it all goes black.

CHAPTER FOURTEEN

2014 – Santana

"Take me to the club," I say three days later to Mack as he prepares to leave.

He turns to me. "Why?"

"It's been three days. He's not spoken to me, and he's not going to unless I go in there and fix this."

"There ain't nothing you can do, short of tellin' him you love him, that can fix this."

I shake my head. "You're wrong."

"I'll take you, but listen to me, Santana," he says, stepping closer. "Don't go in there and make this worse. You wanna be with Maddox, then fuckin' be with him. You don't, leave him be, and make it clear you're not interested. Quit playin'."

I nod. "I swear."

"Fine, then get in the car."

We get into the SUV in the garage, and I drop down as Mack drives towards the compound. We arrive in good time, with no issues. It's just on dark, and the club is in full swing. I get out of the car and walk with Mack inside. I see the guys, and they all give me a grin and a wave as I walk past.

I head straight towards Maddox's office.

I've had a lot of time to think about this, considering it's been three days and he's not said a word. He's right, Mack's right, and I'm an idiot. Maddox does care about me, and if I'm not lying to myself, I care about him. Can it work? I truly don't know. Do I want it to? I don't know that either. All I know is I hurt him, and he deserves me to apologize for that.

I open his office door when I reach it, only to see Krypt and Ash . . . Jesus. I squeal and spin around, pressing a hand to my eyes. "Oh my God, Krypt, I think I just saw your . . . *thingy* . . ."

Krypt laughs, and Ash cries out in shame.

"Lucky girl." He chuckles. "And it ain't a thingy, honey, it's a co—"

"Krypt!" Ash cuts him off with an embarrassed scoff.

"Where's Maddox?" I ask, still covering my eyes.

"Out."

"Okay, carry on."

I step out, closing the door. My God. I'll never un-see that. I walk back down the halls, disappointed. Maddox isn't even here. I go back out and sit at the bar, getting a drink. Austin, the new prospect, comes over and joins me. He's only young, maybe twenty-six, and has messy blond hair and gorgeous brown eyes.

"How you doin', Santana?" he asks.

I shrug. "Not too bad, how are you?"

"Aside from being a biker slave, pretty good."

I laugh. "The life of a prospect, huh?"

He snorts. "Yeah. How's your leg?"

"It's fine." I smile. "All healed."

"Gettin' shot sucks."

I laugh. "Yeah, that's one way of puttin' it."

We chat for more than an hour. Austin tells me about his life, and where he came from. I tell him about mine. We get along quite well. Maddox comes in when I'm on my third drink, and his eyes shoot straight to me. "What the fuck is she doin' here?"

Still mad, I see.

I go to say something, but he storms off. With a sigh, I get up and walk down the hall after him. He's gone into his office, and I hesitate outside the door for a few minutes before going in. He's sitting on the couch, head dropped, a glass of something amber in his hand. He looks up when I walk in, and his eyes are furious.

"Why the fuck are you here?"

"To talk to you," I say, closing the door behind me.

"Nothin' to talk about. Get out."

"Jesus, Maddox, can you stop?"

"Stop," he snorts. "That all you've got to say? Are you goin' to sit here and blame this shit on me, too?"

I shake my head, leaning against the door. "You never told me how you felt."

He glares at me. "And you didn't stop to fuckin' see it."

"I'm not a mind reader," I whisper.

"Doesn't fuckin' matter; it's done with. Now leave. I got pussy waitin'."

"No," I bark. "Don't you push me away!"

"Why?" he roars. "You're fuckin' doin' it to me."

"I'm not pushing you away," I cry. "I didn't know. I . . . I fucked up, Maddox. I fucked up, because I'm scared. I care about you . . . I do . . ."

"Words," he snarls. "They mean fuck all to me. You've done nothin' but make it clear pretty boys are what you want, not some fuckin' biker."

I take a shaky step forward and his eyes widen. "Then I'll show you that you're wrong."

He watches me with that dark, angry expression as I walk towards him. I stop in front of him, and then I slowly climb onto his lap. My heart is pounding—he could throw me off at any second.

Just being settled over Maddox's big body is doing things to me, strange things. I've never felt anything like it in my life. He stares at me, not moving, not even attempting to.

"I made a mistake," I whisper, placing my hands on his chest. "I fucked up, Maddox. The truth is, I was hurt when you were with Ash because I care about you. It confused me, my feelings confused me, and they still do, but I won't deny that it hurt because you matter to me more than I first thought. What I did with Alec . . . it was wrong . . . and I paid for it. He took something from me I can't get back, and the sad thing is I gave it to him. He made it hurt, but I know with you . . . it won't. Show me, Maddox. Show me what we both can't say."

His eyes flash, and the ice in his glass rattles as he reaches out and places it on the small table beside the couch. "There ain't no takin' this back. Once I'm inside you, that's it."

"Show me," I whisper. "Make him go away, make it . . . make it *you* . . ."

"You were a virgin."

It's a statement, not a question.

I nod.

"He hurt you?"

I nod again.

"How bad?"

I open my mouth, and my cheeks go pink.

"How bad, baby?" he demands.

"I . . . it hurt . . . it hurt a lot. There was blood, and—"

"Fuck," he cuts me off. "Can't fuck you, honey. Not when you've been hurt."

I shake my head. "But . . . Maddox . . . we've both wanted this. I want this. With you. I want you to make it feel how it's supposed to."

He takes my hand, pressing it down between us and over his . . . holy shit . . . extremely large cock. "You feel that, honey?" he growls. "Ain't no way that won't hurt."

I lean forward, pressing my forehead to his. "Today, tomorrow, or a month away. We can't change that. I made a mistake with Alec, but I want you, Maddox. I. Want. You."

He pulls back, his eyes hard. "And I'll fuck you, just not here. Not tonight. Not when you're still raw."

I open my mouth to protest, but he cuts me off.

"I don't need to fuck you, to make you scream."

Oh, boy.

I meet his gaze and he gives me a sexy lip quirk that makes me want to lean forward and devour his handsome face.

"Well then," I breathe. "Take it away."

His eyes slide over my body, slowly, and when they meet mine again, they're filled with heat. "Slowly. He fucked up by hurtin' you, sweetheart. I'm goin' to show you just how beautiful this can be."

"O-o-okay," I whisper.

He lifts a hand, running the backs of his fingers down my cheek, so softly and gently it takes me by surprise. He brings his face closer, puffs of breath warming my cheeks. I close my eyes; just taking him in, letting him show me everything he's wanted to show me for so long. His fingers continue to stroke down my face, going down my neck and over my shoulder.

Then he replaces his fingers with his lips, and my entire body comes alive. He scatters the softest, sweetest little kisses over my cheeks and face, gently grazing my lips before moving down to my neck. Tiny prickles of pleasure break out over my skin and warmth shoots through me at the feeling of his lips tickling my neck. It feels amazing, and so damned real.

"Your skin smells like honey," he purrs against my throat, little vibrations travelling through me.

I laugh softly. "It's the soap I wash with."

"Mmmmm," he growls. "Keep washin' with it."

His hands move, sliding up my sides. His fingers tickle over my body, warming a path as they go. Then he glides them over my dress, stroking me, caressing the soft swell of my breasts through the fabric. A whimper escapes and his mouth captures mine, giving me a kiss so mind consuming it takes my breath away. It's so gentle, so perfect…exactly how it *should* be.

I just didn't know I could get what I desperately needed from a biker.

He's being so slow with me, so sweet. His mouth peppers little kisses across my face and neck, his fingers create light touches up my side and over my breasts. My skin is alive, my body is thrumming and it feels amazing. I close my eyes and take it all in, letting him explore my body, letting him bring me alive in a way Alec refused. He's replacing all the bad Alec put on my body, and replacing it with something beautiful, something *Maddox*.

"It's takin' everything for me to hold back," he murmurs against my neck. "You're so damned gorgeous, Santana."

I shudder and he groans.

"That's how it should feel, baby," he growls. "When a man makes you feel something fuckin' beautiful."

"You make it feel," I struggle for breath. "Amazing. I need *more*, Maddox. I need you, now."

He brings his mouth forward and captures my lips in his. Like the first time, the kiss is God damned scorching. His tongue moves past my lips and causes mine to go weak, like it's having it's own wobbly leg moment. His rubble is scratchy against my cheek in the best possible way.

"Fuck," he growls, pulling back. "Never has kissin' anyone felt so damned good."

I stare at him, just taking him in. He's so beautiful. I reach up, stroking my fingers over his rugged face. His eyes search mine, for answers, for hope, I don't know . . . but it feels good. This moment feels exactly how it's meant to. I slide my hands from his face, down his neck and stop when they're flat on his chest.

"What's next?" I breathe.

He lifts me off his lap in one, swift movement, dropping me onto the couch beside him. He turns, shrugging his leather jacket off and tossing it. Then he leans over to me. I put a hand up to stop him. "The shirt," I breathe. "Take it off."

With a grin, he lifts the hem of his shirt and discards it quickly. I take a moment to stare at the pure perfection that is Maddox. Ripped abs, tattoos over tight, smooth skin, and ropes of muscle up his long arms leading to thick, God damned edible shoulders and pecks. He's mouth watering.

I lean forward, pressing my mouth to his skin, letting my tongue slide out to taste him. He growls, throaty and deep, pushing me back. "Who's leadin' this party?"

I smile wryly, leaning away. He reaches for me, taking hold of my dress and pulling it up and over my head until I'm in nothing but a G-string and a bra. A low, guttural moan leaves his lips as he studies me. "You're so fuckin' perfect."

I bite my lip as he takes me into his arms, reaching around to unclip my bra. He drops it off and leans back again, staring at my small, but full breasts. His jaw is tight as his eyes graze over my skin, then he leans down, his hand sliding around my back to pull me closer as his mouth captures my nipple.

"Oh God," I whisper as sensations I've never experienced course through my body.

His tongue swirls the tip of my nipple, causing tiny bolts of pleasure to shoot through me and right down to my sex. I whimper, clutching his arms as he devours one nipple, then the other. His other hand slides down to my panties, taking hold of them and ripping them off in one, quick movement.

Oh, my.

His fingers travel over my pubic bone, and he slips a finger into my damp flesh. I cry out as his thick finger finds my clit, gently stroking it. I squirm in his arms, incoherent babbling coming from my lips as he sucks my nipples and makes my entire body come alive in ways I've never felt or imagined.

"M-M-M-Maddox," I cry out.

"Did he make you come?" he growls.

"No," I gasp.

"Good. I'm goin' to."

He massages my clit softly until little bolts of lightning shoot through my body, erupting like tiny firecrackers. I scream out his name as the most intense, incredible pleasure takes over. I tremble against his body as he shifts me, laying me down onto the couch. Before I've even finished shaking, he's between my legs, lifting my hips and pressing his mouth to my pussy.

Oh, fuck.

"Maddox," I plead as he breathes over my clit, not licking it, just teasing until it hurts.

"You smell so fuckin' good, so fuckin' . . . good," his voice is strained, like holding back is the hardest, most painful thing he's ever done.

"Please," I beg.

"Mmmmm," he hums against my flesh, and it radiates right to my very core.

Then his tongue dives into my flesh and a scream is ripped from my throat. Oh, nothing has ever felt so amazing. Yes. I arch up as he devours me, his tongue flicking, his lips sucking. He tilts his head to the side, running his tongue up my lips before diving back in, capturing my clit in his teeth and rolling it around.

I come again, shamelessly quick. He pulls back, staring down at me, his mouth glistening with my arousal. God, that's hot. His jeans are straining with his cock that so desperately wants to be set free. I want to see it like I've never wanted to see anything in my life.

"I want . . . I want to see it, Maddox," I whisper.

"See what, honey?"

"Your . . ."

"Say it," he growls.

"Your cock."

He moans, throaty and deep. God, he's beautiful. He takes the top button of his jeans and flicks them open. He reaches in and pulls out his cock, his big hand wrapped around it. Holy shit, seeing him holding himself like that is scarily hot. I want to keep watching. I want to see what happens when he comes.

"Oh . . . God," I say, my voice low.

He's huge. Long and thick, an impressive length. His fist is tight around himself, as if he's straining to hold back.

"Will you . . ." I swallow, my cheeks burning. "Will you . . ."

"You want me to stroke it?"

I bite my lip, nodding.

"You want to watch me come, baby?"

"Oh, yes."

He gives me a sexy half-grin, and he begins stroking. His hand moves up and down, revealing the thick head of his cock. It's an angry red—God, it looks like it actually hurts. His hand moves lazily at first, just sliding up and down. His balls are tucked up, only a small flash of them showing every now and then.

"Harder," I breathe.

His eyes widen, but he complies. His hand moves faster, working up and down. God, that's amazing. I sit up, leaning forward, wanting to feel it, to touch it, to see how soft that skin is in my hand. I reach out, tracing my thumb over the thick tip, lifting a drop of pre-cum off and pressing it to my lips. Slightly salty, but all Maddox. I groan.

He hisses.

"Fuck," he growls. "That was hot."

I reach out, offering my hand to him. He stops stroking long enough to take it and wrap it around his cock. He's so hot there, warming my palm as he closes his hand over mine, and begins stroking our joined hands up and down. He's hard, and I can feel the veins pulsing beneath my fingers.

"Fuck, fuck," he pants.

He moves our hands faster, and his cock swells. Then a thick white liquid bursts from the tip, hitting my chin. I stare in shock and fascination as strand after strand shoots out, spilling over me. Maddox groans, low and deep, and it's the best fucking thing I've ever seen in my life.

He softens in my hand, and he lets me go. He stares at me like I'm the most beautiful thing he's ever seen. He reaches up and swipes his release off my chin, and then he brings it to my mouth. I know what he wants from me, but do I have it in me to be that girl? That dirty, erotic girl? I meet his eyes.

"Taste me, honey," he murmurs. "Let me see your mouth around my finger."

That does it for me.

I lean forward and open my lips. He slides his finger into my mouth, and the taste of him swirls over my tongue. I suck him off, taking him, letting him inside me in a way he's never been before. His breathing deepens and a throaty groan escapes his parted lips. He slips his finger from me, curls his hand around the back of my head, and jerks me forward, devouring me with his mouth.

Oh. My. God.

His tongue and my tongue share his taste, swirling it around our mouths. Our groans mingle and I whimper, clutching Maddox's shirt and pressing myself against him.

Then a knock sounds out.

We pull apart, lips puffy, breathing ragged.

"What?" Maddox barks.

"Need a word, bro," Mack calls out. "Now."

His tone sounds quite urgent. Maddox turns to me. "Sorry, honey."

I've already got my panties and bra on. I take my dress and pull it over my head, while saying, "It's okay."

"Hey," Maddox says, doing up his jeans. "Look at me."

I look up at him.

"That was fuckin' perfect. Don't you walk outta here regrettin' it. You hear me?"

I nod.

He steps forward and kisses me, hard and quick.

Then he's gone.

~*~*~*~

MADDOX

"What's so fuckin' important you'd pull me from bein' with that girl?"

Mack turns to me, his face stony. "Got a response from Kennedy."

I tense. I sent word that I wanted to see him, but of course he didn't want a bar of it. Probably thinkin' I was a drug lord comin' to threaten him.

"And?" I prompt.

"He will see you."

I grin. "Fuckin' ripper."

"But he wants Santana there, too."

My blood goes cold. "How the fuck does he know about Santana bein' with me?"

"Prisoners talk. Wouldn't be hard for him to find out who you are. Especially with some of the Tinmen behind bars."

"Fuck," I bark. "No fuckin' way."

"Way," Mack grunts. "And he's threatenin' to get word to her himself if you don't bring her."

"That piece of shit," I snarl, crossing my arms.

"You know what this means, don't you?"

"It means you're goin' to have to tell her," Krypt says, coming into the room.

114

"Fuck off, Krypt. Don't start pushin' me. I just fuckin' got her, and you're both askin' me to break her heart."

"You can't keep dancin' around this," Krypt growls. "She deserves to know."

"And I'll tell her," I snarl. "When I know where her fuckin' sister is."

"Kennedy is the only man who can tell you that, and to tell you, he wants to see Santana."

"Not happenin'," I snap.

"You ain't got a choice," Mack said. "You don't take her, he'll find a way to get word to her. She don't deserve to hear this from him, Maddox."

I run my hands through my hair, growling and sighing. "I need time, give me a few weeks. Get word back to him, tell him I'll bring her in a few weeks, that right now she ain't safe. Might hold him off."

"You're a selfish cunt, Maddox," Krypt barks.

I turn to him, shooting daggers in his direction. "What did you just fuckin' say?"

"You heard me," he says, getting up in my face. "You're a selfish motherfucker. That girl cares about you, you care about her, and you're lettin' her fuckin' get close to you when you know, you fuckin' *know* it's goin' to break her."

"Ain't none of your business," I hiss.

"If you cared about her at all, you'd fuckin' stop until she knows. Not only are you goin' to break her heart when she finds out about her sister, but you're goin' to crush her too, because she'll have fallen for you. Walk the fuck away until this shit has been sorted, you selfish fuck."

He's right. He's fuckin' right. What the fuck am I doing? I'm letting her fall for me, which in turn is only going to break her heart further when she knows what I've done. I run my hands through my hair, and a feral hiss leaves my lips.

"Fuck," I bark. "Motherfucker."

"Ain't sayin' you can't care about her, boss," Krypt says, his voice like ice. "But you need to tell her before she falls for you."

"I'll fuckin' lose her," I snarl. "And she's all I've got."

Krypt shrugs. "You have to live with what you've done. Ain't no one goin' to take that shit for you."

Fuck.

Fuck.

Fuck.

CHAPTER FIFTEEN

2008 – Santana

"Did you get rid of that shit?"

A voice. Barked. Rough.

My head pounds and I roll to my side, blinking rapidly. Where am I? What happened? I see nothing but darkness, even though my eyes are open. I blink again, and a blinding pain radiates through my head. I whimper loudly. God, what happened?

"She's waking."

A hazy form appears in front of me, I can't make him out. He's big, though, his presence strong and dominating.

"Can you hear me?"

I blink again and my vision begins to clear. There's a big man in front of me, his long hair falling down over his shoulders. He's got blue eyes, really, really blue. He's handsome, incredibly handsome, with a big strong jaw, full lips, and olive skin. He reaches up and pushes the hair out of my eyes that I didn't even know was there.

"W-w-w-where am I?" I croak.

"What's your name, honey?"

I stare at him, a little confused. "I . . . it's Santana."

"Santana," he says, testing it on his tongue. "My name is Maddox. I found you convulsing in an alley three days ago. You were high as a kite, nearly dead. Do you know what happened?"

An alley?

My foggy brain tries to piece together what happened. When it does, I bolt upright, crying out in pain as my head pounds. I'm attached to a makeshift drip, which worries me. Why aren't I in a hospital?

"Where's Pippa? Where is she?" I cry.

The man, Maddox, shakes his head. "I don't know who that is. You were alone until those men showed up and . . ."

"Kennedy?" I cry. "Did he come?"

He shakes his head. "No one named Kennedy, but whoever those fuckers were, they were bad news. They were going to snatch you up, take the drugs and leave. We dealt with them."

Cold fear travels through my body as I stare at the stranger in front of me. "W-w-w-who are you?"

"I'm the President of the Joker's Wrath Motorcycle Club. You don't need to fear for your life, darlin'. Those fuckers won't hurt you now."

"But my sister," I cry. "Kennedy!"

"Kennedy sent you out with those drugs to do his fuckin' dirty work?" The biker barks.

"No," I stop. "Yes."

"Bastard. You tell me where he lives, and I'll find your sister."

"Y-y-y-y-you will?"

"Yeah, but don't ask me to take you back to that piece of shit." He leans down close, frightening me. "No one gives an underage girl so many drugs it nearly kills her, and then sends her packing to risk her life for him."

"He didn't give them to me," I whisper the words, low and soft. "I stole them from the package."

118

"You're an addict."

It's not a question.

I nod anyway.

"You got family, girl?"

I shake my head. "They died. My sister and I were in foster homes until Kennedy took us in."

"Well, I'm goin' to get your sister, and then you can stay here as long as you need."

I stare at him. He holds it. There's something very real about this man. He tilts his head to the side, daring me to argue with him. He's also incredibly dominant.

"Okay," I whisper.

"Sleep, Santana," he says, turning to leave. "You've got a long road ahead, judging by those marks in your arm. It ain't goin' to be easy, but we're goin' to get you there."

~*~*~*~

2014 – Santana

Chaos has broken out.

One of the old ladies just found out her man fucked one of the club whores. Fists started swinging. Shit hit the fan. I tried to stay out of it, I really did, until Cacey started mouthing off about YaYa, the old lady who just found out her biker is a prick. I swung the first punch. I won't lie. Then everything just got out of hand.

Cacey hit me.

119

I hit her back.

Suddenly the focus is on us and we're rolling around on the floor. She's gotten two clean punches in, I've gotten three. Now her hands are in my hair and she's tugging, snarling curses at me. I spit them right back, furious. A heavy arm curls around my waist and hauls me backwards, but I use that to my advantage.

My legs swing out, and I connect with Cacey's mouth. A loud crack echoes through the room, and then her screams fill the now silent space.

"Enough," Maddox barks, and I realize it's him who is holding me back.

"You stupid bitch," I snarl at Cacey. "Get your cheap ass outta here."

"Quit swingin' your legs around like a mad woman and stop, fuckin' *now*," Maddox barks, shaking me a little.

His words are like a whip, and my legs drop quickly.

Someone gathers Cacey up and removes her, and I am swung around, still in Maddox's arms, and carried off down the hall. He takes me to the bathroom, his strides angry. He drops me on the sink when we get in, but he won't look at me. Something is wrong.

"Maddox?"

Nothing.

He just soaks a clean cloth and begins wiping my face, his eyes on my wounds and nothing else.

"Maddox?" I try again. "Are you mad at me?"

"No," he says, but his voice is acidic.

"Oh, well, can I come home with you tonight?"

"No."

It hits me then, like iced water to my skin. He regrets what happened. Tears spring to my eyes as I realize what a fool I was. I gave him what he wanted, what he's wanted for years, and he's obviously figured out it wasn't what he'd hoped for. Maybe he had bigger expectations. Maybe I'm just not good enough.

"Okay, well," I croak. "I'll find Mack."

I shove at his chest, but he doesn't move. I look up and his eyes are on mine, and there's pain in their depths, like there's so much he wants to say but can't. The look is gone quickly, covered with that same anger.

"Good."

"If you regret me, why not just say it?" I say, my voice shaky. "Don't treat me like this."

"Never fuckin' said that."

"You don't need to!" I cry.

He glares at me. "You're . . . You're not . . ."

"Oh my God." I laugh brokenly. "Don't, please. I get it, all right? I'm not what you thought. I'm an innocent little girl, not good enough for the mighty Maddox."

His jaw tightens, as if he wants to reply . . . but he doesn't.

"You piece of shit!" I rasp.

I turn and rush out, and for the first time in a long time, he doesn't follow me.

~*~*~*~

121

I don't see Maddox for three long days. He doesn't try to contact me or make any attempt to rectify the situation. To add to that, Mack is being cagey too. Like he knows something I don't. I told him what happened, and he replied with, "Maddox is a prick," before making a hasty retreat.

Something is going down. It's been welling inside me, eating away until I can't take it anymore.

Maddox is not going to do what he did, and then hide from it because he regrets it. He's going to face me, tell me it's done, and then stay the fuck out of my life when I move on. He can't barge in and interfere with my dating life, then turn me down like a spoiled child.

It's taken me days to find the right time to sneak past Mack. I'm going to Maddox's house, whether he likes it or not. I've only been at the club when he isn't there, and he's made sure of that. He's avoiding me, and he's not going to do it any longer.

I can't crawl out my window, because they barred it after my last attempt. I can only sneak out when Mack is asleep. But he barely sleeps—the past two nights he's spent fucking some random chicks, and I can't get out because he's been doing that on the frigging couch. Tonight, though, he came home alone. We shared a few empty words over dinner, and then I said I was tired and went to bed.

Four hours later, he did the same.

I wait for another half an hour before sneaking out of the house. It's easy enough to do, with me disappearing through the back door. I know there are boys out the front. I'm dressed in jeans, a sweater and sneakers. It's not cold out, but it's certainly not warm either. Besides, I need the sneakers to get over the fence.

It takes me half an hour to get out onto the street without making any noise. I catch a cab and order it to Maddox's house. I breathe a sigh of relief when we're on the road, feeling relieved that I made it out safely. What I didn't consider in my plan, is that someone could be watching from somewhere down the street.

I made a huge mistake.

A massive, massive mistake.

CHAPTER SIXTEEN

2008 – Santana

A scream is wrenched from my throat as another tremor takes over. I need drugs. I need them now. I've clawed at my own skin to the point where my hands had to be restrained. Dried blood coats my arms and legs, and even parts of my face. Vomit has become my best friend, and I'm sweating enough to swim in it.

Everything hurts. From the top of my head to my toes, everything inside my poor, broken body burns. It feels as if I've been lit on fire, doused, then lit once more. I can't escape the pain; I can't escape the desperation. I'm trapped, locked in my own personal hell. Nothing can take away my agony, and Maddox won't let anyone near me.

He's been the only person I've seen for the past three days.

And each time I lay my eyes on him, I want to rip his skin apart just to get out of here. I've tried, at least ten times. He's too strong, though. He's attempted to get me out to eat, drink and use the bathroom, but his attempts have been futile. I've pissed myself more times than I can count so now I lay here, drenched in my own urine, crying out for him.

He won't come.

He knows as well as I do that if I don't come down from this, I'll die, and he's making sure that doesn't happen.

~*~*~*~

2008 - Maddox

Her body thrashes and her screams fill the room. I've never seen someone come down so hard before. She's struggling, and her tiny body will go into shock soon if she doesn't start coping. She's begged me so many times to just give her something, and fuck, it's been hard to say no.

She's suffering, and I can do nothing but watch her.

"You need to tell her," Mack says, coming up behind me.

"Look at her, Mack. She's fucked. Her life has been flushed down the toilet. If she knows what happened to her sister, she'll fuckin' die trying to find her. She can't handle that."

"Ain't your choice to make."

"Look. At. Her."

Mack turns his eyes to the girl strapped to the bed, her arms caked in dried blood, her hair a ratty mess, and her clothes soaked with her own urine. She can't know what happened to her sister—she'll set off into the world and be killed or captured before she even leaves the city. She's got no chance.

"She needs time, and right now I've got nothin' to give her. I don't know where her sister was sent, and until I do, her knowing is only going to do severe damage to her recovery."

"What are you going to do?"

"I don't know."

I walk in and stop beside the bed. Santana looks up at me, her eyes desperate. "Please," she croaks. "It hurts."

I lift the cloth sitting in the bowl of water beside the mattress and wring it out, then I wipe her face. "You're goin' to be just fine."

"Please!" she screams.

Her entire body jerks as she tries to get out of her binds. After a few minutes, she slumps down with a ragged whimper.

"Where's my sister?"

I open my mouth to answer her, but stop. She looks over to me, and she must see something on my face, something bad, because she starts to scream. "No, Pippi! No! No! No!"

A lump lodges itself in my throat as she screams for her sibling.

"She's dead, isn't she? No!" she wails. "No!"

I can't move. I can't confirm or deny her thoughts, I just stand there, fucking mute, with nothing to say. She gasps for air and then blacks out. I stare at her, tilting my head to the side as I reach down and check her pulse. It's there, and it's pounding.

God, the poor, poor girl.

CHAPTER SEVENTEEN

2014 – Santana

The first gunshot that's fired hits the car tires, sending the driver into a panic. He speaks very little English and starts rambling in a language I don't understand, but thankfully he doesn't stop when I scream. I throw myself onto the floor, jerking my phone out of my jeans. God, I'm such an idiot.

I try Maddox's number. No answer.

Shit.

Another shot rings out, causing the car to swerve and slam into an oncoming truck. A loud crunch and a jerk sends my phone soaring out of my hand. A scream rips from my throat as half of the car is crushed in. The blaring sounds of horns and screaming fill the small space. I have to get out of here; they're going to kill me if I don't.

I lift my head just enough to see we're near some alleys. If I get out and run . . . I don't think, I just do. I unbuckle my seatbelt and throw the door open, hitting the pavement with a thump. Pain rips up my body as I roll towards the sidewalk. Another shot rings out, missing me through the chaos. I have seconds to get out of sight.

Skin is torn off my legs as I shove my body up and run towards the alley. I disappear down the dark space, crying out as I trip and stumble over unknown objects. I run as hard and as fast as I can, my sneakers pounding, my body aching, and my heart racing.

Cars screech at the end of the alley, and I hear shouted voices. God, they're so close. I run harder, ducking out onto the next street and running towards the closest thing I can. Our local store. It's huge, kind of like Wal-Mart, so I know I can hide well enough in, near, or around it. I decide to go with around it, being that the most obvious choice would be for me to go inside.

I duck around the back, only giving a quick glance behind me. I can't see anyone, but I can still hear shouted voices. They'll appear only seconds after me, of that I don't doubt. I rush through the parking lot and around the back of the building. I see a heap of old bins, but decide to go with the thick bushes surrounding the building.

I shove myself into one, crying in pain as the branches damage my skin even further. My knees and hands are burning in ways I've never felt them burn before. I push right to the back of the bushes and press myself against the wall, ducking as low as I can. Then I pray, I pray because I know if these men get hold of me, I'm dead.

Voices fill my silent space only two or three minutes later. I press my hands over my mouth to steady out my breathing in an attempt to quieten it down as I'm panting from my run. I close my eyes and stay as still as I can, not wanting to rustle one leaf. The sound of boots crunching over the pavement gets closer and closer, until I can clearly hear voices.

"She go inside?" one of them barks.

"I think she did, man," another says.

A snort. "Bet she's in the fuckin' bins."

Breathe. In and out. Don't make a sound. Please don't let them find me, oh God, please . . . don't let them find me.

"She ain't in the bins. I'm sure she went inside. If she was fuckin' smart she would have, probably callin' the cops. We need to get outta here."

"Kent will be fuckin' pissed if we don't come back with her."

"She's fuckin' gone; the bitch can run fast. If the cops show up, we're fucked. We're meant to kill her, not get ourselves locked up."

"Fine, but you're fuckin' breakin' the news that the bitch missed our bullets once again."

"Yeah, fuckin' yeah."

My bottom lip trembles in relief as they disappear. God, they sound so like the Jokers' in the way they speak and act, it's scary. To others, is that how Maddox and the guys look?

I sit in the bushes for an hour, my body seizing, my heart aching with fear. I stand slowly, waiting, just waiting for them to pop out with their guns trained on me. They're not there, though. I manage to get out of the bushes with no harm. I peer around the side of the building, and there aren't a lot of cars left, being the hour of night it is.

I decide to stick to the back road running behind the store, walking down the dark stretch until I find a main drag far enough away that I feel safe. My legs and hands are aching, and when I pass streetlights, I see the bloody mess I've made of them. When I reach a line of cabs, I rush over quickly and jump into one, waiting with fear to see if bullets ring out.

They don't.

I give the driver Maddox's address, and he doesn't even notice me as he drives out. Thank God, he might have thrown me out, or worse, called the cops. I sit in silence the entire way and when the driver pulls up, I pull a twenty from my jeans pockets, grateful I always keep one in my pants. I've learned that lesson the hard way.

The driver still doesn't glance at me as he snatches the money and I get out. He drives off and I rush towards Maddox's house, stopping when I see Tyke and Austin standing watch. Their eyes fall on me, and Tyke wheels himself closer, his face twisted with rage. "What the fuck, Sant . . ."

His voice trails off when I step into the light.

"Motherfucker, MADDOX!"

Austin rushes inside the house as I finally let the tears fall. All I wanted to do was see Maddox, I didn't . . . God, I didn't realize it was this bad. Tyke reaches out, putting an arm around my hips as he forces me closer to the house, his eyes darting about with concern.

"What. The. Fuck?"

Maddox's voice comes out like an icy whip, lashing against my skin and making my tears flow harder. I turn towards him, and his eyes widen with shock and pure rage.

"I . . ."

"Where's Mack?" he barks, looking around. "What happened?"

"I . . ."

"Well?" he roars.

"I snuck out!" I cry. "They . . . they shot at me . . ."

"Get inside," he bellows, so loudly I flinch. "Fuckin' now."

Oh God. I rush past him and into the house. My eyes blur with angry tears as I run towards the bathroom.

"Stop."

His voice, like a damned acid-filled bullet, has me stopping and turning halfway up the stairs.

"Get. Down. Here. Now."

God, he's so angry. With shaky legs, I turn and walk down the stairs, trying hard to even out my breathing. My tears have stopped, and I'm filled with a mix of anger and fear.

"Get on the fuckin' couch!"

I do as he asks, sitting down on the couch. I stare down at my knees and a pained wince comes out as I clearly see the damage done. This takes gravel rash to a whole new level. I've got chunks of blood and road all over my knees. My hands are no better.

Maddox says nothing as he pulls out his phone.

"Mack!" he barks. "Missin' something?"

"This isn't his fault!" I cry, trying to stand. His hand goes to my shoulder and shoves me back down.

"You fuckin' let her out into the night to get fuckin' shot at."

Mack is roaring something on the other end of the phone. I flinch, hating that this ended so badly. I didn't think about Mack when I found the determination to come and see Maddox. I didn't think about how it would affect him.

"Fuck you, bro," Maddox hisses.

Mack says something that has Maddox's face scrunching in pure rage.

"You fuckin' watch your fuckin' . . ."

Obviously Mack hangs up, because Maddox hurls the phone across the room and then spins to me.

"What the fuck is wrong with you? Do you think I'm fuckin' joking when I fuckin' say that you're in fuckin' danger?"

His voice has me flinching with fear. God, I've never seen him so angry.

131

"You selfish, spoiled little fuckin' brat!"

Another flinch.

"Austin!" he roars.

The young prospect rushes in. "Yeah?"

"Clean her the fuck up. I can't look at her."

Then he turns and charges down into the basement where I know he's got a boxing bag that he takes his anger out on. I turn to Austin, my mouth opening but quickly closing again. What is there to say? I'm a God damned fool and I deserve this.

~*~*~*~

Austin cleans me up, and then goes and waits outside. I sit on the couch, staring at the basement door. I've heard Maddox's angry *thump, thump, thump*s as he pounds into his boxing bag. I know I need to go down there, but what do I say? Maybe the truth . . . Yeah, that would be a good plan.

I shove to my feet, groaning in pain at the stiff, achy feeling that radiates through my knees and hands. I hesitantly make my way down to the basement. The noise gets louder and louder as I edge closer. I see the bag flying around before I see Maddox, but when I do lay my eyes on him, I gasp.

God, he's angry.

His huge body is covered in a fine sheen of sweat. He's taken his shirt off, and is only wearing his jeans. His fists are bloody and broken, and his face is a twisted mass of rage. He looks so scarily stunning. He notices me before I can open my mouth, his blue eyes cutting through me like razor blades.

"I fucked up."

Thump, thump, thump.

"I'm sorry, Maddox. I just . . . I wanted to see you."

Thump, thump, thump.

"I shouldn't have done it, I deserved everything I got."

Thump, thump, thump.

"For fuck's sake!" I scream, losing my shit. He pauses for a minute, but resumes his thumping. I resume my yelling. "You pissed and moaned about me dating Alec, you made it clear you didn't like it, you put your . . . *body* all over mine, and we have a big-ass moment, and then you switched off. You just fucking switched off. You don't get the right to do that, you giant . . . fuckhead."

He stops hitting and stares at me, his face expressionless.

"You done?"

"No!" I snap. "I'm not done. I came out tonight because you haven't spoken to me for three days. I'm tired of this fucking game we continue to play. You either want me, or you don't. Make up your fucking mind. If you decide you don't, then stay the fuck out of my business."

He's in front of me in a flash, causing me to take two quick steps back. His eyes flash with rage as he glares down at me.

"You could have gotten yourself killed, because you don't fuckin' listen."

"I know that," I say, keeping my voice strong.

We stare at each other for long, long moments, saying nothing, but feeling *everything.*

"You touched me," I say, my voice low and broken. "You made me feel incredible after he . . ." My voice wavers, "hurt me. And now you're treating me like I don't matter."

133

His face softens, but it's still so hard. He says nothing, but I can see the internal battle going on inside him. For whatever reason he's holding back, and I'm tired of it. I'm tired of dancing around this. I take a step forward and reach up, placing my hand on his damp, hard chest. He flinches, and his eyes close.

"Maddox," I breathe. "Stop hiding from me. You want this as much as I do. I can feel it."

His lips thin out, his jaw flexes, and his eyes remain closed. I step even closer, pressing my lips to his skin. I let my tongue slide out, tasting the salt. I let out a little, satisfied moan and step even closer until our bodies are molded together. He doesn't move; he's stiff as a damned brick wall.

I don't back down, though.

I press my open mouth against his chest, and blow hot puffs of air against his skin. He shudders, but still, his hands aren't on me. He's not pushing me away though, so I'm not going to stop. I gently lower my body down his, sliding my mouth over his abs which are super hard from his work out.

I reach his jeans and take the top button, trying to ignore the pain in my knees as I squat. I can't lean on them; this is the best I can do. I've always wondered what it would feel like to have a man's cock in my mouth, and now is my chance for that. I undo the top button, my heart quickening at the realization of what I'm about to do.

No words are shared between us as I slowly lower his zip. His cock is hard. I can see it straining against his jeans. *Yum.* I lower the top of the denim just enough for him to spring free. God, he's huge. I stare at the long, thick length in front of me for a minute, before reaching up and wrapping my fist around it. I try not to wince in pain at the movement of my bandaged hand, and I pray I don't hurt him with it.

He finally hisses.

I guess it doesn't hurt.

His hands are clenched by his sides, and he's panting, both from his exercise and what we're doing. I lean in close, breathing him in. *Slightly salty, all man.* I slide my tongue out, shivering when it touches the soft, silky skin. He growls, low and deep. I lick around the crown of his cock, before tilting my head, and slipping him into my mouth.

"Fuck," he snarls, finally speaking.

I suck, feeling my lips stretch around his impressive length. His hands twitch, and he finally raises one to my hair, tangling it through the lengths and tugging softly. I take him deeper, sucking my cheeks in to give him the best I can. He hisses and groans, jerking his hips forward. I swirl, suck and lick, until he's rasping my name. He takes my arms suddenly, pulling me to my feet.

His lips crush down over mine, and he kisses me with such ferocity it takes my breath away. I shake, melting into him, pulling his hips closer and loving how heavy his cock feels against my belly.

"No more wasting time," I whisper against his mouth. "I want you to fuck me, Maddox."

"Fuck," he breathes. "You're fuckin' killin' me."

He backs me up until my body is pressed against the cold concrete walls. I whimper as he runs his hands up my sides, causing little goose bumps to break out over my skin. His fingers knead my flesh as he moves up, reaching for my shirt. He lifts it and removes it quickly, before making light work of my pants and underwear.

Soon, I'm fully naked in his arms. He lowers his head, capturing a nipple between his teeth and rolling it about. The stiff peak almost hurts it's so damned hard. I cry out, but it's not in pain, it's in pure pleasure. Maddox clutches me with a ferocity and passion that has my heart pounding so hard it hurts.

He puts a hand to my belly and slowly lowers to his knees, using that hand to hold me against the wall. With his other hand, he takes my leg and lifts it up and over his shoulder. Heat floods my cheeks as I realize what he's about to do. He doesn't allow for protest, because his mouth is against my pussy in mere seconds.

"Oh God," I cry out, arching towards him.

His mouth devours me, every stroke like fire against my exposed core. His tongue goes up to lazily circle my clit, while his finger gathers the moisture at my opening, rubbing it up and down, up and down, preparing me. Just as I start to clench with pleasure, he slips one finger inside me.

I squirm, feeling a slight burn as he rotates it around, stretching me, preparing me for what I know is coming. He keeps sucking my clit, bringing the pleasure to the surface again. I'm mumbling his name through moans, and God, he looks good down there, his big body crouched, devouring mine. When his finger is slick with my arousal, he slides a second in.

"M-M-Maddox," I whimper.

He says nothing, he just holds his finger still while he continues to lick and suck my aching nub. Finally, when I've stopped clenching around him, he moves his fingers gently until they're sliding effortlessly into my pussy. He tilts them, rubbing over a bundle of nerves inside me that has my knees going weak.

Then he stops, pulling his fingers out and removing his mouth. He stands, steadying me with one hand while the other strokes his cock, preparing it. "You're goin' to come around my cock," he breathes. "Not my fingers."

I stare at the thick length, then back at the blue eyes I trust so much. He reaches into his jeans pocket and pulls out a condom, tearing the packet with his teeth and rolling it down his length. He doesn't take his eyes off mine, and I know he can see how nervous I am.

"It's gonna burn, baby," he says, lifting my leg and putting it around his hip. "But it won't burn for long."

I nod, biting my lower lip as he gently pushes up. His head probes my opening, encouraging it to take him. I close my eyes, terrified after my last ordeal. Maddox is gentle, though, pushing in slowly. His entire body is straining, and I know it's hard for him, but he doesn't hurry it up.

My pussy stretches around his length, burning and protesting as he fills me deeper. "I'm in, honey," he rasps. "Fuck. You're so fuckin' tight."

I open my eyes and stare at him. He looks so incredible, looming over me. I stare down at our bodies, joined for the first time, and my heart warms. I didn't realize until this moment just how much I've wanted this. Maddox slowly pulls out, sending a fresh burst of pain through my body, before sliding back in. He does this over and over, so slowly, so beautifully, until finally I grip his arms, my breath coming out in short bursts.

"F-f-f-fuck me."

He makes a low, throaty sound and gradually picks up the pace, thrusting his hips in and out, warming me, filling me. I whimper, my fingernails sliding into the flesh on his shoulders as I tilt my pelvis up to take him deeper. Our moans tangle together, increasing as his hips thrust harder and faster.

Until finally, he's fucking me.

And God, does Maddox fuck good. His big powerful body is overwhelming in the best way, surrounding me, all hot and hard. His muscles flex as he moves his hips so skillfully it sends me climbing higher and higher, my body burning for more. His mouth is everywhere—on my throat, on my nipples, and his finger is on my clit, rubbing and stroking.

"Maddox," I cry out. "Oh God. Yes."

"Hang on for me, baby," he rasps. "Hang on."

He fucks me harder. His fingers on my hips will no doubt leave bruises. His cock swells inside me, and he barks out, "Now, come now."

I was already there before the last word left his lips. I come hard, so hard my world goes white for just a moment. I've never felt something so incredible in all my life. My pussy hugs his dick, clenching and unclenching, milking his cock. His bellows are deep and throaty, the veins on his neck bulging as he releases into me.

I come down from my high first, dropping my head into his chest. My God, that was everything I ever dreamed and more. He runs his hand down my back softly, before slowly pulling out of me. "You hurtin'?" he croaks, his voice husky.

I shake my head, even though I am a little sore.

"You're a bad liar," he murmurs, pulling the condom off and tying it, before throwing it in a nearby trash can. "Come on, lets get you cleaned up."

He takes my hand, pulling me close to him. His lips rest on my forehead for a moment before he helps me get dressed. We walk up the stairs and towards the bathroom, where I get undressed all over again. I'm not complaining though, not even a little bit.

Because I spend the next half an hour running my hands all over Maddox's hot, wet body.

CHAPTER EIGHTEEN

2014 - Santana

I sleep in Maddox's bed that night, his arms wrapped around me, his soft breath against my ear. By morning, my body is stiff and sore. My knees and hands hurt, but I've had worse. I realize when I roll, that Maddox is no longer beside me. Sitting up, I glance at the time, it's past ten a.m.—I must have slept longer than I'd thought.

I throw my legs out of the bed, and dress myself. Then I make my way down the stairs, throwing my hair up in a messy ponytail. The moment I reach the bottom, I stop, and my cheeks heat. We have visitors, and I'm in Maddox's shirt, panties . . . and nothing else. Everyone at the table turns when they hear me, and my cheeks grow warmer.

Maddox, Mack, Krypt, Tyke, Ash and two of the old ladies from the club, Indi and Petra. Maddox grins lazily as his eyes rake over my outfit. I'm glad he finds this amusing. I wave lamely. "Ah . . . hi. I didn't know . . . I mean . . ."

Mack laughs, loud and boisterous. I shoot him a glare.

"You are fresh fucked, *chante*, and nothin' you can say will hide that."

I cross my arms, but say nothing.

Maddox stands and walks over, wrapping his big arms around me and pulling me up to his mouth. My feet dangle as his lips crash down over mine, and he kisses me with such ferocity I lose my breath. I'm dizzy by the time my feet hit the floor again. I grin up at him. "Good morning to you, too."

He lets me go and leads me back to the table, pulling me down on his lap. "So," I begin. "What's with the family gathering?"

Mack is still grinning at me. Krypt isn't. His face is a hard mask, and it immediately worries me. "Krypt, is everything okay?"

He turns to me, piercing me with those devastating eyes. "Fine."

"You don't look fine . . ."

"She's right," Ash says, staring at her man. "You don't look fine."

"He's just broody," Maddox grates. "He'll be fine."

"Okay," I say, still not convinced. "So why are you all here?"

Maddox runs his fingers up my bare thigh and I shiver. "You've been busting for company, and I've got business to take care of. You get the girls, and, lucky for you, Mack . . . and Krypt, Tyke and I are gonna go do what we gotta do."

"You could have just taken me to the clubhouse . . ." I point out.

"Yeah." Ash grins. "But there we can't paint our nails, do our hair, talk about girly things and eat chocolate while drinking wine."

I grin. "Girls' night?"

Petra grins. She's a really pretty girl in her late twenties. She's got short, pixie-cut black hair and green eyes. She's a busty girl, but it somehow suits her personality, which is big and bubbly. "Girls' night!"

I turn to Maddox, grinning up at him. "You're giving me a girls' day?"

He leans down, brushing his lips across my ear. "Mmmm."

"And I have to baby-fuckin'-sit," Mack grunts.

"Sendin' somethin' your way later, bro." Maddox laughs. "Don't worry."

"It better have tits, an ass, and a fine pussy."

"Aw Chief," I tease. "We could do your hair, if you like?"

140

"Ohhh," Indi finally pipes up. "He does have nice hair."

I laugh and high-five her. Indi is close to my age, which is nice. She's only been an old lady for about six months, but she's good value. She has to be, to put up with Zaid. He's a grumpy fool, but he loves the little blond bombshell. And that's exactly what Indi is. Blond, blue eyed, big breasted and super fine.

"I'll fucking drop you, Santana," Mack growls. "You fuckin' brat."

I laugh. "You love me, Chief. Don't worry, we'll make sure your hair looks a million bucks."

Maddox pinches my thigh and I squeal. "Hey!"

"Don't tease the man."

"You offering to take his place, handsome?"

He snorts. "No fucker is touchin' my hair."

"Aw, precious."

He slaps my thigh now, and Ash laughs hard. "Come on, Maddox. It'll be fun."

He grunts and stands, putting me down. "I'm gettin' a coffee, then gettin' the fuck outta here."

We all laugh as the guys stand, Krypt taking Tyke's chair and wheeling him out. I rush over to him before he reaches the door. "Hey, Krypt."

He turns, staring at me, but not before I see his eyes flicker to Maddox. I put my hand on his arm. "Are you okay?"

He nods. "Fine."

"Krypt . . ."

He stares at me. "I'm fine, Tana. Just . . . be careful, okay?"

Careful? With what?

"I'm safe here . . ."

"Not with that." He stares up at Maddox. "With him."

Then he pushes Tyke out the door. Ash comes over and we both watch him go to load Tyke on the bike.

"I don't know what's wrong with him . . ." she says. "He's been off for days."

"Yeah," I say, watching him. "I hope he's okay."

"He'll be fine," she takes my hand. "Come on, we've got the best day planned."

I smile. "I can't wait."

~*~*~*~

The guys leave a few minutes later, and we're left alone with Mack. He doesn't give us the chance to taunt him, he just disappears down into Maddox's basement, no doubt to punch the shit out of the punching bag to save his sanity. Poor Mack, he gets left with the girls more often than not.

"So," Ash says, laying out bags of food on the counter. "Where do we start?"

I stare at all the food, hair and make-up products, and movies she's got laid out.

"Jesus . . . you thought this through."

"Of course we did," Indi says, pulling out the wine. "You've been prisoner for a while now. We wanted to make being imprisoned fun."

"Besides," Petra adds, "We want gossip on you and Prez."

I snort. "There's no gossip."

They all stop and raise their brows.

I laugh. "Fine, there's a little."

Giggles break out between them, and we begin preparing food to nibble on.

"You finally took the next step, then?" Ash asks, emptying a packet of crackers onto a plate.

I flush. "Ah, yeah."

"Well!" Indi encourages. "Come on!"

I shake my head with a laugh. "I need liquid courage before I tell that story."

"It's too early in the morning for wine," Ash pouts. "We have to wait until at least lunch time for that. You can't leave us hanging."

I snort, crossing my arms. "Fine, but it's graphic . . ."

They all laugh and we take the plate of food and beauty products to the lounge, where we all throw ourselves down. I get the beauty treatment first, with Petra doing my nails, Ash doing my toenails, and Indi doing my make-up.

"Come on, you're killing us . . ." Petra says, filing my thumbnail.

"Okay," I sigh. "It was amazing."

"More," Indi encourages. "Where did you do it?"

"The basement." I giggle.

"The basement?" Ash squeals. "Where?"

"Against the wall. God, it was hot. He was so angry at me, it was kind of like make-up sex . . ."

Indi fans herself. "Oh boy, I can just imagine. Give us a mental image now."

"He had been punching the boxing bag. No shirt, lots of sweat."

"Swooooon!" Petra groans. "Maddox is fine."

"And his . . ." Indi says, wiggling her eyebrows.

I share a look with Ash, so much passing between us. She knows what Maddox packs, and at the thought my chest clenches. I have to let it go, it isn't her fault, but it still hurts like hell when I think of it. She gives me a sympathetic expression, but I decide I'm not going to let it affect me, not today.

"It's huge." I laugh, glancing at Indi. "I mean . . . whoa!"

They all squeal just as Mack emerges from the basement, sweaty, shirtless, and panting. We all stop and stare at him. Holy hell, Mack is fine. All that lean muscle, no markings on his gorgeous olive skin . . . His pants are dipped low, showing us a nice V. He narrows his eyes at us, and I whistle at him, a big, loud, wolf whistle. "Chief, you fine!"

He shakes his head, walking past us.

"Holy, he can paint my skin any time," Indi calls out.

"He can paint me with his man juice," Petra adds.

Mack grunts as he nears the stairs. He knows they're joking.

"Come and play with us, Chief," I call out.

"Go away, brat."

"Aw, he's still angry that he's babysitting."

144

He glances at me over his shoulder. "I've just listened to you describe my brother's cock, and how he fucked you in the room I was just in . . . pretty fuckin' sure that's enough to scar me for life."

I laugh. He shakes his head and disappears up the stairs.

"Damn," Petra says focusing on the task at hand. "He's fine."

"Agreed," Ash says. "I've never seen a Native American man look that good. All that muscle and olive skin . . ."

"And his hair!" Indi sighs. "Jealous."

"Right!" We all say it at once, then burst into yet another fit of giggles.

We continue our beauty treatments right into the afternoon, when Mack's little present arrives. Maddox had Austin bring over one of the club whores. Ew. Seriously. Not that I can argue, poor Mack has been stuck listening to girl crap for hours, and it's sending him over the edge.

"Ugh, of course you bitches have to be here."

Ah, Sandra. She's the club whore who gets into more fights than it's worth, because of her big mouth. The only reason the guys keep her around is because apparently she's a wild cat in bed. Gross. She sashays in, her tiny hips swinging as she walks into the kitchen and picks up a bottle of wine, popping the top and taking a drink.

I stand, walking over and snatching it out of her hand. "Ew, get your mouth off my wine."

"Fuck you, Santana. Maddox invited me here, so you don't get to say what I do."

"He invited you here to get your ass pounded because Mack is bored."

She grins. "He invited me here because I fuck like a God damned warrior."

I laugh, loudly. "Seriously? A warrior?"

She crosses her arms. She's actually a pretty enough girl, she's just got a disgusting attitude. Her pale blue eyes and honey-colored hair compliment her fair skin. She's got . . . ahem . . . enhancements in her breasts, making her look curvier then her short five-foot frame really is. Today she's wearing a tiny bikini top and a short skirt. I suppose she doesn't really need anymore, it's only going to come off.

"Fuckin' finally," Mack says, coming into the kitchen.

"Gee, Chief, good choice," I point out. "Warrior here should keep you entertained for a few hours."

He gives me a confused expression, while Sandra glares at me. "You've got a bad attitude, Santana," she spits.

I laugh. "Aw, I'm sorry, is my bad attitude offending you? Why don't you go lie on Mack's bed with your legs apart. After all, it's the only reason you're here."

"Oh, I'll be doing that. And you'll be hearing me scream while he fucks me, because," she curls herself around Mack, "didn't you know . . . the Indian fucks good."

My mouth drops open. Nobody . . . nobody calls Mack an Indian. His jaw ticks, but he says nothing.

"Seriously, Chief?" I say, my mouth open. "You're going to let her insult you."

He steps forward, flicking her off before curling his hand around the back of my neck. "I've been listenin' to shit for hours now, I'm pissed off, I'm horny, and I couldn't care if she came in dressed like a God damned Indian

146

princess to impress me. I'm goin' to take her upstairs, fuck her a few times, and throw her ass out. End of story."

I narrow my eyes at him. He grins at me.

Then he lets me go and takes hold of Sandra's arm. "Move it."

She flicks me a smile before disappearing up the stairs with him. Ew. I join the girls again, and we pop our second bottle of wine.

"She's such a . . . tramp . . ." Indi mutters.

I laugh loudly. "Indi, honey . . ." There are more giggles from the girls. "I think that's the point."

CHAPTER NINETEEN

2008 – Santana

Three months.

I've been here now for three months.

It's been three months since my sister's life was so cruelly taken.

I don't want to go on; what's the point? I just want to join her, taking myself out of this misery. How could Kennedy have let anything happen to her? He was supposed to take care of her. He promised . . . he . . . *promised.*

The pain in my soul hasn't numbed. It hasn't done anything but grow inside me, until taking my life is all I think about. She was the only thing I was fighting for. Without her, I have nothing. No one. I'm just an empty shell of a person, living each day because no one will let me go.

Maddox . . . he's amazing. He takes care of me, holds me when I cry and soothes away the nightmares. He can't bring her back, though. He got me clean, even though the days are still so hard. He gave me shelter, but it's not *home* without Pippi. He gave me a friend, but that's not something I can return.

"That's it!"

The loud shout of a man has me turning my head towards the door to see it swing open. It's Mack. He's Maddox's adopted brother, and I haven't really had a chance to get to know him. He's just been here helping Maddox since I came in. He's spent a lot of time barking at Maddox to get me off my ass and stop letting me wallow.

"Get up," he barks, charging over to the bed and taking hold of my skinny arm, hauling me up. "He might baby you, but I'm not going to. I've sat here and watched you wallow for fucking months, feelin' sorry for yourself. Get your ass up, and get out and fix your fuckin' life."

I'm in shock for the longest moment; I just stare at him as he pulls me towards the door. Then my resistance kicks in, and I push my heels into the carpet. "No! Let me go!"

"No fuckin' way. You've been sittin' here refusin' help for too long, now."

"That's how I want it to be," I scream. "I never asked him to save me. I never asked to be here. I want to die, but none of you will let me."

He lets me go so suddenly it scares me. I stumble a few steps before steadying myself. He spins around, taking an angry step forward while pulling his gun from his pants. He points it at me. "You want to fuckin' die? Huh? You want to fuckin' die?"

His eyes are two deadly daggers, shooting into my body, daring me.

"Yes!" I scream, dropping to my knees. My ratty hair falls around my face. "She was all I had. I'm nothing without her."

"I'll kill you, if that's what you want. I'll pull this trigger and put a bullet through your skull right now-"

"Yes."

"But tell me somethin' real before I pull this trigger. Is this what your sister would want for you? Would she want you to die for her? Would she be proud of you for letting me shoot you? Would it make your family look down on you with honor to see you on your knees, weak, pathetic, and broken . . . begging to end your life?"

I look up at him, trembling. He doesn't understand. He's probably never felt this kind of desperation before. Never felt the way it eats at you, burrowing into your soul and taking everything you are, crushing it until all that's left is an empty shell.

"They wouldn't . . . They couldn't . . ."

"Is this how you want to honor your sister's life?" he barks, cutting me off. His face is a mask of the worst thing a person can see—disappointment. He's disgusted in me for letting myself get so low.

"No!" I scream, tears streaming down my face.

"You have a fuckin' second chance that she didn't get. You goin' to throw it in her fuckin' face by wastin' it away like a fuckin' coward?"

"Stop!" I cry, pressing my hands to my ears.

"Well?" he bellows, taking a demanding step forward and causing little whimpers to leave my throat.

"No," I scream so loudly my voice cracks. "No . . . God . . . *no.*"

"That's what you'll be if I pull this trigger. I'll do it, if it's what you really want . . . or . . . or you can get off your knees and start piecin' your life back together without the danger of the past loomin' in every corner. Maddox has given you a home, a family, safety and comfort. You decide how you want to honor the work you've put into your life so far. You give it up, or you get up, take my hand, and keep fuckin' fighting."

I lift my head brokenly and stare up at him. He's got the gun pointed at me with one hand, and his other hand stretched out, offering me a second chance. His words burn into my soul, they burn in a way no words have ever burned before. I have a choice. I have a choice Pippi didn't have. It's up to me how I choose to use it.

To go on or to end.

I reach up, curling my fingers around his. He closes his eyes for a second, breathing a sigh of relief. I've no doubt Mack would have shot me, if that's what I'd have really wanted, but it would have ruined him, and he knows it. He curls his fingers around mine, too, and pulls me up. I fall into his chest, exhausted.

It's time to piece my life back together. For Pippi.

~*~*~*~

2014 – Maddox

I throw my leg over the bike, kicking the stand down and shrugging off my jacket as I stare up at the walls of the prison. Fuckin' huge, fuckin' *awful*. Krypt pulls in close beside me with Tyke. They get off and he hands Tyke the crutches he uses when he doesn't want to use his chair. A shudder goes through Krypt as he stares at the place he's more than familiar with.

"Ready?" I ask, reaching into my jeans and pulling out a cigarette. I light it, taking deep drags and letting the burning smoke fill my lungs to calm me, before dropping it. Fuck. Here goes.

"Yeah," Krypt grunts, shooting me a hostile glare.

He's furious at me, I already know he is, but there isn't time to go over it right now. I need him beside me, and he fuckin' knows it. He can throw a fuckin' tantrum later, when this shit isn't so raw.

"Let's do this."

We go through intense security just to get in for a visit. We're scanned, felt, asked basic questions, and sent through metal and drug detectors. We're not allowed to wear our colors in the prison, so we're in basic clothes. When security is done, we're lead through cramped halls and given angry glares as we make our way to the visitors' room. We're here to see Kennedy. It'll be the first time I lay eyes on the man who fucked my girl's life.

"Second booth," the guard barks. "Two of you only."

"I'll sit here," Tyke says, nodding at a chair.

I jerk my chin at him, and then turn to Krypt. "Don't say anythin' unless you need to, got me?"

He nods. "I fuckin' know how it works, Maddox."

"I know that, boy," I hiss, leaning closer. "But you're goin' to fuckin' humor me anyway."

He shoots me an angry glare, but doesn't argue further. We walk to the second booth and sit down. It's a basic communication center. Bullet-proof glass, ensuring we can't access the prisoner on the other side. Phones—two on my side, one on his. Nothing more. No pens. No papers. Nothing.

We sit for five minutes before two guards appear holding onto a prisoner. I stare at the man, shocked. Not what I expected. Fuck, not what I expected *at all*. Aside from his prison outfit, he is the meaning of sophistication. Salt and pepper hair, eyes the color of champagne, a chiseled jaw, and straight posture. In a suit, he'd be the perfect lawyer.

I expected a roughed up, tattooed bastard. Not this. Definitely not this. He sits down, meeting my expression and a slow smirk appears on his lips as he reaches out, lifting the phone. Krypt and I do the same.

"Well well," he says, his voice a low, professional purr. "I've wondered what you're like. After I heard who you were, it got me curious."

"Yeah," I grunt. "Ditto."

He drums his fingers casually on the bench. "How can I help you, Maddox?"

"You know exactly why I'm here, Kennedy. Don't play coy with me. I'm not goin' into details," I say, flicking my eyes to the guard standing in the corner. "But you know what I want."

"And you know what I wanted," he lets his eyes flick around behind me, "but she isn't here . . ."

"Santana doesn't wanna see you."

He narrows his eyes. "See, you're lying now. I know that's not true. If you've told her the truth then you and I both know she wouldn't ignore me, because she knows I'm the only one who knows what happened to Pippa."

Fucker is right, and he knows it.

"She's..." I can't tell him she doesn't know. "In a bad way right now. She ain't ready."

He laughs, low and throaty. "You haven't told her yet, have you, biker?"

Then the fucker *tuts* at me.

"Poor Tanie. And to think she probably trusts you."

"Don't fuckin' call her that, and you ain't no better than me, asshole. Leavin' her to die."

He flinches. "I never wanted to hurt her. I loved her. She was precious to me in a way you can *never* understand. I wanted to see her, and you didn't bring her to me."

"I said I'd get her to you, and I will," I lie. "But first I want to talk."

He stares lazily at me. "About what?"

153

"Where is Pippa?"

"I don't know what you're talking about."

My jaw grinds. "You want to see that girl, Kennedy, you'll tell me what I need to know."

"She'll see me regardless."

I lean forward, and even though it really does nothing in regards to threatening him or making him feel intimidated, I do it anyway. "See, that's where you're wrong. Santana and I . . . we're lovers, she's my old lady, which means if I don't want her to come here, I'll make sure she doesn't."

His face pinches, and something truly broken washes over his expression. "You're a liar."

"Am I? How much are you willing to bet on that? After all, it was me in her bed last night. You tell me what I want, Kennedy, or I'll make sure she never steps foot in this prison."

His jaw ticks. "Peter Caler."

I tilt my head to the side, giving him an expression to encourage him on.

"Find and speak to him. He has some information you'll need. I'm not giving anything else until I see the girl."

He won't either, I can see it in his eyes.

"Fine, then we're done here until next time."

"Better hurry, biker," he says, a slow smirk appearing on his face. "You ain't the only club lookin' for Pippa."

Then he slams the phone and stands, and my world fuckin' spins.

154

CHAPTER TWENTY

2014 – Maddox

"It's fuckin' Howard, I know it," I bark, pacing up and down the side of my bike.

"Don't fuckin' matter who it is," Krypt snarls. "Someone else is lookin' for that girl."

"Why, though?" I bellow, clenching and unclenching my fists.

"Because there is no better way to fuckin' bring you down than to destroy her . . . People have figured out she's important to you, wouldn't be hard to dig up shit about her past and find what they needed. It would destroy you if something happened to Santana, and therefore the club would suffer and become weak . . ."

"Fuck," I snarl. "Fuck, fuck."

"You gotta tell her, Maddox. This shit needs to end before her or her sister, or fuckin' worse . . . *both* . . . are killed."

"I know, and I will."

"Fuck." He runs his hands through his hair with a growl. "How much is it gonna take for you to see shit is bad?"

"I fuckin' know," I roar.

"No," he barks, taking a step closer. "You fuckin' don't. You're a selfish bastard who is thinkin' about his cock, and not his girl."

I swing my fist, and crack him hard in the jaw. My temper has finally weakened its restraints. He goes back a few steps before gathering himself and lunging forward. His fist hits my jaw, hard and fast. It makes a horrible fucking crunching sound as my head swings to the side. *Fucker can punch.*

"Enough!" Tyke yells.

Krypt and I circle each other, blinded by rage.

"You need to stop bein' a fuckin' selfish, motherfucker!" he spits, baring his bloody teeth.

"And you need to keep your fuckin' nose outta my business."

"It's fuckin' club business now, people's lives are at fuckin' risk, and you need to fuckin' sort it."

"What do you fuckin' think this is?" I roar, lunging at him again.

We go down in a heap in the dust, fists flying. Tyke tries to pull us apart and ends up on his ass in the dirt, the only thing that stops us. Krypt snarls, shoving me back harshly, and helps him up. His face is covered in dirt mixed with blood, and I've no doubt mine is the same.

"I'll fuckin' do it, understand?" I growl.

He doesn't answer me. He helps Tyke on the bike, and shoots me a truly feral glare before climbing on his. I do the same. Fuck this. Fuck it all. I'm going to lose her before I've even had the chance to have her.

CHAPTER TWENTY-ONE

2014 - Santana

We're well on our way to being drunk when Maddox, Krypt and Tyke return. Mack hasn't once emerged from his fuck-fest in the bedroom and we're in the kitchen, giggling and laughing like children. We hear the bikes, and Ash squeals happily that her man is finally back. It's just hit evening, and they've been gone all day.

Krypt comes in first, and we all stop what we're doing.

He's beaten up. Seriously. I blink a few times, shaking my head. His lip is split, his eye is puffy, and he's covered in dirt. Ash rushes over, her face a mask of concern as she stops, putting her hands on his chest. "What happened?"

Krypt stares over at me for a second, before muttering, "Got into it with Maddox."

Tyke comes in then, and aside from being dirty, he's not hurt.

"Where is he?" I ask, watching the door, waiting for him to come in, but he doesn't.

"Sulking in the garage."

I shoot him a glare before putting my wine down and walking out into the garage. Maddox is on his bike, staring down at the gas tank. His big body is covered in dirt, and he's got dried blood on what I can see of his face. He looks up when he hears me enter, and our eyes hold and meet.

"You okay?" I ask.

He shrugs. He's not okay. Whatever happened between the two of them has upset him. I make my way over to him, stopping when my thighs hit his bike tank. I reach out, running my fingers down his dirty cheek.

"You two got into it good, eh?" I ask.

He shrugs again.

Music above begins to play, and I realize it's the sound of Mack singing. He has somewhat of a talent with the guitar, and he writes his own music. His voice flows down into the garage.

There is nothing more defining than the moment your lips find mine . . .

I swallow and take the hem of my shirt, lifting it up and over my head. Maddox looks up. "You wanna shower with me, big guy?"

God there's something in his eyes . . . something so truly broken. What did they do today? What hurt him? Who upset him so badly? My heart aches to see him like this. I reach over, running my fingers down his scruffy cheek. He leans into my hand, almost affectionately, tilting his head and rubbing his cheek against it.

He stands up, not asking me to take anymore clothes off, and not taking his own off, either. He reaches out, taking my hand, and pulls me against him. Then we're dancing to the soft sound of Mack's voice above, our bodies moving together, our eyes locked. His hand slides down my back and rests against my hip, using it to drive our swaying.

This moment, oh this moment, babe, it changes time.

I slide my hand up his arm, over his muscled bicep and up onto his shoulder. I squeeze, loving how the muscles feel flexing and pulling. He presses his forehead to mine, his expression saying so much more than his words ever could. I can feel what he's trying to put across, and I hope he can feel how much I'm giving it back.

When you tell me, oh, oh, it makes it all so real. Show me, baby, don't tell me, it's time to let me feel.

Mack's voice fills my ears as we dance, our bodies pressed against each other, our breaths nothing more than warm puffs against the other's lips. Maddox closes his eyes, his fingers flexing on my hip as he pulls me closer. I reach down, taking hold of his shirt. He steps back for a second, letting me pull it over his head and toss it to the side.

Make me understand, oh baby baby, show yourself to me. Show me what's real.

I lose my pants in a matter of seconds, and soon I'm naked in Maddox's arms as he backs me towards his bike. He lifts me, placing my bottom on the warmed leather seat that only minutes ago he was on. I reach my hand out, pressing it against the candy-apple red tank, feeling the warmth there, too.

Maddox reaches to his jeans, popping the top button as he steps between my legs. He frees his cock, and his gaze drops to my exposed pussy and he growls, low and throaty. Then he takes hold of my leg and wraps it around his hip at the same time as he steps into me, his cock pressing against my heated, waiting flesh.

There are times, oh there are times, when your love feels like a dynamite.

I close my eyes, letting my head fall back as Maddox pushes into me, slowly, filling me with painful bliss. My sex burns as it stretches around him, still living in sheer remembrance of the last time he was there. Slowly, inch by inch, he slides in until our bodies are fully connected. My heart pounds at the intensity of this moment.

Dynamite. Dynamite. Baby, you're a dynamite.

His hips slide back, painfully pulling, before he thrusts back in. Our foreheads press together, and his hand supports my hip as he begins to move, slow, yet so deep. My whimpers blend with the sound of Mack's singing, and we make a melody all of our own, even if the singer doesn't know it. Maddox doesn't kiss me, but I can see how his jaw flexes with pleasure like this.

"Maddox," I whimper. "More."

He hisses, low and husky, and then he begins flexing his hips, driving deeper and deeper until I cry out his name and clutch his shoulders with pleasure. God, he feels so good, so amazing. I'll never get enough of him, never get enough of drowning in everything that he is. I close my eyes, my mouth open on a moan, and I arch my hips up to meet his thrusts.

His bike holds us as he becomes more frenzied, fucking me without a word, using his body to show me what he's too afraid to tell me. I can feel it in him right now, I can feel how much I matter, how much he's let me into his heart. Maddox loves me, I have no doubt of that right now, in this moment.

"Tell me," I cry out. "Tell me what you're too scared to say."

"No," he grunts, sharing the first word he's said since he's been home.

I want to protest, but the pleasure is too strong. Maddox fucks me harder, deeper, until I'm forced to reach out and hold onto the bike. I stare down as he steps back, holding my hips up and watching as his cock slides in and out of my heat. My cheeks flush at the sight of his hard, thick, wet length driving in and out of me. God, that's hot.

My orgasm creeps up upon me, shocking me with its intensity. I don't move my eyes from his cock as I come, trembles of pleasure shooting through my body. He reaches down, running his finger over the glistening base of his cock, then he lifts it and presses it to my mouth, his eyes intense.

I open my mouth, letting him slide his finger into my waiting lips. The taste of us combined is such a turn on, my nipples form hard peaks and my sex clenches in response. Maddox's eyes drop closed, and his jaw becomes a tight ball of muscle as he fucks harder and harder, until his lips part in a gasp and I feel him explode inside me.

God, that's a truly beautiful sight. His straining neck, his tight jaw, his flexing muscles . . . like *that* . . . he looks like heaven. He pants out my name, slowing his thrusts. When he finally looks down at me, his eyes are blazing with an intensity I've never seen coming from him. I reach up, cupping his dirty face, and we just sit like that, staring at one another until he finally pulls back.

"Are you okay?" I ask, watching as he jerks his jeans up and hands me my clothes.

I take them, getting dressed quickly. Maddox isn't looking at me; he's just staring at his boots. Something is wrong. The only word he shared with me during our love making was "no". I bite my lip, contemplating my next move, then I do something stupid . . . I ask him what I've been so desperate to know.

"Do you love me, Maddox?"

His entire body jerks and he turns, staring at me in . . . God, if I didn't know better, I'd say it was horror. His face is scrunched, his lips curling and his eyes narrowed. Then he grates out a hoarse, "You deserve someone better than me to love you."

"That's not what I asked," I say in a small voice.

He sighs. "Not right now, Santana. Please."

God.

Rejection hurts.

I nod, turning and walking towards the stairs. "No problem."

"Tan—"

I don't hear whatever else he says, I'm already halfway up the stairs. He can have it his way, I'm not going to push him right now. Obviously something is going down, because there's a darkness eating away at him, and he doesn't need me making that worse.

I just hope it won't ruin what we're fighting so hard to keep.

CHAPTER TWENTY-TWO

2010 – Santana

I twirl in my blue dress, smiling at the reflection in the mirror. One of the club's old ladies got it for me. I'm going on my first date tonight, with a guy I met while working at the local café. He's sweet, kind and cute. I reach up, tucking a strand of dark hair behind my ear. It's looking so much healthier now—in fact, *I* look healthier now.

I've been with Maddox and the Jokers' for just under two years now. It's been a hard journey. First, I had to grieve my sister's death, and that took a long time. There are still days I miss her so much it burns. Coming down from the drugs was another big challenge, but as time has gone on, things have gotten easier.

I got a job two months ago, deciding it was time to get my life together. I've been sitting around the clubhouse for too long now, watching and living in their dark world. I need to start creating a life of my own, and getting a job was the best way to do that. Then I met Thomas and now, for the first time since Pippi's death, I feel like things are looking up.

"How does it fit?"

I turn and smile at Penny. She's not an old lady, but she's close with Krypt, another one of the club members, and she and I get along quite well.

"I don't know," I say. "Do you think it looks okay?"

She smiles, her blue eyes sparkling with happiness. "It looks gorgeous. He'll never know what hit him."

"Santana!"

The sound of Maddox's booming voice fills my room, and I roll my eyes. Did I mention Maddox is controlling? Well, he is. He's always been protective, since the moment he picked me up off those streets, but he's also a biker . . . which combined makes things very . . . *painful.*

"Up here," I call.

"Why the fuck is there a fuckin' boy at my door?"

Shit.

I quickly put the clip into my hair, and rush out of the room and down the stairs. Maddox is standing at the bottom of those stairs, his big arms crossed over his chest. Maddox is an impressive man. There are many times I've had to stop myself from staring at his beauty and rugged good looks. He's tall, broad, and has a face that belongs on the cover of . . . *Biker Weekly* . . . only the good one.

He's stunning.

Blue eyes travel down over my dress, and then flick back up to mine. His jaw tightens and he turns to stare at Thomas, who is standing at the open door with his mouth slightly agape. Oh yeah, I forgot to tell him I live with a biker. A big, pissed off biker. Maddox's leather jacket squeaks as he turns back to me and walks over, stepping up so we're face to face.

"No."

I cross my arms. "Don't, Maddox. I live here, but you're not my father."

"Not fuckin' old enough to be your fuckin' father, so stop insulting me. What I am, though, is someone who cares about you. You've lived through a lot of shit, and that fucker looks dodgy."

I snort, tilting my head to the side. "Unless he was wearing leather, riding a bike and swearing, you'd think he looked dodgy."

He grins, and I shake my head with a sigh.

"I met him at work. We're going out for lunch."

"No, you ain't."

"Oh yes, I am."

I try to step past him, but his hand lashes out, taking hold of the railing and stopping me.

"Maddox," I protest. "Why the hell won't you let me have a life?"

"You got a job?"

"Yes!"

"Friends?"

"Yes!"

"Then you've got a life. That—" He jerks his finger towards Thomas. "—is a cock wanting in you . . . not a life."

"Oh my God," I cry, throwing my hands up. "Why do you have to be so vulgar?"

Maddox turns to Thomas. "How old are you, boy?"

"Nineteen, ah, sir."

He turns back to me. "Nineteen year old boys think about nothin' more than their cocks and their stomachs."

"Maybe they do, but I don't think about those things. Do you think I can't take care of myself?"

He tilts his head to the side, studying me. "I know you can."

"Then start showing it. We're going to lunch, Maddox. We're not going to some back road to fuck."

He flinches, and his eyes harden. "Don't fuckin' say shit like that."

I sigh and push at his chest. "Move, I'm going out. I'll be home in a few hours."

"Fine, but Krypt is goin' to send a boy to trail you."

"He is not!" I cry, stepping past him when he moves.

"Keep it in your pants, boy," Maddox barks at Thomas as I reach the door. "I have many awful things I can do with it if you don't."

"Yes, sir," Thomas splutters.

Oh God.

Who said bikers were cool?

~*~*~*~*

2014 Santana

The club is pounding at full force when I step through the front doors. Waves and shouts are thrown in my direction as I pass the drunken bikers, club whores and old ladies all milling about. I head right for Maddox's office, needing to see him. After last night, I just want to make sure everything is okay with us.

I knock on the door before entering, but no one answers. Hesitantly, I open the door. He's not in here, which either means he's not at the club, or he's somewhere else…possibly down at the sheds. "Ain't there, princess."

I turn and see Tyke wheeling down the hall. I smile at him. "No problems, has he been gone for long?"

"Nah, just an hour."

"Right, I'll wait for him in here, then."

He flashes me a smile before disappearing down the hall and back into the chaos. I step into Maddox's office and close the door behind me, then I sit down at his desk, putting my feet up on it and leaning back in his chair. I do this for a few minutes, then I resort to swinging in circles before sighing and stopping.

There's nothing on his desk, really, aside from a few papers and pens. He doesn't have a computer or anything special like that. I decide I'll organize it for him; it'll give me something to do. Maybe I'll even spread myself out on it for when he returns. I gather all the papers into a file, and stack them, sorting them from A to Z.

I glance around, wondering where he keeps them, when I notice a filing cabinet. It would be there, surely. I get up and walk over, pulling the drawers, but they're locked. Hmmmm. I go in search for a key, finding one in the safe sitting on a shelf. It's cracked open slightly, which is strange. He must have grabbed something out of it and hurried off, not locking it correctly. From the looks of it, there's nothing special in there anyway.

I pull out the key and rush back over and test it in the filing cabinet, and sure enough, it unlocks it. I pull it open, glancing at the unlabeled dividers. Great, he doesn't put anything away properly. *Fine, I'll do it myself.* I pull the small stack of papers out and walk back over to the desk, dropping them.

I begin to sort. It's mostly invoices, things like that. I come across a yellow folder at the bottom, labeled *Santana*. Curious, I flip it open. It's a few police records in regards to that horrible night, as well as some prescriptions. Things like that. I keep flicking through until I come across my sister's name. It's only by pure luck that I see it, but it stops me, and I pull out the bundle of papers attached to it.

God, I wonder if it's her death records.

I flick through. There's strange information about illegal farms and slaves, as well as some with contact names and dates. Kennedy's name pops up and I find a newspaper report on his arrest, saying he was taken in for drug possession. A pang radiates through my chest at the thought that Kennedy is now in prison.

I want to hate him and feel as though he deserves that, but I just can't. He was good to me—maybe to others he was a monster, but he gave me far more than the streets ever could. Yes, my addictions came from him, but I had a roof over my sister's head and someone who cared. We couldn't be too picky when negativity surrounded us, could we?

I flick past the article and stare down at some printed emails. They're from about two years ago, sent from Maddox's email address. I am about to flick past them when I catch the topic. It's my sister's full name and date of birth. Unable to put them down, I sit back and start reading them. The first, or the one on the top, is an email from Maddox. I read it, and my world changes.

To: Cane Earnest

From: Joker's Wrath MC

Subject: Information on Pippa Lexus

Cane,

I'm contacting you for help with some information. A girl in my care went missing late 2008. From what I've been able to gather, she was sold in a drug deal and sent to a farm as a slave. I've not been able to find out which farm or to whom she was sold. I've been told you have information on these things.

She went missing on November 12th 2008 at around six p.m. I found her sister, and by the time I went back, she was gone. After intense

168

research, I found out what happened to her. As far as I know she's still alive, and I need to find her. Any information you have on her would be helpful.

Maddox.

I gasp in pure agony, pressing a hand to my throat as I continue to flick through the emails. The man replies with information stating that a girl of that name and birth date was in fact sold overseas only days after, however he had no further information as to where.

No.

No.

I stumble backwards, the papers slipping from my fingers. This has to be a lie. Maybe Maddox was confused. *He wasn't confused, because he told you she was dead. That he found her dead.* How could he have possibly confused something like that? It only leaves one, horrible, gut-wrenching truth.

Maddox lied to me.

I don't realize I'm panting and sobbing until I stumble forward and land on my hands and knees because my eyes are so terribly blurred. I gasp and cry out for my sister as I crawl out into the hall, rage and pure heartbreak fighting to win through. I shove to my feet, wailing in agony as I run.

I crash into a hard, lean chest. Strong hands curl around my shoulders and push me back. Through my blurred vision I see Mack, staring down at me with a confused, worried expression. "*Chante*, what's going on?"

"Is it a lie?" I scream so loudly everyone in the room stops.

"What? Honey, what's going on?"

"My sister, is she fucking dead?"

169

He flinches and I can see it, I can see every answer I need in his eyes. I pull my hand back and I slap him so hard pain radiates up my arm. "You all lied to me?" I scream so loudly my own ears protest against the invading noise. "You fucking lied to me!"

"Santana," he says, carefully. "It's not what you think. Let me call Maddox and . . ."

"Go to hell!"

I run past him, tripping and stumbling a few more times before I get to the door. The pain in my heart can't be controlled. It feels like someone has shoved a hot poker into my chest and ripped it out, crushing it and stomping on it, before shoving it back in. Pippa. My poor, sweet sister. All along I've been living a happy, loving life while she's been someone's slave.

At that very thought I collapse to the floor, screaming, my fingernails going to my cheeks and tearing at the skin there as reality crushes me. She's been alive all this time, scared and alone, living in pure hell while I've been enjoying my lying lover. Strong arms go around me, but I squirm in protest, crying out profanities as my feet kick about.

"Calm down, Santana, *calm*," Mack yells.

"Let me go, you lying son-of-a-bitch!"

"You need to hear him out, you need to understand—"

I jerk forward, forcing him to let me go. I spin around, charging towards him, fists clenched. "Understand?" My voice is a frantic, desperate scream. "Understand? You want me to understand that the man I love lied to me for five years, and that everyone I thought was my fucking family stood by and let it happen? She was alive all this time, and you all let me believe she was dead!"

"It was for the best. If you'll calm down enough to let us explain—"

I don't listen to anymore; I just turn and run towards the gates. Mack barks a curse, calling on the guys to "stop me". I'm a fast runner, faster than most of these bikers. I'm out the gate and across the road in the thick forest before they've even had the chance to reach the gates.

I shove through the thick bushes and trees, tears pouring out of my eyes as my heart falls into a thousand more pieces. Not only have I found out the girl I fought so hard for has been alive all this time, but the man I have fallen in love with knew. He knew. Oh God, he knew. A strangled bellow of raw anger rips from my throat.

I don't know where I'm going. I don't even know what I'm going to do.

Right now, I have no one.

CHAPTER TWENTY-THREE

2014 – Maddox

My phone rings, and I glare at the man over from me. He's got information, but gathering it is proving to be fuckin' hard. He refuses to give me answers, even with Krypt's persuasion in the forms of punching, stabbing, and burning.

We've been at it for two hours, and the fucker refuses to give us what we want. Kennedy's lead is a fuckin' flop, and our next best option is killing the fucker. My phone stops ringing, for less than a second, before it starts again. Fuck, someone wants me.

I lift it out, not taking my eyes from the bloody, battered male in front of me. "What?" I bark.

"Maddox, we have a huge fucking problem."

It's Mack, and by the sounds of it, the man is frantic.

"What's goin' on?"

"Santana came by . . . She was in your office and decided to start organizing papers. You left your safe open and she went into the filing cabinet . . ."

I'm already rushing forward, even before the words leave his lips.

"She knows, Maddox."

No.

Fucking no.

"Where is she?" I bark.

"She ran. I've got the guys looking for her but so far, we've not been able to find her."

"Well fuckin' find her," I roar. "I'm on my way!"

I throw the phone so hard against the wall it smashes. Krypt turns to me, his eyes narrowed.

"What's goin' on?"

"She knows, she fuckin' knows."

"Shit."

"We gotta roll; kill that fucker. I don't have time for this shit."

"What?" The man croaks. "No."

"You gonna tell me what you fuckin' know?" I bark, pulling out my gun.

"I can't . . . they'll . . . they'll kill me."

"Then allow me to make it easier for them."

I lift the gun and I shoot him right in the middle of the eyes. I don't even watch the blood explode from the back of his head before I turn and charge out of the room with a bark to Krypt. "Clean that up."

I have bigger things to worry about, including how the hell I'm going to get my girl back.

CHAPTER TWENTY-FOUR

2014 – Santana

My hands tremble as I shove my clothes into my suitcase. I'm not sure where I'm going to go, but I'm not staying here. I can't be at Mack's house, and I certainly can't go back to Maddox's. I need to find somewhere to base myself before I get to work on finding my sister. I won't leave her in hell a second longer than necessary. I've let her down.

This is all my fault.

"Santana!"

Maddox's booming voice fills my ears. I don't move. I don't even look up when I hear his booted strides coming up the stairs. My door swings open, and my fingers tremble as I try to avoid staring at the man who broke my heart. He stops, and the room is so silent I can hear his panting breath.

"You're leaving."

It's not a question, but even if it was, I wouldn't answer it. I don't owe him any explanations. I just keep packing with shaky hands, trying to keep the hysteria inside.

"Santana, I know you're hurtin'. I fucked up lettin' you believe Pippa was dead, but you need to understand it was the best thing at the time."

I say nothing. My fingers clench around the shirt in my hands, but I don't answer. *Be calm. Leave. Don't get into it with him.*

"You were in a bad way. I went looking for her and she was gone. When I found out what'd happened, I came back to tell you."

Breathe. Breathe.

"You were scratching your arms to pieces, screaming and thrashing. I knew then and there you couldn't handle it. If I'd have told you, you would have rushed out, desperate for drugs, and killed yourself before you could ever help her."

I begin to shake all over.

"So I told you she was dead. I wanted you to get better. That was the only way you would pick up your life. I never stopped lookin', not even for a fuckin' second. I was going to tell you when I found her . . ."

I turn, my eyes wild, my body shaking with rage. Maddox is standing at the door, staring at me, his hands in fists by his side.

"It. Wasn't. Your. Right," I spit at him.

"No, but I was doin' the best I could at the time."

"You told me she was dead," I scream, finally losing my cool.

"Because you would have fuckin' killed yourself if I didn't. Then where would that have left her?"

I charge towards him, my fists flying towards his chest. He catches them in his big hands, holding me as I thrash.

"She's been alive all this time, all this fucking time. She's been suffering while I've been living a wonderful life. You might have had your reasons for keeping it from me at first, but for five fucking years?"

"I wanted to get information. I wanted you to be able to find her easily, not run around the fuckin' world lookin'. You would have done that; you would have carried on and rushed out with no information, puttin' yourself in a deadly situation."

"Of course I would," I scream, angry tears sliding down my cheeks. "She's my sister."

"Yeah," he barks. "And who would have helped her if you got yourself killed? Huh?"

"You kept something from me that you had no right to keep."

"That's not what I fuckin' asked," he bellows, jerking me closer. "I ask who the fuck would have helped her if you had jumped out into that fuckin' dangerous world and gotten yourself killed? Because you fuckin' would have, Santana. It's more dangerous than you could ever fuckin' understand."

"It still wasn't your right," I yell, kicking out and hitting his shins. He bares his teeth at me in a deadly hiss, but doesn't let me go. "I mourned her. I cried for her. You let me believe I'd fucking failed!"

"No," he barks. "I let you believe she was in a better fuckin' place so you could pick yourself up and put your own life together."

"But she wasn't in a better place, was she? She was suffering."

"I've spent five fuckin' long years searchin' for her, Santana. I never stopped, not for a fuckin' second. Do you think you would have had the contacts I've got, if you had have gone out on your own?"

"Even if that's true," I whisper, my body slumping, "you still lied to me. You still kept something from me. You could have held me back, you know you could have, but instead you chose to lie. You let me fall for you, and all along it's been a big, fucking lie."

"No," he rasps.

"Let me go, Maddox. We're done here."

"No."

"Let me go!" I scream. "I said we're fucking done."

"What're you goin' to do?" he snarls. "Run out there and try to find someone whose situation you know nothing about?"

"She's my sister. Of course I'm going to fucking find her."

"You'll fail," he barks. "You know why? You have no contacts and no leads. If you want to find her, there's only one way to do that, and it's through me. You want to find her, you stay here and you find her. You wanna do it alone, then run out there, but you won't be gettin' shit from me."

The bastard.

"You're blackmailing me," I whisper, staring up at him in horror.

"No," he says, his voice low and throaty. "I'm givin' you a choice."

"If I walk out, you won't help me. You're using the information you have to keep me here. That's blackmail."

"Or maybe I'm just not ready to let you go."

I look away, anger and pain fighting inside me. Anger at him for lying to me, and pain because I don't want to spend my life without him.

"You don't get a choice."

He lets me go, his body stiff. He steps back, letting his arms fall by his sides. "Whatever you think I did, you're wrong. I only ever had one goal, and that was to keep you safe. I did what I had to do to make that happen. Hate me, go ahead, but if you want my fuckin' help, you'll stay."

Then he turns and walks out, slamming the door behind him.

I fall to my knees, and for the hundredth time today. I cry.

~*~*~*~

177

2014 - Santana

I know he's right.

I don't have a choice here, not really. If I go out on my own, I could easily get killed, or worse, sold too. Maddox has information, leads and contacts. He's the only person who can help me with this, and he's the one person that makes it so hard for me. I don't want to be near him, and yet the very thought of him makes my heart burn with want.

I'm curled in my bed at Mack's house. I've cried myself into exhaustion. My heart hurts, my body aches, and I'm so damned confused I don't know which way to turn. All I know is that I have to help Pippa, no matter the cost. If it means I have to work with Maddox to do that, then I will. If it means I'll save my sister, then I'll do whatever I can.

My door creaks open, and I roll over to see Mack standing with a sandwich in one hand and a soda in the other. He walks in, placing the items down on the bedside table. "You gotta eat, or you'll crumble."

I nod, turning away, tucking myself back into a ball.

"You take the time to hurt, Santana; you have the right to do that. But eventually, you're going to have to pick yourself up and decide what to do. I know you're angry at Maddox, again, you have the right to be, but you need to understand that everything he did, he did because he loves you. Hate him for it if you must, but just remember that with each cruel word, you're breakin' his heart as much as he's breakin' yours. You gotta decide where you want him, and leave it there. He doesn't deserve this either, because no matter what you believe, he's worked his fuckin' ass off to find that girl."

Then I hear him leave the room, closing the door softly behind him. More tears leak out of my eyes, because I know he's right. Maddox didn't do it to hurt me; he did it to protect me. I know that, but right now everything inside

178

my body hurts. It hurts so badly. I don't want to let go of my anger just yet, but at the same time, it hurts to be so in love with him.

I close my eyes, so exhausted. The blankets around me don't have the same warmth they usually have. The pillows aren't comforting, and the soft sounds of Mack talking downstairs bring me no relief. My heart aches in a way it's never ached before. A huge part of me wants to crawl out of this bed and find Maddox, wrapping myself in his arms. The other part refuses to let him in.

The last thought in my mind is of my sister, and how she must be feeling in this moment. Is she scared? Is she happy? Is she even alive? I wish I had the answers I so desperately need. Instead, I'll go to sleep tonight not knowing if she's going to be okay, and hating that there's a small chance that I'll never find her.

Nothing feels okay right now.

CHAPTER TWENTY-FIVE

2014 – Maddox

"How you doin', Prez?"

Krypt hands me a beer. I take it, swallowing it down, not tasting it but relishing the warmth it brings to my broken, aching body.

"Fine."

"It's goin' to be okay. It's all out there now."

"Bet you're fuckin' real happy about that, ain't ya?" I snap.

He crosses his arms, glaring at me. "I'm not happy to see you hurt, or her, but this shit had to come out, and you know it. Have some fuckin' faith; that girl loves you. She'll hurt, but she'll come around."

"You didn't fuckin' see how she looked at me. There ain't no way she's comin' back."

"She's asleep."

We both turn to see Mack enter the room, beer in hand, tired expression on his face.

"Poor fuckin' girl," I say, my voice tired. "If I had to hear her sobs a second longer, I'd fuckin' die."

"She's hurt, but the pain will ease soon, and she'll want to find her sister. You just gotta be there for her."

Yeah, and not blackmail her because the very idea of losing her is like someone taking my heart out and crushing it.

"I'm gonna be there, I'm gonna find her sister, and I'm gonna give her the last honest thing I can before she steps away from me."

Mack sighs. "She cares for you, bro. I don't think she's just going to run."

I stand, not wanting to hear anymore of their "she'll come back" bullshit. I broke her. I fuckin' tore her heart out and stomped on it. She ain't comin' back; I saw it in her eyes. I drop the beer in the bin as I pass them and walk up the stairs.

"Night, Prez."

I don't answer.

I walk down the long hall and stop at Santana's door. I take the handle, pushing it open softly. I stare at the girl curled in a tight ball on the bed. Her tiny body is tucked up to protect itself from the cold. Her dark hair is fanning out over the pillow, and her eyes are clenched closed, like even sleeping hurts.

I step in, lifting a blanket from the pile of linen sitting beside the bed on a desk. I drape it over her, watching with a broken expression as her fingers go out to grip it, pulling it up under her chin. She doesn't open her eyes, but a huge part of me wishes she would. There's so much I want to say, but I'm too fuckin' broken to let it out.

I leave the room, closing the door softly behind me.

I've lost her, I just fuckin' know it.

I've got no one to blame but myself.

~*~*~*~

2014 – Santana

"Here."

I look up to see Ash and Indi, both smiling. Ash pushes a coffee towards me, and I take it gratefully.

"How are you feeling?"

I shrug. "As good as can be expected, I guess."

"I'm so sorry," Indi says. "I can't imagine how it feels."

I don't know how to answer her, because I'm barely able to filter through my own emotions, let alone trying to explain how it feels to someone else. Instead, I offer her a weak smile and sip the coffee. Mack comes into the living area a moment later, shirtless and carrying a heap of papers. Maddox comes in close behind him, also shirtless. His eyes flick to me, but I keep mine facing the coffee cup.

"We've got information. You wanna hear it?" Mack asks me.

I nod, and am grateful when Ash puts her hand on my shoulder and whispers, "I'll come with you. It's okay."

I stand and follow them to the table, where we all sit down. I keep my eyes off Maddox as I stare at the mass amounts of information presented to me.

"This is what we've got," Maddox begins, and I can feel his gaze on me. "As far as we know, Pippa was sold as a working slave. We've narrowed down a few locations, however we're relying on the help of Kennedy to give us the exact point."

"Kennedy?" I gasp, lifting my head.

Maddox nods. "He's in prison. He knows where Pippa got sent, because he's the one who sold her."

What.

Kennedy . . . sold her?

No. He wouldn't.

"I don't . . . I don't understand."

Maddox sighs. "When you went missing and the drug lords came after him, Kennedy had nothing to offer them. So he sold Pippa to them, knowing they'd get a good buck for her in one of the overseas slave markets."

"But . . . he wouldn't," I whisper, staring at the papers so no one can see the pain in my eyes.

"He did," Maddox says simply.

"Then why haven't you gotten the information from him?"

"Didn't know he was in prison until recently. Been to see him once, he refuses to hand anything over unless . . ."

"Unless what?" I snap.

"Unless he sees you."

My jaw tightens. "He wants to see me?"

"Yeah," Mack grunts. "The fucker is greedy."

"Then why haven't you taken me?" I cry. "If that's all that's been between me and finding Pippa?"

"Wasn't that easy," Maddox grinds out.

"No, because you wanted to fuck me first."

He flinches. "You fuckin' know that ain't true, and if you so much as think it again, I'll pull this fuckin' case and you can do it on your own. Be angry at me as much as you fuckin' like, Santana, but don't you dare, not for one fuckin' second think I used you."

I stare at him, and I can see the pain in his eyes as he speaks. I drop my head.

"When can we go see him?" My voice is broken, like a shaky rasp.

"Today. Now."

I stand. "Then let's do this."

~*~*~*~

We make it to the prison three hours later. Maddox had to work out some details first. I rode with Mack, not wanting to be on the back of Maddox's bike. Being that close to him is too much right now.

Only Maddox, Krypt and Mack came for the journey. The less bikers, the less suspicion raised as to why we're already visiting Kennedy, considering they were only just here.

The security is quite intense, and by the time we're let into the visitors' area, I'm overwhelmed. Maddox stands in front of me, refusing to give me access until he needs to. Mack pats my back once before sitting down with Krypt. A loud buzzer goes off, and then I hear Maddox mutter, "There he is, the fucker."

I peer around him, my heart going a million miles an hour. I haven't had the chance to process the fact that I'm about to see a man I once loved again, and the butterflies and anxiety filling my stomach are enough to make me want to run out and throw up. My hands shake as I catch sight of the man who, more or less, changed my life.

Very little has changed about Kennedy. He's still got salt and pepper hair, and a sophisticated look that even his prison outfit doesn't take away. His eyes fall on me, and I can see him suck in a breath, his hand going up to his heart. Tears well in my eyes, and I'm not sure if they're happy tears or angry tears. Maddox walks over, and I follow closely behind, not touching him, but near enough that I can smell him.

"Sit," he orders, and I do as I'm told, sitting beside him.

I haven't taken my eyes off Kennedy this whole time, and my fingers flinch as I reach out for the phone. Maddox does the same beside me and Kennedy on the other side. I press the cool device to my ear and listen as Kennedy's voice fills the line. "Tanie, oh, sweet Tanie. How I've missed you."

I open my mouth but nothing comes out. A small part of me still feels like a fragile child around Kennedy, but the other part is so angry at him for what he did to Pippa.

"It's okay, sweetheart," he soothes. "It's okay. I'm here now."

His words have my eyes fluttering closed as old memories fill my head. The comfort he gave me, the feeling of his soft hands stroking me to sleep. Then there are the dark memories, where he plunged that needle into my arm, watching the drugs consume me. I shudder and tears trickle down my cheeks.

"Say something, sweetheart, let me hear your voice. It's all I've wanted to hear for so long."

"You sold my sister," I croak.

I finally open my eyes, and Kennedy's expression is pained.

"I thought you were dead, Tanie. I thought—"

"You promised me that you would take care of her. No matter what."

My voice is a rasp of pain, causing even Maddox to flinch beside me.

"I know, but . . . they were going to kill me, Tanie. I had no choice."

"There's always a choice," I cry, meeting his gaze.

"You don't know how hard it's been for me. For so long I thought you were gone . . . until . . ." He looks to Maddox. "Tell me you're okay; tell me everything has been good for you, Tanie."

In other words, tell me the man beside you hasn't caused you pain.

"Everything is fine, but it'll be better when I can find Pippi. Please, Kennedy, if you care about me at all . . . tell me where she is."

He closes his eyes, exhaling loudly, before staring at me again.

"Just let me see you for a minute longer, just a minute. As soon as I tell you, then you're going to walk out of here, and I'll never see you again."

"Just fuckin' speak," Maddox barks.

"It's okay," I say softly, giving Maddox a look. "We're in no hurry."

I'm not saying this because I want Kennedy to feel good; I'm saying it because I don't want to make him angry. I want him to tell me anything he can about Pippa, no matter the cost.

"Thank you," he breathes. "You've grown into such a beautiful young woman—I always knew you would. Tell me what you've been doing, Tanie. Tell me."

I can feel Maddox's glare burning into the side of my face, but I don't look at him. I just focus on Kennedy. "Maddox saved me. I've been with him since. There isn't much to tell, aside from the fact that I'm happy."

Kennedy stares at Maddox, his face full of disgust. "He isn't the type I would have picked you to go for, Tanie. I hope he's good to you."

I can hardly say, "oh no, he's not" or "actually we're not together anymore" because that will give the wrong impression. Instead I force a smile and mutter, "He's fine to me."

Kennedy narrows his eyes. "You don't sound convinced. If he's hurting you, just say the word and . . ."

Maddox snorts loudly, cutting him off. I close my eyes, gathering my calm, before saying, "He's good to me, Kennedy. He's the first—" My voice trembles. "—the first man I've ever fallen completely in love with."

Maddox turns to stare at me, his eyes saying so much, even though his mouth is tight. We hold each other's gaze for a long moment, before I turn and face Kennedy again. He's watching us, suspicion filling his features.

"I don't have long left, Tanie," he finally says. "We only get so much time. I'm so glad I got to see you; I want you to know how sorry I am. I let you down, and for that, I'll never forgive myself."

If he doesn't have much time, I don't want to waste another second. I don't forgive Kennedy for what he did, but I want information, so I smile and whisper, "I forgive you, Kennedy."

He beams, his eyes filling with tears. "You've just set me free."

"Now set Pippa free, for me, please," I plead. "Tell me where she is."

"I don't know where she is; I didn't sell her as a slave. I do know the man I sold her to, however. It's him who would have sold her as a slave."

"Then give me his name."

He sighs. "Jamie Whitman."

I smile through my tears. "Thank you, Kennedy."

"Come and see me again, Tanie. Please?"

I nod. "Of course."

Then I hang up the phone, knowing as well as he does that we'll never see each other again.

CHAPTER TWENTY-SIX

2014 – Santana

"Where's Maddox?" I ask, walking into the main room of the club house.

"No idea," Tyke says, lifting a smoke to his lips and inhaling.

"Thanks," I mutter.

"He's drinkin' himself into a stupor."

I turn to see Krypt with Ash, his arm wrapped firmly around her middle, holding her close to him.

"Oh, right."

"Not sure goin' to see him is the smartest move, Tana. You don't wanna tango with Maddox when he's drunk, and believe me, sweetheart, he's drunk."

I sigh, running my hands over my face. I'm tired. It's been a long, draining few days. Tomorrow we're going to see Jamie Whitman, to see who he sold Pippa to, and whether or not we have the chance to get her back. I know sleep won't come easy tonight, because if the news is bad tomorrow, we're back to square one.

Each day we waste time, she's stuck in that hell for longer than she needs to be.

"I need to talk to him about tomorrow."

"I'd leave it," Krypt advises, his eyes narrowing in warning.

"Maddox doesn't scare me," I say, waving a hand. "Drunk or sober."

"No, but he can be a fucking asshole, and you don't need anymore shit."

"He needs to know I'm leaving, Krypt. You know he won't like it if I go without telling him. I'll be a few minutes."

"Your funeral," he mutters.

"Just be careful, honey," Ash says, forcing a smile.

"I'll be fine."

I disappear down the halls, checking the rooms as I go. Nothing. Maddox isn't in any of them. I decide to check the sheds down the back. He isn't in the first one, but upon entering the second, I see him. He's standing in the corner, half-empty bottle of whiskey in his hand. I hesitate at the door, not entirely sure what to say.

He looks up when the door closes behind me, and the expression on his face breaks my heart. He looks like he's just lost his best friend. He sways slightly on his feet, his blue eyes narrowed in pain and his mouth a weak line on his face, as if it's too hard to scowl or frown. He's drunk, beyond it in fact. I can see it in his eyes. The bloodshot depths have the answers even before he opens his mouth.

"What do you want?"

His voice is a low slur, not defined, but there all the same.

"I . . . I wanted to see you before I went."

"Fuckin' why?"

I cross my arms, tired of arguing. "Because I know you'd want to know."

"What I want," he grates out, "don't fuckin' matter."

"It wasn't my mistake, Maddox. Don't make me suffer for it."

"No." He laughs bitterly. "It wasn't your mistake. You've made that fuckin' clear, over and over again for the past few days. It's all on me, and we're done. So why the fuck are you here?"

An angry pang invades my chest, but I push it back.

"Don't," I warn. "Don't make out like I'm being the selfish one here."

"Aren't you?" he snarls, lifting the bottle to his mouth and taking a long draw from it. "Far as I can see, you're blamin' this shit entirely on me. Not once have you stopped and seen that I fuckin' worked my ass off for you. I didn't have to pick you up off that street; I didn't have to support you all these years, I didn't have to work to find your sister. I fucked up, but you're equally as selfish as me."

"Really?" I say, my voice low. "You're going to throw this back in my face because you're guilty."

He snorts. "Fuckin' yeah."

"You know what? If you want to sit here and drink yourself into oblivion . . . go right ahead. I don't have time for your bullshit games."

I turn to leave, but he's behind me before I reach the door. His hand lashes out, curling around my arm and spinning me so hard I stumble, falling into his chest. With an *oomph*, I gather my footing and push back, but his arm is firmly around my waist.

"Let me go," I grumble against him.

"Here's how this is goin' to go. You can either forgive me, Santana, or you can't. I ain't gonna sit around and play fuckin' games. It's never been the way I roll. You decide what I mean to you, or you walk the fuck outta here and this ends now."

190

"Don't threaten me into deciding right now," I growl, trying to step back, but he's holding me too firmly.

"It ain't a threat, it's a choice. You need to make it."

"You hurt me, you lied, you let me fall—"

I stop talking. I can't say it. Not when we're like this.

"What?" he growls. "Go on and say it."

"It won't change anything."

"Won't it?"

"No."

We're silent for a minute or two before he mutters, "For what it's worth, I fuckin' love you too, Santana."

Jesus. Why did he have to do that? Why did he have to break every restraint inside me? I squirm furiously, angry, hurt, and confused. He lets me go, and I step back, shoving at his chest over and over. He doesn't stop me, but lets me go until my wrists burn from the impact.

"How dare you?" I cry, tangling my fingers into his shirt. "How fucking dare you drop that on me? You broke my heart. You lied to me. You let me believe the only person I loved was dead."

"How long are you gonna hate me for that?" he barks, curling his fingers around my wrists. "I fucked up, but I did it because I care, not because I wanted to hurt you. Do you have any fuckin' idea how hard it's been on me to keep this from you? I knew, I just knew I'd lose you when you found out. Do you know what that did to me? Do you know how much it killed me inside to know I was goin' to lose the only fuckin' thing I fought for?"

"Maddox," I croak. "Don't."

"You've been my life for a little over five years, and I've fought with everything I am for you. I fucked up, I lied because I wanted to protect the broken girl that stumbled into my life. I didn't do it for pain. I've spent every fuckin' day tryin' to find that girl, because you're every fuckin' thing to me, and leaving you without was never an option."

"Maddox."

"So go ahead and fuckin' hate me. Make me suffer for what I did. But know this, Santana: I'm gonna love you for every minute, every hour, every day, every month and every year for the rest of your life, because you're the only person in *my* life that's worth fightin' for."

Tears cascade down my cheeks as I stare at the man who has caused so much emotion in me. From love to hate, he's had it all, but the thing that stands out the most about all of it is that he's not once left my side. In all my years of pain, heartache, loss and growth, Maddox has stood by me, helping me through it, protecting me. He made a mistake, a huge one, but he did it because he loves me.

How can I hate him for that?

"I—"

I don't get to finish my sentence, because he tugs me closer to him, growling a fierce, "No more," before crushing his lips down over mine. His scent surrounds me, alcohol mixed with a smell that belongs to Maddox and Maddox alone. I open my mouth on a moan, tilting my head back to let him take me deeper.

My back hits the wall a second later, and then Maddox's hand is going down the top of my pants. His warm fingers find my clit while my hands fumble madly at his jeans, needing him out of them and inside me. He growls when I slip my hand in, wrapping it around his cock.

"Hurry," I plead.

My pants are gone a second later, and his jeans are jerked down, his cock freed. He growls, low and deep, as he lifts my leg up around his waist and plunges inside me with little warning. God, yes. I cry out his name as I push my hips forward. I don't care about the pain, or the burning sensation spreading through my limbs. All I care about is how good it feels to have him inside me.

"Harder, God, fucking *harder*," I scream.

He fucks me harder. He thrusts until our skin slaps together so fiercely it burns. My fingers claw at his back, tearing into his skin. I come so God damned hard my vision blurs and for a moment, I don't hear my own screaming. Maddox growls his appreciation and then suddenly he's pulling out of me, fingers tangling into my hair to force me to my knees.

"Taste it," he orders. "Taste your cum on my cock. Taste. It."

I open my mouth on a gasp as his glistening cock nears my parted lips. It presses against me and I open for it, letting him slide it in my warm, waiting depths. I moan at the taste that invades my mouth—salty, a little sweet, all Maddox and I. He lets out a ragged hiss as his fingers tangle into my hair.

"Suck baby, suck hard."

I do. I suck hard, my cheeks hollowing around his thick cock. He lets me do this for a few seconds before pulling his cock out and taking it in his hand, running it up and down my cheeks, swirling it around my lips, and then plunging it back in.

"Where am I goin' to blow, baby? You tell me where."

"My . . . f-f-f-face."

"Dirty, filthy girl."

I suck him harder, groaning when I feel him swell in my mouth.

"Coming, fuck . . ."

He pulls out swiftly, and his hand works furiously over his cock. A few pumps later, he explodes, his hot release hitting my mouth and cheeks. He barks a few choice words as he watches his cum hitting my skin.

"Looks so fuckin' good against your skin, so fuckin' sweet."

He drops to his knees in front of me, still stroking his cock. He uses his other hand to take a drop of his cum, then he slips it into my mouth. I whimper at the taste, sucking his finger until he groans my name. He carefully tucks his cock away, before taking hold of the closest item of clothing to wipe my face clean.

Our eyes meet. So much passes.

"Tell me you're goin' to be by my side, now and after we find Pippa."

I stare up at him, still on my knees.

"Tell me, baby," he rasps. "I need to know. My club has been all I've had for so long—it's been all I've worked for. Then I found you. Tell me I get to keep you, tell me this hasn't all been for fuckin' nothing."

I push to my feet, reaching out and taking his face in my hands. "You're not the only one who found something to keep."

He closes his eyes, almost as if my words hurt him because they bring him such relief. He brings his forehead to mine. "I'm an asshole, I'm overbearing and controlling, and I'll drive you fuckin' crazy. But I can swear I'll fuckin' lay my life down for you, honey. Anytime. Anywhere."

"I know that," I whisper. "Because you've proven that to me with how hard you've worked to find my sister."

"I fucked up, I know that. I'll try not to do it again."

"You might have fucked up, but in the grand scheme of things . . . I think you saved me, Maddox. You're right; I would have run after her, not thinking. I would have made it less than a day before my addiction would have crippled me. I owe you my life, and when I find her, she will owe you the same."

"We will find her, one way or another."

I know what he means.

Dead or alive, we'll find her.

I'm not entirely sure that brings me the comfort I need right now, but it'll have to do.

~*~*~*~

2014 - Maddox

"Say nothin', let me fuckin' speak," I growl in Santana's ear as we near the old, fucked up house that holds Jamie.

"I won't," she promises, but I can see her fingers fumbling together with nerves.

Krypt trails me, Mack by his side. I didn't want to show up on a tonne of bikes with demands that would piss this fella off. All I want from him is an answer, and I'll be on my way. I have no fuckin' idea what we're walkin' into, though. Usually I wouldn't bring a woman on club business, but Santana knows more about Pippa then any of us. He might need her to refresh his memory.

We make our way up the rickety steps of the house. My hand stays firmly on Santana's wrist, holding her slightly behind me as we near the front door. I knock loudly, and the old door creaks in protest with each pound of my fist. No one answers for a solid five minutes.

"No one here," Krypt mutters.

Then I hear the back door slam.

"Fucker is around the back, go," I bark.

Krypt and Mack take off before I've even finished my sentence.

"Stay behind me," I bark to Santana, pulling out my gun.

She does as she's told, staying directly behind me as we round the side of the house. Krypt and Mack have a scrawny, greying man on the ground, his hands pulled tightly behind his back. The man is growling protests and spitting nasty words in our direction. I stop in front of him, glancing to make sure Santana is behind me, before stepping on the man's fingers, causing a cry to escape his lips.

"Tryin' to run is a really stupid fuckin' move."

"I don't have your information. I told your boss that. I've given you all I have."

I narrow my eyes. We've never seen this man before. Then it clicks; Kennedy's words ring out in my head. *"You ain't the only ones looking for that girl."*

Fuck.

Looks like the Tinmen have been here first. Not wanting to alarm Santana, I play along.

"I didn't get any fuckin' information. My men mustn't have passed it on."

He stares up at me, his eyes narrowing.

"You're not . . ." His eyes flick to my patches. "You're not them. Who the fuck are you? What the fuck do you want?"

I grin. "Your worst fuckin' nightmare, if you don't tell me exactly what you told them."

"What the fuck is with this girl? Has she got a golden fuckin' pussy or something?"

"You piece of shit!" Santana cries.

I turn, shooting her a glare so deadly her mouth closes and her big brown eyes widen. Smart girl keeps her mouth shut as I turn back to the man.

"I don't have a lot of patience. You either tell me what I want to know, or I'll end shit for you right now."

"End it then," he dares me. "I don't care!"

I drop down in a flash, my gun pressed to his temple.

"Fine by me. I don't need scum like you around."

"Maddox," Krypt warns. "We need this one alive."

Krypt knows me too well; he knows how to scare the fuck out of the bad guy when I need him to.

"Last man you killed had valid information. Don't lose your temper on this one."

"I don't care about this one," I sneer, baring my teeth. "He's a waste of my space."

I flick the safety off my gun. It's all it takes.

"Don't," the man pleads. "I'll tell you, fuck, just let me go."

197

"You tell me what you told them, I'll let you go. I find out you're lying, I'll come back and I'll make it fuckin' burn."

"I-I-I got the girl off Kennedy. He owed me serious cash, she was his payment. I didn't need her, had enough pussy to last me a lifetime with all the drug-fucked whores about."

I hit him, so hard his temple splits open and a piercing scream leaves his throat. Santana gasps behind me, but she says nothing.

"Why the fuck did you do that?" he cries, squirming.

"I'll do worse if you disrespect women like that again."

"Fuck, dude," he grunts. "If you'd let me finish, I could tell you what you clearly want to know."

"Hurry it up."

He glares at me, but continues. "I had the girl, but I had no use for her. Sure, I could sell her as a prostitute, but I wasn't interested, and she was too young. That would cause too much shit. I had contacts, people that brought strays to work overseas. I got a good buck for her, being young. Not as good as I would have got if she was a male, but it covered Kennedy's drug debt."

I glance at Santana, whose fists are tight. Her face is white and she's trembling slightly. I give her a slow nod, letting her knows it's okay.

"Who did you sell her to?"

"Atreau James. He buys slaves and divides them out between farms, making a profit off them. Powerful man, deadly, too."

"How long ago did you share this information with the other club?"

"Y-y-y-yesterday."

"And where can I find Atreau?"

198

"Outside of Mexico. He runs a business on the side, called Trea's Tilts—it's not for money, it's just a cover-up."

"That it?"

"Yeah," he mutters. "I don't know what happened to her. I don't check up on the people I get rid of."

I grin at him again. "No matter; you won't be doing it again."

I point my gun at him.

"You said . . . you said you wouldn't kill me!" he squeals.

"You sold someone important to the girl I love, you use women, you're a dirty scumbag the world will be better without—let's call it an act for humanity, shall we?"

"No," he screams, squirming. "Don't."

I turn to Santana. "Turn away, baby."

She shakes her head. "No. I want to watch him die for what he's done."

Her face is determined and steely.

"Turn, Santana," I warn.

Mack lets go of the man, leaving Krypt to hold him down. He takes Santana and forcefully presses his hand over her eyes.

"Let me go!" she cries.

He nods at me.

I turn and pull the trigger, one clean shot through the forehead. The man's squealing stops and he slumps to the ground, lifeless.

"Deal with that. I'm organizing flights for tonight. We don't have time to wait. If Howard's guys found out before, they're likely on their way."

"On it," Krypt says.

I turn and Mack spins Santana around, letting go of her eyes but holding her shoulders so she can't turn. I take her, pushing her forward. She don't need to see that shit.

"They're after her too," she whispers. "You didn't tell me that."

"Wasn't sure, Tana," I mutter, pushing her towards the bikes. "But I am now. Chances are they're trying to organizing a way to get to her. We're goin' to leave tonight. I have contacts, luckily for me."

"Contacts?"

"I've got a man that owns a plane. For the right price, he'll take us."

"You know a man that's got a plane?" She gasps.

I grin at her. "Baby, I'm a biker. I know everyone."

She nods. "What if they've already left? Why didn't they kill him, Maddox? They left him open for you to find and get information from . . ."

"Could be a set up, could be that they want us to chase them overseas, could be as simple as them thinkin' we didn't know about him."

"Two of those are dangerous . . ."

"Riskin' it, babe. Don't think we've got any other choice."

I pull a helmet over her head, nodding to Mack.

"Finish up here. I'll go back and organize some solid men to take."

"On it, boss."

I climb onto the bike, starting it. Santana's arms go around me, and I can feel her hands shaking. I wrap my fingers around hers, squeezing.

"It's goin' to be okay, Tana."

"I hope so," she whispers.

Me fuckin' too.

CHAPTER TWENTY-SEVEN

2014 – Santana

"It's going to be okay," Ash says as I throw some clothes into a suitcase.

"They're after her, too. They're going to get to her before us and . . ."

"Hey," she says, taking my shoulders and turning me towards her. With a soft expression, she whispers, "Trust in Maddox. He's going to make sure she gets home."

"He's not God," I say in a shaky tone. "If they get there before us, they're going to take her, and do God knows what else."

"They might not have left yet. We could be in for a head start."

"Maybe," I say, staring at the faded red shirt in my hands. "God, if something happens to her before I can get to her . . ."

"You're thinking too far ahead. For her sake you need to stop doing that, honey. It won't help anything. You can't change what happens, but you can change how you think about it. Be positive; she needs that from you."

I nod, swallowing back the tears threatening to escape. "Thank you for helping me pack, I needed a break from the drama."

She waves a hand. "Always."

We hug once more.

"Ready to go?"

We both turn to see Maddox and Krypt at the door. Maddox is dressed all in black, his long hair pulled away from his face allowing me the full, perfect view of his chiseled jaw and the way it shapes his gorgeous face. I nod softly, throwing the shirt into the suitcase and zipping it.

Maddox comes in, lifting my luggage while his other hand finds my chin. He tilts my face up, his blue eyes intense. "It's goin' to be okay."

"I know," I whisper, even though I don't really believe it.

"There's still a good amount of activity at the Tinmens' compound, which means there's a good chance they haven't left. We're goin' to get her back, I promise you that."

I nod. It's all I can do. He leans down, pressing a hard kiss to my lips before letting me go and turning towards the door.

"Let's do this."

Yes, let's.

~*~*~*~

The plane is actually quite nice. It's older, but the inside is clean and tidy. It has one row of seats along the left side, and on the right are some beverage and refreshment carts, as well as blankets, pillows and other such comforts. The toilet is right up the back, and is typical for the plane's tiny size.

We didn't take a whole lot of bikers, being that the plane only carries ten people. That made it difficult to take anymore than that. Maddox took his finest, though. His finest being himself, Krypt, Mack, Ryhder, Tyke, Austin, Grimm and Zaid.

I'm not entirely sure why he brought Tyke, being that he can only stand for so long before needing to sit from the pain. My guess is that he doesn't like to leave him out, and that Tyke is one of his closest friends. Plus, he'd make a good watch, and the man is killer with a gun—probably better than most of the club members.

"What's the plan when we get in, boss?" Krypt asks.

"We've got an address. Not sure if it's still his, but it's worth a shot. We tracked it down from the business and went from there. He lives outta town, so it makes sense that it'd be the place."

"How are we goin' to go in?"

Maddox has a glint in his eye when he answers. "We're goin' to go up to the door and ask for the girl, gauge his reaction. Best case scenario, he hands her over. Worst, he has a fuck-load of people that will put up a fight. That's why we're takin' a whole lot of weapons."

"That's so dangerous," I say.

Maddox reaches over, taking my hand and squeezing it. "No other choice. A surprise attack is the best we've got."

"What if . . ." I hesitate. "What if I went in and pretended I was lost . . . I could see if she was there first."

"No fuckin' way," Maddox growls. "I've sent you in as a plant before; didn't like how it ended."

"It was fine," I protest.

He flashes me a wild glare. "You were hurt, and it fuckin' scared you. Not happenin'."

"You could get her killed," I say, my voice firm. "If you go in and just demand her, he might make a call that will end her. Then what?"

Maddox leans in close. "You need to trust me, Santana."

"You've hardly made that easy."

He flinches, and everyone else stares at the walls as if they've suddenly changed color. Maddox gives me such a pained expression my heart explodes as he stands and disappears to the small space at the back of the plane. I sigh, dropping my head into my hands. God, I don't mean to be such a brat. I'm scared for my sister. If this goes wrong . . .

God.

I push to my feet, avoiding the stares as I head down the hall. A hand lashes out as I near, and I stare down to see Mack is holding onto my arm. His expression is firm, but gentle. "Be careful about the words you use in there, Santana. He's tryin' the best he can to get that girl back."

"I know that, Chief," I whisper. "I know."

He gives me a sympathetic look, and then surprises me by standing and wrapping his arms around me. I fold into him, sighing and forcing down the wall of tears building up.

"We're all goin' to do the best we can, *chante*. Don't doubt that."

"I don't," I whisper. "I'm just scared and being a brat. I'm sorry."

"Not me you need to say that to," he murmurs, letting me go and staring down at me with those piercing brown eyes.

"I know."

I give him a weak, but grateful smile before disappearing into the same space Maddox went. I find him standing, staring out the small, oval window. His fists are tight balls beside his body, and his face is a mask of anger, frustration and hurt. I don't hesitate—I walk over and wrap my arms around his waist, pressing my tiny body against his big one.

"I'm sorry, you know I didn't mean that."

"I don't know what you fuckin' mean anymore. If you're goin' to punish me for what I did over and fuckin' over then maybe we're wastin' our time here."

My heart twists.

"No," I whisper. "No that's not . . . that's not . . ."

He turns to me, forcing my arms to drop from his waist. "Isn't it?"

"No," I whisper. "If I didn't have you, Maddox . . . I wouldn't . . ." I swallow. "I wouldn't be me."

His eyes soften, and his hand curls around my chin. "Then stop fuckin' punishing me. I'm doin' everything I can."

"I know," I say, reaching up on my tiptoes to press my lips to the side of his mouth. "I know, and I love you for it."

His hand goes out and curls around my waist. "Say that again."

"I love you."

His lips come down over mine in a kiss that has my toes curling. It's all tongues, heated passion and desperation. I press my body to his, feeling the bulge of his cock against my belly. I rub against him, whispering his name as my tongue slides over his bottom lip.

"Fuck, stop, baby," he growls. "Or I'll bend you over here and put my cock deep inside your sweet cunt."

"Do it," I whimper.

"Can't," he grunts. "I'll make you scream so loud the pilot will crash this fucker, and we'll never get to where we need to go."

I lean down, nipping his neck softly. "I have plenty of places to smother my screams."

"Fuck."

"Fuck me, Maddox. Make it all go away."

He does.

He jerks my skirt up, pulling my panties aside. Then his big fingers are inside me, thrusting while he uses his other hand to free his cock. My face presses against the window, my pussy clenching with need. Someone could come in any second, and that thought doesn't do anything but turn me on. God, does it turn me on.

"You're so fuckin' wet on my fingers, honey," Maddox rasps. "So sweet."

"Hurry," I plead. "Maddox, hurry."

He removes his fingers, leaving me bare and cool. That doesn't last long—soon his cock is inside me, deep and hard. I stretch around him with a whimpered plea. His fingers dig into my hips hard enough to bruise and then he's fucking me from behind, my face still pressed against the glass. He fucks me with a brutal force that has my back arching.

I bite my lip so hard I draw blood. God, it feels so fucking good.

"Yes," he grunts. "Fuckin' yes."

In and out, his cock burns its way into my soul. Just like he's found his way into my heart. My pussy acknowledges the invasion with excitement, squeezing and clenching around him until I'm forced to bite my arm to stop the desperate scream from leaving my throat. I come so hard around him he's forced to slow his thrusts because I'm squeezing him so tightly.

"Holy fuck, your cunt is squeezin' me so tight it fuckin' won't let me fuck you harder."

I mewl at his words, clawing at the wrists that are attached to my hips. He hisses when my nails break his skin, as my orgasm rocks me.

"Baby, I'm goin' to come. Fuck, yes. Squeeze your little cunt around me again, oh . . . *yeah* . . . that's it."

He explodes inside me with jerky thrusts and angry grunts. He pumps his cock into me until he's milked every last drop from his body, then he slowly slides out, pulling me back so he can wrap his arms around me. He nuzzles my neck while his fingers run down my belly, swirling through my arousal before lifting it to his lips and sucking.

"We taste fuckin' good together, honey."

"Yeah we do." I smile softly.

"You two done there? I need to fuckin' piss."

Krypt's voice comes from behind the curtain. My cheeks burn and I turn, burying my face in Maddox's chest. He chuckles softly, while straightening my skirt and pulling up his jeans. He pulls me out, looking over me before yelling out to Krypt. "Yeah, we're done."

"Fuckin' thank God," Krypt mutters, coming through the curtain. He gives Maddox a wry smile before going into the toilet.

"That was fun," I murmur, horrified.

Maddox laughs. "Not like he can say he's never done it."

Krypt snorts from the toilet. "Not in a small, confined space with fragile ears around."

"I believe I recently busted you and Ash goin' at it," I call out.

He laughs. "Touché."

Maddox leads me out and past all the smirking faces. Magic, they all heard us.

"Feelin' better?" Mack grins.

"Bite me, Chief."

He throws his head back and laughs. Rhyder actually lifts his hand to give me a high five. At my look, he lowers it with a chuckle.

"Someone kill me now."

Maddox puts a big arm around me with a laugh. "You're doin' me proud, honey."

Oh, I just bet I am.

CHAPTER TWENTY-EIGHT

2014 – Maddox

The property is located about two hundred miles from Mexico City. We arrive in the early hours of the morning and check into the hotel. None of us sleep incredibly well, and by mid-morning we're all itching to get to the property to find out if we're too late. Santana insists on coming, even though I don't want her there, but like before, she's the only one who can identify the girl.

The ride out is long, and fuckin' horrible. I've kept a brave face for Santana, but the truth is I have no fuckin' idea what we're about to walk in to. It could be a fuckin' big trap, or the girl might not even be here. Then we're back to square one. That shit won't go down well for me, but I might not be able to avoid it.

When we're close enough to large acreage, I pull the car off the road down a small dirt track. The others follow suit and then we all climb out, staring at the miles and miles of fields. I can see hints of a house in the distance, but it's well hidden. I pull out weapons, loading them into my pants. We're all carrying at least two guns and a few knives.

"Are you sure this is it?" Santana asks. "I'd hate to ambush the wrong house."

"This is it, all right."

"So do we just . . . walk in?"

I tuck the last gun in my jeans. "Yeah, we just fuckin' walk in."

When we're loaded up, I give Tyke instructions to alert us of any newcomers. He nods, assuring me he's got it covered. Then we make our way towards the fences surrounding the property. We find a break in one to the far left, and after a bit of reworking, we manage to slip through. The driveway is blocked with a large electric gate, no doubt equipped with cameras.

When we're all in, we begin the long trek towards the house. My hand stays near my gun at all times, on alert. Santana stays by my side, but she's barely said a word all morning. I know how she's feelin' inside; this is fuckin' killin' her.

"See the house," I murmur to the guys, pointing.

"Looks fuckin' big," Krypt mutters.

"Jesus," Rhyder comments. "I wonder how . . . *many* he's got there."

"Probably a good fuckin' lot," I grunt.

When we reach the thick trees surrounding the house, we all gather. I point to the front door, which appears to have no one near or around it.

"Oh my God."

I turn at the sound of Santana's voice; she's staring through a gap in the thick trees. I step closer to her, seeing what's got her so upset, her face white as a ghost's. What I see has a curse ripping from my throat. There's around twenty men and women working in a field of tobacco crops. They're all quite skinny, and their skin is olive from hours in the sun.

Guess that means we've found the right place.

"I . . ." Santana's voice trembles. "Oh God."

"Hey," I say, turning and taking her face in my hands. "You want to come with us, you need to get it together. I know what seein' that does to you, but I need you to keep your shit under wraps. I need you alert and ready. If you're cryin', then you ain't watchin'."

She nods, straightening her back and swiping away her tears. I'm fuckin' proud of her in that moment, so fuckin' proud. I press a kiss to her forehead, before turning back to the group.

"Right, we've got two options. We ambush, or we walk right up to the door and just knock – see how we go."

"I say we go right to the door," Krypt says, thumbing the gun in his pants.

"I agree," Rhyder says, staring at the large house.

"We're stupid to start an attack if there's a chance we can just get the girl back with a bit of force," Zaid mutters, staring at me.

"Right, then lets do this. Santana, you fuckin' stay behind me at all times. Don't move."

She nods, her face still pale. She's fuckin' terrified, but she's holding it together…*for now*. I hope I didn't make a mistake bringin' her here.

"Let's move in," Krypt says. "Maddox, you go first. Santana can go behind you and we'll tail her."

"Let's do it."

We all move towards the front of the house. There seems to be nobody around, except for the people in the fields, the house seems almost dead. It's a massive home, somewhat castle like with it's square, jutting stone tops. The house is all a grey looking brick, no porches, few windows. We're only twenty or so meters from the front door when they appear.

They come from behind trees, from inside the house, from the back. Every fuckin' where. About ten, maybe fifteen, of them…I don't know. They're all armed, *guns*, and from the looks of them, we've just made a huge fucking mistake. Fuck. I go to clutch Santana's hand, but one of them barks, "Move, I'll blow your fuckin' brains out."

Shit. Fuckin' shit.

"Set up," Krypt growls.

A tall man with blonde hair, scattered with tiny pieces of grey, appears through the armed men. He's got a small smirk on his face as he takes us in, his eyes particularly trained on Santana. He crosses his skinny arms, and his grey eyes twinkle with victory. This must be Atreau. Motherfucker.

"Well, isn't this interesting," he says in a low, girlish tone. "Butch said you'd show up, but I really didn't think he was right."

Butch.

FUCK.

It all falls into place like a fuckin' bomb going off inside my chest. I close my eyes for a brief second, fuckin' sick to my stomach with the reality of the situation I just put my boys, and my girl, in. This was a big, fuckin' set up. The Tinmen weren't chasin' Pippa to get back at me, they were chasin' her to get me here.

"I don't really know what's so good about the girl, that would make all of you would show up, but I'm not sad about it. I need some new workers, and all this muscle will do the job."

"Like fuck," Krypt growls.

Atreau laughs, looking around him as if to say, "Are you serious?".

"One click of my fingers," he laughs joyfully, "and you're all minced meat on the ground."

I can feel Santana behind me, her fingers trembling as she places them on my back. I've fucked up. Now we're all going to pay for it. The only good news we have is that he wants us as slaves and not to kill us here and now, that gives me some hope that the boys will come for us.

"Don't say another word, Krypt," I mutter, low and deadly.

Atreau laughs again, fucker. "Yes, you should listen. I've been known to kill men for less. But, like I said, I could use your kind of muscle. So, if you will…"

He waves a hand towards the door. That's when Mack shoots. I don't see it coming; he's behind all of us. But suddenly he's firing, shot after shot into the men surrounding us. It takes them a moment to respond, by this time Krypt, Zaid and Rhyder are all shooting. I spin, pulling out my gun, shooting a man aiming at Santana. His brains scatter as his body falls into a heap on the ground.

"Fuckin' run!" I roar at her.

She doesn't hesitate, she knows better. She turns and runs towards the thick trees we came from. One of the men raises his gun and shoots at her, he's not quick enough to hit a vital part, because I blow his fuckin' brains out. I can't tell if it's a graze or if he got her good, because she disappears. Her scream rips a fuckin' hole in my heart, but I can't go to her. If I do, we're dead.

"She can't go alone, Mack," I bark over the gunfire. "Go after her."

Mack, two guns in his hands, doesn't hesitate. He disappears into the trees, too. There's only a few of us left now, and a whole lot of them still standing. Atreau must have made some sort of call, because suddenly another twenty or so men appear.

"You fucking put those guns down, or we'll blow you to fucking pieces," he roars.

Machine guns. They've got machine guns. We're no match for machine guns.

"Drop the guns," I growl, low and throaty. My leather is covered in blood splatters.

Zaid, Krypt, Rhyder, Grimm and Austin all drop their guns. Atreau steps forward. "Get on the fuckin' ground!"

We do as we're told, lowering to our knees. My pride rips to pieces as I get closer to the grass.

Turning to his men, Atreau roars, "Go and find that fuckin' girl, now."

About six of the men run off in the direction Santana went. My heart tears to shreds. Please, Mack. Fuckin' make sure she gets to safety. Atreau's boots crunch in the dirt as he nears.

"You just killed eight of my best men, I can't let that go unpunished. I need your muscle, but not all of it. Which one of you will pay for the lives you just took?"

My stomach coils and I lift my head. "Don't you fuckin' kill them. You want revenge, you kill me."

"That would be no fun. I mean, you're the President after all. Isn't it your job to protect them?" he laughs high and delighted. "I think you need to watch one of them die. Now, which will it be?"

His eyes scan over my guys. My hand goes to my gun, and he spins back to me. "You fuckin' put that down, right fuckin' now, or I'll kill the fuckin' lot of them and let you watch. What's it goin' to be?"

"Take me," I growl, my voice a low hiss.

He ignores this, turning back to the guys. My heart races and my entire body feels like it's going to explode with rage. I shoot, they kill us all. I don't, they take one of my men. I have to come up with something else, something better, something he wants more.

"I've got girls," I bark.

He looks down at me, his face serious a moment. I want to bellow with relief when he laughs, no longer amused, but deadly. "I've plenty of girls, biker."

Then he turns his gun, without hesitation, and he pulls the trigger. An agonized cry rips from my chest, as Rhyder slumps backwards, his head no longer whole. Agony, the kind I've never experienced, rips through my body, collapsing me to the ground. Krypt bellows in rage, and if it weren't for Ash, he would charge...life or not.

Zaid, Grimm and Austin have their heads bowed, their bodies shaking. With rage or emotion, I don't know. My chest heaves with emotion, swirling with the rage inside, making me want to kill every fuckin' one of them. I can't do that, though. I can't leave Santana. I drop my head, letting a single, agonized tear slide down my cheek for my brother.

They will pay for that. I vow it.

"Get them inside, now!"

Someone grabs both of my arms, jerking me up. The butt of a gun connects with my temple so fuckin' hard my world goes black.

CHAPTER TWENTY-NINE

2014 - Santana

My leg burns like it's on fire as I head into the thick trees to the west of the property. I don't think the bullet went in, but it kills all the same. I can't run to the driveway, the land is open and I've not doubt someone has come after me. If I'm in an open field, I'll get shot before I make it. The sounds of gunfire still echoes, breaking me with each loud, ringing shot.

"Santana!"

I hear a familiar voice and turn to see Mack running towards me, two guns in his hands. He's covered in blood and his hair is whipping wildly in the wind. He stops when he reaches me, staring down at my bloody leg. "Fuck, you're fuckin' bleedin'. We gotta get outta here, I don't have time to stop and fix that. Can you run a little further?"

I don't hear his words clearly; my eyes are trained on the field of workers behind him. I let my gaze settle on one in particular. A small blond girl. I can't be. I start running in that direction without thinking. Gunfire and shouted voices are all I can hear, but I don't stop. Mack grabs my arms, but I shove him away so forcefully, his fingers drop away.

He turns, shots ring out, and then he barks, "Santana, we've got company."

My mind is in a haze, the blond girl...*so familiar*. I don't think, I don't feel, I don't fucking care. I turn, pulling my gun from my pants and I shoot the two figures in the distance that are running towards me. I hit them with a precision I shouldn't have. Their bodies drop into the overly long grass.

"Fuck me," Mack mutters.

I charge onto the field, not caring if I get shot. Not caring about anything but the blond girl I'm getting closer and closer to with each step. I can't feel the pain in my leg anymore; the only thing letting me know I'm still here is the pounding of my heart.

The fields are filled with lines of stout trees. Slaves are scattered through them in groups of four or five, all chained together by the ankles. They're all working, and I see the reason they can't go far, is because their chains lead to a massive post at the end of each line of trees, stopping them from being able to run.

They call out to me, pleading voices, but I only have eyes for one. The blond girl turns as I near closer and I know, *I just know*. A pained cry rips from my throat as I take her in. Ratty, damaged blond hair, a body so tiny she's undoubtedly mal-nourished, and the biggest, bluest eyes I've ever seen.

"T-T-Tana?" she croaks.

Her voice is like music to my ears. I skid to a stop when I reach her, my arms going out to launch her tiny body into mine. She's so skinny, God, so skinny. Agonized cries leave my throat and my legs go out from beneath me, taking her down into the dirt, too. Her tiny arms are around me, her crying loud and pained.

Gunfire erupts.

"We gotta go!" Mack bellows, reaching me.

I pull back, and through blurred vision stare down at Pippa's chains.

"We need to get them off…we need…"

The other slaves attached to her, are staring at us, their expressions a mix of shock and confusion. I look at them, then to Mack.

"Hurry!"

He growls, "Move!"

218

I do, and he aims his gun at the chain, pulling the trigger. It explodes. It takes a few shots to get the second one, but in seconds, Pippa is free. She launches herself into my arms, sobbing hysterically. I could nearly lift her she's so tiny. Mack does just that, sweeping down and lifting her into his arms.

"Santana!" she screams, so loudly and so full of fear it makes my entire body ache, knowing what she must have been through.

"He won't hurt you, but we have to go. It's okay, *shhh.*"

She stops screaming, but her tiny body continues to shake. I turn to Mack, hearing voices getting closer and closer. We're protected from the trees right now, but it won't take long for them to figure out which row we're in.

"Please!" One of the slaves calls. "Please help us."

"You have to help them," I cry.

"No," Mack bellows, taking my arm and jerking me away.

"Mack, please!"

"We take them, we're fuckin' dead. Not to mention the shit they'll do to the guys if they come out and find their slaves gone. You wanna risk Maddox?"

I can't argue. I turn to the slaves, calling, "We'll come back, I swear."

Their cries trail after me as we disappear into the thick trees only twenty or so meters away. A shot hits the trunk right beside my head just as I get in. I scream, and Mack pulls me harder and faster. The pain in my leg is back with full force now, burning to the point vomit rises in my throat and escapes my mouth before I can stuff it back. I don't stop running, Mack doesn't even notice.

He pulls us through the trees with a ferocity I'm not sure I'd have without him. More shots ring out, coming too close. I smother my cries, forcing my legs to move when they really don't want to. We run towards the road, trees and rocks causing damage to our bodies as they scrape along our skin. We reach the massive fence and Mack doesn't hesitate, he lifts Pippa and throws her over.

"Mack!" I cry, hearing my sisters pained wail as she lands on the other side.

"No time to fuckin' wait," he barks, lifting me and hurling me over as if I weigh nothing.

I land on the other side with a thump; my arms go out, finding Pippa. She clutches me and we watch as Mack hauls himself over the massive fence, dropping on his feet. He reaches down, scoops Pippa up, and runs towards the car sitting over the other side of the road. We reach it, flinging the door open just as a few of the men appear, aiming their guns at us.

"Fuckin' go!" Mack roars.

He's just barely in when the shots ring out, smashing the windows. Tyke doesn't hesitate; he plants his foot to the floor and skids off onto the road so fast my body is launched backwards into the seat. I cry out, clutching my leg. My jeans are soaked in so much blood it's alarming. Pippa shakes, her eyes wide as she stares around. She's in shock.

"It's okay," I soothe, pulling her close. "It's okay. You're okay."

"What happened?" Tyke roars over the screaming of the engine.

"Set up," Mack grinds out. "Tinmen set us up, they didn't want the girl at all. They wanted to fuckin' take Maddox down and they succeeded."

"Fuck, no," Tyke rasps.

"They ain't dead, at least, I don't think they are. We got out, but I don't know how shit is goin' to go down. We've gotta get a fuck load of men, and we gotta do it fast."

"Makin' the calls as soon as we stop."

"We need a hospital, but it's the first place they'll look."

Tyke nods as I stroke my fingers over Pippa's hair. My relief is smothered and drowning with my fear for Maddox and the guys. Tears leak out of my eyes and I begin to shake, too. Mack notices and his arm goes around me, pulling both Pippa and I closer to him, until we're all bundled together.

"There's another town around about four or five hours from here – I checked it out before we came. We'll go to the hospital there."

Mack nods, I can feel it against my head. "Just hurry."

~*~*~*~

My leg burns in a way I've never felt before. I've tried, tried to hold it back, but I can't. I begin sobbing about an hour into the trip, biting my lip to stop it from becoming wailing screams. My mind is spinning, my body aches, and it feels like my leg is on fire. My vision is starting to waver, and my heart is pounding so hard it's starting to scare me.

"You're going to be okay," Mack soothes. "You're going to be okay."

"It…hurts…" I wail.

"I know, darlin'. I know."

He strokes my hair; it's all he can do. Pippa is dead still in my arms, but she's breathing and that's the main thing. I can't focus enough to move my mouth anymore. I close my eyes and let darkness take me; the pain goes away there.

CHAPTER THIRTY

2014 - Maddox

The dried blood on my face makes every movement painful, even blinking feels like running a God damned marathon. My cheek bone is broken, my nose is broken, and I wouldn't know, but I could guess I've got a fuck load of slashes on my face. My ribs, collarbone, and arm have also been snapped.

They didn't go easy on us.

The moment they put us down in this cramped little cell, they beat the fuck out of us. I got it the worst, because I was the one who threw myself in front of every punch. I'd do it again, over and fuckin' over, if it meant protecting my boys. Krypt got it hard when I fell to the floor. He's nearly as beaten as me. His face a mass of puffy, red welts and slices.

The other guys are all sitting on the floor, staring at their hands. They've been like that for hours now. We're too hurt to be hungry, but that will come soon if they don't feed us. We've already had to resort to pissing in the corner, causing the musky, dark room to smell even worse. Austin is pissing serious blood, and that bothers me, but there's fuck all I can do about it right now.

I have to hold onto hope that Mack and Santana got away. The very idea that something might have happened to her makes me feel so fuckin' sick my insides twist angrily. That girl is the first thing that's made me smile in a long, *long* time. If I lose her now...*fuck*...I just can't. I can't lose the one thing I've fought so hard for.

Loud voices force my head up. I blink through the haze that seems permanently covering my eyes. Krypt lifts his head, too. His black eyes are so swollen I'm almost sure he can't see clearly, but he turns his face in my direction, anyway. He raises a hand, winces in pain, and drops it. This isn't how it's meant to be, bikers that are some fuckin' sicko's slaves.

We fucked up.

No, *I* fucked up.

I put them in this position; I was the asshole who kept this for so long. If I'd come out and opened up from the beginning, Howard and his goons might not have found out about Santana's sister, and we wouldn't be here. This is my fuckin' fault, and I'm takin' full responsibility for it. I'll lay my life down to get my boy's outta here, and I *will* get them out.

"What the fuck do you mean she's fuckin' gone?"

I tilt my head, listening to the voices drifting in.

"Chain blown clean off, they fuckin' took her."

"Well, did you fuckin' find them?"

"No, by the time we got to a car, they were far outta sight. The guys are still lookin'."

"Use your fuckin' brains and think about it, you fuckin' fools. Where would they go with a severely underweight girl and another with a fuckin' bullet in her leg?"

"The hospital. We checked. They weren't there. My guess is they'll go far, far away before checkin' in. They're not stupid."

"Fuck!" he barks. "Keep lookin', we need to find them. They'll bring re-enforcements and a biker club isn't someone we want to fuck with."

"And if we don't find them?"

"We kill these fuckers and then I kill you. Now move – cover the airports while you're at it. Leave nothin' uncovered."

"On it."

I turn my eyes towards Krypt, and I know he's thinking what I'm thinking.

We don't have much time left.

~*~*~*~

2014 - Santana

It takes me a moment to register that someone is speaking to me. I open my eyes and through blurred vision I see a Mexican nurse. She's speaking in faint, poor English, waving her arms around and asking me questions I can't understand. I'm in a bed, and from the feel of it, my leg is tightly bandaged. I rub my eyes. Where's Pippa? Where's Mack?

"Leave," a voice calls.

I turn to see Mack standing at the door, looking worse for wear.

"Mack," I croak.

He comes closer, his hand going out to stroke my hair. "You're okay, the bullet didn't go in, but you had a serious gash. I know you need to recover, but we have to get the fuck outta here. I've got everything you need."

"I understand," I whisper. "Where's Pippa?"

"She's doin' okay. Sweet kid. She's been on a drip for twelve hours; given her some color back. She even ate some soup. She's been in and out, checkin' on you. They put a fair few stitches in your leg, so it's goin' to be sore. I'd love to leave you here, but I can't risk it."

"I know."

He kisses my head, and then he leaves the room for about half an hour. In this time, the nurse helps me clean up and gives me some fresh clothes. I've no idea where she got them from; maybe Mack got some when I was out. I

225

make my way down the hall with one hell of a limp. Mack is coming my way, with Pippa by his side.

At the sight of my sister, fresh tears spring to my eyes. Now she's cleaned up, I can really see her. The blond hair that was ratty before is now brushed, but it's still dull. Her blue eyes look too big for her face, she's still a mass of skin and bones, but her cheeks are pink and she seems to have come out of her shock.

I reach for her and pull her into my arms, breathing her in, so grateful she's alive. Fresh tears burst from my eyes and my body trembles. So long I've believed she was gone, and now here she is. "I'm so sorry it took me so long to get to you, Pippi," I whisper. "God I've missed you. I thought…I thought…"

"I missed you too, Tana," she croaks. "You were the only reason I kept fighting. They told me you were dead, but I didn't believe it…I *didn't*…"

I did.

I'd believed she was gone, yet she'd held hope for me. Guilt washes through me, but I don't have time to think about it now. I have to figure out how to help Maddox and the guys. When we get home, *if* we get home, then I'll tell Pippa everything but right now we don't have the time.

"We're together again now," I croak. "It's going to be okay."

I keep my arms around her as we walk down the halls. Mack has a handful of pills, and a bag of food. He leads us out the front doors and to a car I don't recognize.

"Where's the car?"

"Got Tyke to change it over, they know what we're drivin'. This might throw them off for a bit."

226

Good idea.

The car is bigger, a massive SUV that has a good amount of backseat space. It's been stocked with food, water and clothes. There's a pillow each for Pippa and I, plus a big, warm blanket. Mack helps us into the car, and then climbs in the front, taking over the driving. Tyke can drive, but I know the time it took to get here has done some serious damage to his already sensitive legs.

"Are you okay?" he asks, turning and staring at us.

I nod. "I'm okay," I whisper.

"And you," he turns to Pippa.

She stares at him, her eyes wide, her mouth slightly agape. He gives her a smile, a warm smile that melts my heart. Her cheeks grow pink, but she is unable to answer.

"She's okay," I say for her.

He smiles and turns back to the front of the car. After a moment, his voice grows serious. "I called the club, they're on their way."

"How long are we lookin'?" Mack asks, pulling out onto the road.

I reach over and take Pippa's hand. It's late at night; I don't know what hour. I'm not feeling any pain in my leg because of the strong meds, but that'll wear off soon. I wasn't happy about taking anything, but I was out of it and didn't get a choice.

"They'll be here in a few days."

"How many?"

"The entire club and anyone else they've been able to rally. Maddox left instructions, he's a smart fuckin' man. He had plans organized, and weapons. We gotta be thankful he's ahead of every situation."

"What if we're too late?" I whisper.

Mack doesn't look at me, but I swear I see him flinch.

"We're goin' to do everything we can, but you're goin' to stay away when we do it."

"But-"

His voice allows no argument as he snaps, "You don't get a fuckin' choice. What the fuck do you think you're goin' to do with a fucked up leg, aside from get us into more strife?"

I've got nothing. Pippa squeezes my hand and I close my eyes. Don't cry; be strong for him. He needs you to be strong. I can't be there, I know that, but an idea comes to my head all the same. I snap my eyes open and start rambling.

"No, you're right. I can't be there; I can't run fast enough. But I can be a distraction. If we're seen, we could lead some of them away. They might think we haven't gotten our backup."

"No," Mack barks.

"It's not a bad idea," Tyke mutters. "If they think we're still alone, they're going to be off guard. If they spot us, or even the girls, they're goin' to send men."

"It's too risky," Mack argues.

"Maybe, but it'll take five or so of the men out of the picture. It's worth a chance."

Mack says nothing more, but I know he's considering it. He's a smart man; he knows he has to consider everything when it comes to a good plan.

"You girls get some rest," Tyke offers. "We've got a fair bit of drivin' to do. We're five hours or more away from the house now."

"I thought you said it was only four?" I ask.

"Misjudged, took us five hours to get to that hospital. We're not goin' all the way back, because they'll be lookin' for us. We've looked up maps and found a twisted route, not back roads, but not the highway either. Best you can do is sleep, you're gonna need it."

"Mack?" I whisper in the darkness, hating his silence.

"Yeah?"

"Thank you."

"Don't thank me," his voice is low and dark. "It ain't over yet."

CHAPTER THIRTY-ONE

2014 - Maddox

A booted foot connects with my ribs, hitting what's already broken. I have no fight left. The pain has gone far and beyond. Now I'm drifting in and out of an agony induced haze that has me teetering on the edge of passing out, yet my body seems to want to keep putting itself through hell by keeping me awake.

I wish the fuckin' darkness would come.

"Get up, you piece of shit," Atreau barks. "You're not so tough now, are ya?"

Arms curl around mine, jerking me up. There are two men holding me, straining with my weight. I spit blood in Atreau's face, earning me a jaw crunching punch. I bare my teeth at him; grateful I've still got them all. He gets up in my face, his vile smelling breath making my empty stomach coil.

"I could beat you more, but I've got a load of crops that need to go out. You and your boys start work tomorrow, aren't you lucky?"

"Fuck you, cunt," I hiss.

"Oh, I forgot to tell you…we found your precious girlfriend. Looks like they didn't get back up, after all. My men are moving in first thing; they're at a hotel. Can you believe? And here I was thinking they were smart. Looks like they're not, because they came back."

My mind swims and my stomach continues its destructive path, twisting and turning. Mack wouldn't be so fuckin' stupid as to get caught…he knows better. He should have gotten the guys. What the fuck is he doin' at a hotel? Krypt growls from his spot in the corner, and Atreau laughs.

"I thought bikers were smart, the *ultimate*. Looks like you sent the wrong guy to look after your girl. Don't worry, you'll see her tomorrow."

"Why tomorrow?" I croak, my voice barely there.

"There are too many people there tonight. A wedding. I can hardly send my guys to go in and get them now. We're watching them, though. They won't get out without passing my men."

Fuck. *No.*

"You fuckin' certain they're alone?" I challenge.

His eyes flicker. "We saw them, smart ass. They're alone."

"You'll fuckin' pay for this. I'll cut your fuckin' dick…"

He hits me again, so hard I spin and the men let me go. I land on the floor with a thump. Pain rips through my body, causing a tortured bellow to leave my lips. I might be tough, I might have lived with pain, but this…*this* is far and beyond anything I've ever lived through. It fuckin' burns.

It doesn't stop me from opening my mouth and snarling another insult.

I'm rewarded with a kick to the nuts.

That's when darkness finally takes me.

~*~*~*~*

2014 - Santana

"They've seen us," Mack mutters, pacing the hotel room.

I'm on the bed, my hands clutching Pippa's. She's watching Mack and Tyke, confusion flickering across her face as he rambles and storms across the room. He's not happy with the plan, to say the least, but there's really no other choice. They need to think we're alone, that we've got no backup.

"That's the point," Tyke mutters from the couch. He's leaning forward, his elbows on his knees, watching Mack pace.

"Don't fuckin' care," Mack barks. "I don't like this fuckin' plan. They could bring ten or twenty men, maybe even fuckin' more. Then what hope have we got? We'll have our brains blown out before we can move."

"They won't kill us," I say, my voice scratchy, my throat sore.

Mack shoots me a glare. "What makes you think that?"

"They want us as slaves, if they wanted to kill us they would have done it right away. We're worth more to them alive."

Mack shakes his head, contemplating this. "Possibly, but we can't just risk it and assume we're right. We could get ambushed at any moment."

Pippa makes a strangled sound and her eyes dart around the room.

"Must you!" I snap, tired, terrified and sensitive.

Mack storms forward. "We wouldn't even be in this fuckin' mess if it wasn't for you and your family. I don't fuckin' care if what I'm saying bothers you. I could lose the only fuckin' family I've ever had because of you," he roars so loudly I flinch.

I stare at him, my heart breaking in half, my lip trembling. I've held it together, I've stayed strong, I've forgiven Maddox for what he did and I've gotten my sister back...but my fault? No...*no way*. I let go of Pippa's hand and stand on shaky legs. Giving Mack a look that tells him just how much he broke me, I turn and disappear into the bathroom.

I'm not going to yell and scream, or carry on. What will it prove? My heart aches so badly I can't afford any more pain. I lower down onto the floor, the cool tiles causing my leg to ache when I stretch it out on them. Tears break lose and spill over, running down my cheeks. It fucking burns.

If I lose Maddox, the only man I've loved with all my heart, I'll never recover. I don't know what's happening to him. I don't know if he's okay. I don't even know if I'll ever see him again. That thought alone has a sob ripping from my throat. I can be strong, but I can't stand the thought of losing him.

The door creaks, but I don't look up. A small frame pops down beside me, her tiny arms going around me. Together we cry, both of us living with our own demons. By the time our tears are dried up, the sun has begun to go down. Which means the guys will be here soon.

"Tell me about him?" Pippa asks, her voice low and soft.

I smile at her, my lips trembling.

"He saved me. He picked me up when I passed out on the mission Kennedy sent me on. I woke with him. He took care of me for five years."

"Did he tell you about me?" she asks.

I swallow, shaking my head. "He told me you were dead. I only recently found out about you being alive. He was trying to search, for years he got leads and lost them. He said he was protecting me...I was in a bad way. I'm so sorry, Pippa. I should have been there...I shouldn't have believed-"

"No," she says, her voice the strongest it's been since we found her. "He gave you a gift, Santana. I saw you; I saw what was happening. You weren't there; you had gone. He's right...he was protecting you. You would have come after me, I know you would have...and you would have gotten killed."

"I thought you were dead," I say, my voice breaks and a ragged sob tears from my throat.

"I'm okay," she says, her own voice breaking once more. "They didn't hurt me, because I always did what I was told. I never fought. What was the point?

233

Until I found another way, that was my life. I worked hard, I was hungry, but mostly…I was safe."

"You were a slave for five years while I was living with a man, having a good, solid life!" I cry, clenching my fists.

"You didn't know. How could you have known? He told you I was dead, and I'm glad he did. You laid your life on the line so many times for me. You kept me alive; you protected me. You deserved five years of happiness, because Tana, you gave me more than that…"

I wrap my arms around her, holding her close, thanking God for bringing her back to me.

"I'm never letting you go again."

She laughs hoarsely. "I don't think I'll be in a hurry to let you lose me again."

We laugh brokenly together and then pull apart.

"Do you love him, Tana?"

I swallow down more tears, and nod. "I do, very much."

She squeezes my hand. "Tell me about them…"

"The club?"

She nods.

I smile.

"They're the best family…not better than Mom and Dad of course, but they're so loyal. They drive you crazy, but they'd lie down and die for you. I adore all of them."

"Do you think…do you think…" she looks away.

"They're going to love you, honey," I soothe. "I promise."

There's a knock at the door that has us both looking up. Mack comes in, his face regretful.

"Mind if I have a chat with Santana?" he asks, his eyes trained on Pippa.

She nods, standing. I give her a weak smile and watch as she leaves. Mack hesitates at the door, but with a sigh, steps in and crouches in front of me.

"I don't do this a lot...I don't even fuckin' know how, but..." he runs a hand through his hair. "I fucked up, Santana. This ain't your fault – I'd do the same thing for a woman I loved. Maddox made the choice to take care of you and put his time and effort into looking for your sister. I can't judge him for that, and I sure as shit can't judge you. So...I'm sorry."

I stare up at him, my eyes softening. I reach out, clutching his hand. "I know."

He closes his eyes for a minute, and then in a raspy voice he mutters, "I'm scared. So fuckin' scared. He's all I've got..."

His voice breaks and my heart goes right along with it. Maddox is everything to Mack. He's the only family he's got. I know how much he means to him, and how close the brothers are. They've got the kind of bond that even some blood related brothers don't have. Mack drops down to his knees, his head bowed.

"We're going to get him back," I say, taking his other hand. "We're going to fight this."

He seems to gather himself, because when he looks up, the emotion is gone from his face. Mack has always struggled with emotion, and he finds it hard to let people see the real man that's inside.

"Come on, you need to eat and so does Pippa. Then we're going to find out where the guys are. It's time to end this."

He helps me up and we head back out into the room. Pippa is sitting on the bed, having a shy conversation with Tyke. I smile and sit down beside her. My leg is aching, but I'm not going to be a cry baby and whine about it. I'll survive. Mack lifts the phone that's in the room, and puts it to his ear, turning to us.

"What do you girls want?"

I turn to Pippa and her cheeks grow pink.

"Is there something you want?" I ask her.

"There is…I've dreamed about it for so many years."

I nod in encouragement.

"A cheeseburger," she admits.

Tyke laughs and even Mack cracks a smile.

"Two cheeseburgers," I say to Mack.

He turns and orders four, one for each of us. The food arrives only twenty minutes later. I'm hungry, but after four or five bites, I can't stomach the heavy beef, cheese and bread. It would seem I'm the only one. Pippa devours hers like a starving child and of course, the men gobble it down in a few big bites.

Then Mack makes the call.

"You in?" I hear him ask.

He nods a few times.

"Morning, night attack is too dangerous. We shoot the wrong fuckers and we'll pay for it."

Oh God.

"No, don't come here. We need them to keep thinkin' we're alone. I'm goin' to leave the girls with Tyke then I'm goin' to sneak out, there's a back entrance. I'll ring you and we'll go in."

My stomach coils - that cheeseburger threatening to come back up.

"Stay low, I'll call first thing."

Then he hangs up. Turning to me, his eyes are full of fear, tension, rage and...if I'm correct...pain.

"Is it all ready?" I ask.

He nods. "We're set."

"What if...what if they're expecting you? What if you don't make it out? What if-"

Stepping forward, his hands shoot out and curl around my shoulders. He shakes me, just slightly, making my mouth snap closed.

"What if's are only going to cause problems. We don't have time for what if's. I'm goin' to get those guys out of there, no matter what it costs me."

"Mack-"

"They're all I've got, Santana. Nothing will stop this."

I nod, even though fear has curled itself around me, choking, suffocating...

"What now?" I ask, my voice low.

"Now we wait."

~*~*~*~

237

Mack leaves the moment the sun is up and the call comes in. I've felt fear in my life, but watching him sneak out is up there with some of the scariest moments. We watch from our window as he creeps past the pool and gardens. He has to go down the back, over the fence and through the trees a long while before he makes it out onto the road. He needs to get far enough away that they won't see him exit.

I hugged him eight times. A full eight. I smothered my tears, staying strong. He needs me to be strong. He needs us all to be strong. I've said more prayers in the past twenty-four hours then I've said in a lifetime. Over and over I've prayed for the guys, but mostly, I've prayed for Maddox. I've tried not to dwell, but there's no switching my brain off.

He's everything.

Tyke sits beside me, squeezing my hand. He's got guns readily available in case these guys decide to bombard us. I really hope that doesn't happen. We're hoping that as long as we're in here, they'll think we're plotting. I've got Tyke's cell phone clutched in my hand, waiting for the text from Mack.

Thirty minutes later it comes.

M – I'm out.

I breathe a sigh of relief, but it lasts only a second.

This is just the beginning.

CHAPTER THIRTY-TWO

2014 - Maddox

So fuckin' thirsty. Everything in my body burns, like someone has taken a match to my organs and lit it. My throat has a scratchy, dry sensation that refuses to leave because there's no longer saliva to ease it. I'm covered in dried blood, and my broken bones have gone far and beyond aching, instead they're numb.

"Maddox?"

It's Grimm. His voice as hoarse as mine. I want to lift my head, but there's no fuckin' hope of that happening any time soon. I answer anyway, even though my voice is barely a rasp. "What?"

"G-g-g-gunfire. Can you hear it?"

I close my eyes, trying to focus. All I can hear is the loud, continual ringing in my ears. With painful effort, I reach up with a groan and press my hands over my ears. Still nothing. It only makes the ringing louder.

"I can hear it," Krypt rasps from the corner.

"Me, too," Zaid grunts.

"I can, as well," Austin whispers.

It takes me longer than them, but after a few minutes, I hear the faint cracks of guns being fired. I shove myself up, growling in pain as I shift into a sitting position. The gunfire comes closer, and I hear shouts, also getting louder as the minutes tick by. Krypt is on his feet, the other guys following quickly. Austin and Zaid reach down and lift me, all of them listening intently.

"Get the fuckin' bikers, and blow their fuckin' brains out. We're not lettin' these fuckers take them."

Fuck.

Krypt turns. "We're about to get visitors. Guys, put Maddox over in the corner that's hardest to access. We're going to have to jump them. I know you're all fucked, but if we don't, we're dead."

"Do you think it's Mack?" Zaid asks.

"Yeah," I grunt as they put me on the floor.

A door creaks, booted strides fill our tiny space, and I know they're comin' down. I hate, more than anything that I can't get up and fight. Those are my boys, and here I am with more broken bones than I can count, wanting to stab some fucker in the face but unable to do it. The guys stand either side of the door, waiting for it to open.

When it does, they lunge. Gunfire rings out, grunts fill the room, and all I can see is a tangle of fuckin' limbs as they drag three men down. Zaid gets hold of the gun, after receiving a brutal kick to the stomach. He rolls, groaning in pain as he lifts it with a shaky hand, pulling the trigger. He hits the first guard right in the back of the head.

Krypt has the other man in a death grip, his arm pressed under his chin, tilting his head back. "Shoot him!" he roars.

Zaid doesn't hesitate. He takes the gun and aims it at the guard's heart. He goes down as quickly as the other one. Austin takes that guard's gun, and he shoots the last one without hesitation. Krypt spins around, makin' me fuckin' proud as he takes on my role with a force that makes my heart clench.

"Austin, Grimm, get Maddox up. Zaid, you're comin' forward with me. If it ain't ours, kill the fucker. Let's go."

The two guys raise me up, and they drag me out of the cell and up the stairs. I've forgotten the pain in my body as I force my legs to work enough that they're not taking all my weight. Gunfire is loud outside, but the shouting is louder.

"Front," Krypt barks.

He's exhausted, damaged and fucked, but it's clear adrenaline has kicked in. He won't have his normal fight, though. I can only fuckin' hope Mack got a good load of men. They take me through the front door, and the sun burns my eyes as I squint to try and get a clear picture of what's goin' down.

Dead bodies fuckin' *everywhere.*

So many of them.

Mack is amongst my other members, and there's even more back up then I thought he could wrangle. His eyes lift to me, and his face turns murderous as he takes me in. With a violent side I've rarely experienced with Mack, he shoots the fuck out of anyone who comes close enough to feel his wrath.

"Where's Atreau?" Krypt bellows, raising his guns and shooting like a mad man.

"No fuckin' clue," Mack roars.

He's got blood pouring from a wound in his leg. He's been shot. I count four men from my club on the ground, dead. My chest twists and rage rises in my body to the point I begin to tremble.

"Find that fucker," I growl. "And bring him to me. I'm goin' to fuckin' make him scream. Injured or not."

Krypt barks the order to three of the guys, and they disappear into the house, looking for him.

"Give me a gun," I order.

Austin hands one to me without hesitation, and the guys adjust me so I can use it. I start shootin'. I might not be able to fight, but I can shoot. There are few of Atreau's men left, maybe six.

"Mack!" Krypt barks. "Behind you!"

Mack spins from his shooting and narrowly misses a shot to the head. This is gettin' too close. It needs to end. Two more of my guys have gone down, and the more I see, the wilder I get. I begin shooting with every piece of rage inside my body, blowing Atreau's men into bloody pieces.

"We got him, Prez."

My boys come back with a panting Atreau. He bares his teeth at me in a snarl, and I return the favor.

"He was in his car about to leave. Made some calls. Don't know to who."

"Who did you fuckin' call?" I bark.

"I'm not tellin' you, piece of shit!"

I raise my gun. "I'd love to kill you slowly, makin' you scream beneath my hands, but I don't have fuckin' time and my men are dyin'. I'm going to make this simple by blowin' your fuckin' brains out."

I press my finger to the trigger and gunfire sounds out...but it isn't mine. The bullet hits Greg, one of the members holding Atreau. Roaring in pain, he lets go. Everything happens in a blur. More gunshots, then Atreau is lunging at me, knocking my broken body back. I don't lose my gun as I land on my back, roaring in pain as my bones stab into things they shouldn't be stabbing into.

Then, before I've got the chance to fight, he's got a knife in my chest. My mouth opens; an agonized bellow leaves my throat as blood fills my mouth. Pain unlike anything I've ever experienced tears through my body. He twists

242

the blade and my world spins. "I'm not as good as you," he growls. "I won't make it quick."

I don't know where I find it, maybe it's the pictures flashing in my head of Santana, but I lift my gun and I shoot him. He rolls off me, dislodging the knife. A gurgling, squelching sound fills the air. More gunshots ring out, and the shouting voices around me fade into dull hums. My eyes shut and the pain slowly leaves my body.

This must be what it feels like *to die*.

CHAPTER THIRTY-THREE

2014 - Santana

Two hours into our guard, the guys that have been watching us, leave.

That must mean Mack has made it and a war has begun.

Another four hours later – my world crashes.

It crashes because they bring Maddox to me…broken, bloodied and barely alive.

~*~*~*~

He's in the back of an SUV – his body covered in blood. So much so I can barely see any skin, and the skin I do see is battered. The voices around me drown out as I stare at the man I love, so broken and weak in the back of the car. My fingers won't stop trembling and there's so much emotion swirling inside me that I've gone beyond wanting to cry, and instead gone straight to feeling numb. I can't…I *can't* be weak.

He needs me.

Needs. Me.

My knees tremble and I use my hands to steady myself against the car as I stare down at Maddox. If he dies…no…*no*…I can't. I can't think like that. If I give up on him, where will that leave me? I'll fight for him the way he's fought for me. I won't shed a tear, not a damned tear, until he's looking into my eyes again.

"We've got to move out, now!" Krypt barks.

"We gotta get him to a hospital," Mack argues.

"Riskin' too fuckin' much takin' him to a hospital. One of those men could have gotten away, or worse, the cops could show up. We don't want to be anywhere nearby if that shit goes down."

"We left over fifteen dead fuckin' bodies," Mack growls. "It's going to be found by the cops, they might even find evidence, but they're goin' to find enough out about Atreau to keep them busy. That fucker is dead – we need to get Maddox to a hospital."

"No," Krypt barks, his fists clenching. "He's goin' to be in for a solid week, if not two. We can't risk bein' around here long. Besides, a man comes in, in his condition, and news hits about Atreau…you think they won't piece it together?"

"I won't fuckin' let you load my brothers half dead body onto a plane. He'll fuckin' die."

"We gotta protect this club. This is what he'd want!" Krypt snarls.

The two lunge at each other, fists begin to fly. I stare at them, my expression blank as I watch them pummel each other into the ground. I turn and stare at Maddox. His breathing is ragged. He could die at any second. I close my eyes, fighting back my emotion as I try to think with a clear head. What would Maddox want?

I already know.

He'd want us home – for safety.

But taking him home could mean stealing his life. He's barely hanging on. My mind swims and my chest feels like someone has dived in and ripped my heart out. I'm selfish, I don't want to lose him, but I also love him and know where his heart lies. His heart is with his club…that leaves only one choice.

"Enough," I yell, so loudly they stop fighting. "Krypt is right, Mack. We can't stay here. It's too dangerous and we can't afford to be arrested in another country. We've got one choice, and that's to take him home."

"He'll fuckin' die-"

I cut Mack off.

"No," I growl. "No, Mack. Because we're going to find a doctor, I don't know how, but we are. Someone to fix him in private for a whole lot of money."

Krypt's face is bloodied all over again. He is also in bad condition, so he couldn't afford to be beaten again.

"And if you two hit each other again, I'll find a God damned knife and stab you so fuckin' hard you'll take Maddox's place. Your brother and president is lying there, fucking dying. Pull your heads out of your ass and fucking figure something out," I step forward, my hands shaking. "I won't lose the man I love because of you two."

Both men stare at me, but it's Mack who speaks first. "You're right, I'm sorry. Tyke," he barks. "Make a call, find a fuckin' doctor and do it fast. I've got a whole lot of cash, I'll pay whatever it takes."

Tyke nods and pulls out his phone.

I stare around at the broken men – battered, bloody and standing like they're lost. I count them. I don't know who they had here, so I don't know how many are missing, but I do notice one. "Where's Rhyder?"

Krypt's face drops, if it could, his expression would break to pieces and fall to the ground. My heart clenches. I know what he'll tell me even before he says it.

"He got shot. He's dead."

My mind swims, twists and turns until I'm forced to my knees, vomit rising up my throat and rocketing out all over the pavement. Pippa is by my side in a second, her hands rubbing my back. "It's okay," she soothes. "It's okay."

I vomit until there's nothing left. Tears leak out of my eyes because of the exertion, but I squash them back down. I have to do this for Maddox, for Rhyder. God, Rhyder. He was such a good guy. I liked him, a lot. I hadn't spent a lot of one on one time with him, sure, but he was there for the last five years and he was part of the family.

"Come on."

A rough hand is on my shoulder, but it's offering the softest touch. It's Krypt. He helps me up and his arms go around me. I give myself a moment to bury my face in his chest, breathing him in. Just taking a second to allow comfort into my heart. He holds me like that for a few minutes, before pulling back.

"We're goin' to fix this."

"It's all my fault," I croak. "If it wasn't for me-"

"Don't fuckin' do that," he warns. "Don't you dare put this shit on yourself. Maddox found you, Maddox made it his mission to find your sister, you can't start doin' that blame game. We need you strong."

I swallow and nod, forcing my emotions back down. I return to the SUV, crawling in beside Maddox. I don't care about the blood, or the smell, or the fact that he's hurt. I tuck myself into his side, and I don't move until Tyke brings the doctor.

~*~*~*~

"There's too much injury. He needs hospital."

There's a tall, fat Mexican doctor examining Maddox in the back of the car. Mack paid good money for the man to come out here.

"Listen to me, buddy," Krypt growls, getting in his face. "You do what you can to hold him out or you don't get the fuckin' cash."

The doctor stares at him, his eyes narrowed, but does as he's told and turns back to Maddox.

"I can stitch…and align bone…but there might be bleeding…"

He's got a thick accent, and not so great English…but it's enough.

"Do what you can."

Krypt turns, not giving him another option. The doctor does what he can, cleaning Maddox and stitching wounds. He puts any broken bones he can in bandages after aligning them, and gives him a few injections. I don't know what, but they seem to calm his breathing.

"This all I can do," he says.

Mack hands him a fuck load of cash, I stare with wide eyes but don't argue. The doctor takes it, nods, and leaves. Krypt turns to the group.

"Time to go home. It's also time you all fuckin' pray that he makes it."

I'm praying.

I haven't stopped.

CHAPTER THIRTY-FOUR

2014 - Santana

I'd never thought being home would bring me so much joy. The relief I feel when we touch down is so overwhelming, I drop my head into my hands and force my emotions down. Pippa is beside me, here eyes wide as she takes it all in. The pilot's second in command, and the owner of this plane, comes out, glancing down at Maddox once the plane has touched down.

"If I didn't respect him so damned much, I would have never let him con me into flyin' you mob over there."

I don't know much about Jeremiah, the man who owns the plane. All I know is he's got a fuck load of money and travels the world for work. He doesn't like flying airlines, so he got his own plane. Maddox helped him at one point, and Jeremiah owed him. I'm thankful for him, regardless of how he feels about us now.

"Thank you," Mack says, offering his hand.

Jeremiah takes it, and glances at Maddox who we had to strap down to the floor so he wouldn't be jerked around with turbulence. "Take care of him," he says. "And tell him he owes me, now."

Mack nods, and orders the guys to get Maddox off. I don't leave his side; I help them down the stairs. The moment we're out, I see Ash and Indi, both of them waiting anxiously. The moment Ash sees Krypt she lets out a pained cry and runs towards him. They meet in a tangle of arms and legs. My chest aches.

Indi stares at Zaid, her eyes watering, her hand over her mouth. He stares right back at her, and then she drops to her knees. He's by her side in a second, scooping her into his big arms and nuzzling his nose into her neck.

She's holding him tightly, I can tell even from this far. A cool hand slips into mine, and I look down to see Pippa, holding onto me.

"He's going to be okay."

I nod, my eyes burning…but no tears slip out.

"I know."

He's made it this far. It was a bumpy ride, and a few times on the flight his breathing become gurgled and shallow. I held onto his limp hand, begging him to keep fighting. I lay awake with him when everyone else slept, my hand never leaving his. I don't care if I die from exhaustion, I won't leave his side.

Ash lets go of Krypt and rushes towards me. The moment she reaches me, she throws her arms around my neck and I let her. Indi is there in seconds, and together we all hold each other. I bite back my tears, still not letting them go. *Not until he's safe.* We finally pull apart and Ash turns her eyes to Pippa, and they soften.

"You must be Pippa," she says, extending her hand. "I've heard a lot about you. I'm Ash."

Pippa hesitates, staring at me. I nod softly to her and she takes Ash's hand, shaking it wearily. Ash doesn't hold back, she wraps Pippa in a hug. The look on my sister's face would make me smile any other time. She looks both overwhelmed and humbled. Ash pulls back but keeps an arm around her. "Come on, I'll bring you back to my place and you can rest."

Pippa looks to me again. "It's okay, honey. Ash will take good care of you, I promise you that. I'm going to be at the hospital."

"I promise I'll bring you as soon as you've rested," Ash assures Pippa.

Pippa nods. "O-o-okay."

I hug her, whispering into her ear, "Trust them, they'll be as much your family as they are mine."

She squeezes me tighter, but she's a strong girl. Stronger than she looks. She pulls back and Ash gives me a warm smile before leading her away. We all separate then – Krypt calling an ambulance. They arrive twenty minutes later, asking a lot of questions but not getting a lot of answers. They take Maddox all the same. Mack and I follow in a cab and the guys that are injured come along also. Austin is quite sick, so he went in the ambulance. The rest of them go back to the club.

The moment we arrive at the hospital, doctors swarm Maddox, whisking him off. A tall man, probably around fifty years old, stops me before we make our way to the waiting room. His cool fingers curl around my arm. "Miss, I'd like to ask you a few questions."

Mack steps in. "She ain't givin' you any information."

The doctor flicks his eyes towards him, but I step in before he can say anything.

"About his condition, I'll answer your questions."

The doctor nods, still giving Mack a weary look. He turns to me. "Can you tell me what exactly happened to him?"

"There's only a few people that, ah, know," I turn to Mack. "You might need to call Krypt."

He nods, taking out his phone and disappearing.

"He's been stitched, his bones very basically aligned. Who did that?" The doctor asks when Mack is gone.

"I can't tell you that, but he was a doctor."

"You don't need to be afraid of me, I can help…"

"Please," I say, giving him a hard stare. "I'm safe and well. I need you to focus on that man in there."

He closes his eyes a second, opens them and takes a deep breath. "Very well. Can you tell me as much as you know?"

I do. I give him everything I've got. Mack comes back twenty minutes later with a list that makes my stomach turn. Kicked, punched, starved, broken bones, and a stab wound that was explained so horrifically, my legs give way. Twisted. Inside him. Oh God. Mack kneels when my knees hit the cold tile, and his arm goes around me. "She needs help, too."

"Bring her in, I'll check her over," the doctor says.

Mack lifts me, carrying me into the room. I don't fight. The very thought of Maddox having a knife driven into his chest, and twisted, makes my stomach turn so violently, I gasp out, "I'm going to be sick."

The doctor has a little bag in front of me in a matter of seconds. I throw up into it, Mack still holding me. He lays my body down onto the bed, and the doctor checks me out. He's happy with how my leg has been dealt with, but says I need to spend at least a night. That's fine; I wasn't planning on going anywhere.

"When will he get out of surgery?" I croak before the doctor leaves. "How long until I know if he's okay?"

"It's going to be a good, solid four hours. Get some rest. I'll let you know the moment I know anything."

I nod. "Thank you."

He nods in return, and leaves. Mack pulls the covers back, not giving me a choice but to lay in them. A nurse comes in a few minutes later, connecting me to a drip at the doctor's request. She also gives me an injection. When she's gone, I slide into the cool sheets. Mack sits beside me, and he looks exhausted.

"Your leg?" I croak, noticing on the plane that he was injured.

"It's nothin', I'll get it fixed soon."

"Mack…"

"Sleep," he says, ignoring my protest. "You need it."

"I can't…if I close my eyes I'll see him like that and-"

My voice breaks.

"He's in the best hands now. You gotta rest, Tana. If he wakes and you're not…"

"I know," I whisper.

He strokes a thumb over my cheek.

"Mack?"

"Hmmm."

"Will you…please…just lie with me?"

He doesn't hesitate; I guess he just knows I need it. He climbs into the bed, tucking me into his arms.

And together, we sleep.

Still praying.

CHAPTER THIRTY-FIVE

2014 – Santana

I curl against the man I adore, my fingers running up and down his heavily bandaged chest. I've been sitting with him for three hours now, at least, that's how long I think it's been since he came out of surgery. The doctor said he's critical, but stable. The next twenty-four hours will tell. Hell, if he wakes up will be a big enough sign of things to come.

I'm tucked into him, tubes and wires gently resting on me. The doctors tried to move me; I told them there was no way in hell I was moving and that they'd have to carry me out. They adjusted things around me and this is where I've been sitting since. I still haven't cried. Ash and Krypt came in, and Ash told me just how bad it is that I haven't cried.

I know.

But he needs me to be strong.

Ash told me Pippa is at Maddox's house, with four of the guys standing guard. Indi is with her, but apparently she fell asleep and has been that way ever since. I'm glad she's getting rest. I'm just glad she's with me. Things have been so hard; I can't lose the man I love when I just got my sister back. I won't trade one for the other.

Ever.

He has to make it.

I close my eyes, breathing him in. I've been praying for him to wake, hell, to move. He hasn't. He's been steadily breathing, though. I figure that has to count for something. Mack has been in and out; the poor man looks exhausted even after our sleep. None of us will get the rest we need until Maddox wakes.

Mack told me the club has been informed of Rhyder's death. They're preparing a funeral now for him and the other men lost. My heart aches at the very thought. Poor Rhyder. He didn't deserve that. Non of them did. Maddox will be devastated when he's forced to wake and attend a funeral. I can't change it though, I can only hold strong for him.

It's all for him.

"*Chante?*"

I turn my face to see Mack standing by the bed, a coffee and bagel in his hand.

"You need to eat."

He's right. I do…but I don't want to.

"Please," he says.

If it wasn't for the fact that his eyes are so exhausted and broken, I would have refused. Instead, he helps me slide out from my spot beside Maddox and sits me down on a nearby chair. I sip the coffee, barely tasting it.

"You should go and rest."

He shakes his head. "Can't leave you or him alone, not now."

"There are other guys, Mack. They can watch the door."

His eyes grow hard. "I said no, end of discussion."

"Mack…" My voice is soft, and at the sound of it, his eyes soften.

"Can't leave him, Santana. You know that."

I nod because I do know that. There's no way I'm leaving him, and I shouldn't expect anything different from Mack.

"Eat," he says, pointing to my bagel.

I lift it, taking a small bite and struggling to chew it. I manage, though. Half way through, I can't push anymore down. I place it on the tray and continue to sip my coffee. A nurse enters, her eyes travelling over Mack and I. She smiles, and goes over to Maddox, checking his vitals. Satisfied with his progress, she leaves.

"How long until he wakes up?" I whisper to Mack.

"The doctor said it could be any minute, or it could be days."

"Do you think he will?"

"Yeah," he responds, his voice hard. "He fuckin' will."

I nod, swallowing back my emotions as I stare at the lifeless body in the bed.

"You should go catch a shower," Mack says. "Get some fresh clothes and come back. I'll stay with him."

I hesitate. I don't want to go home. I don't want to leave his side...but I do need to shower and freshen up.

"Can anyone take me?"

He lifts out his cell. "I'll call Tyke."

"No," I say quickly. "He's probably sleeping. Call someone else."

He nods and calls another club member. When he arrives, I stare at Maddox, then to Mack. "Please, call me if anything changes."

"You know I will."

I hug Mack and then...*hesitantly*...I leave.

~*~*~*~

256

Pippa is awake and sitting at the table with Ash and Indi when I come in. I smile at them, allowing hugs all round before taking a few steps back.

"How's Maddox?" Ash asks.

"Nothing has changed," I answer, tucking Pippa into my side.

"I'm sorry, honey."

I can offer nothing more than a grateful smile.

"Mack sent me home to shower and change, I won't be here long," I turn to Pippa. "Are you okay?"

She smiles up at me, looking better than I've seen her since she's been back. She's clean, her hair soft. Her eyes are bright and her cheeks pink. It's going to take a long time to take the dullness from her locks, and put some flesh on her bones, but at least she's home and she's safe.

God answered one of my prayers.

"I'm fine," she says in a small voice. "Ash is really nice and Indi said she'd stay over, we're going to watch movies."

I give the girls a grateful look, and they both smile warmly at me.

"We're going to have a great time," Indi announces.

I love them in that moment, more than I ever thought I could. They're worried about their men, no doubt wanting to hold them for days on end, yet here they are supporting me. I let go of Pippa and hug them again, forcing my tears back.

"It's okay," Ash says, even though I haven't said a word. "Our men are home, safe. Yours isn't. We're going to take care of Pippa until he is."

My nostrils burn and my throat constricts. Not now, Santana. Not now. I pull back, nodding because it's all I can do.

257

"Shower," Ash says softly. "I'll get you some clothes."

I nod, turning and rushing off up the stairs. I skid to a stop when I reach Maddox's room. With shaky legs, I enter. I sit on the bed, pulling a shirt into my hands that had been tossed onto the dark covers. I breathe it in, and the burning in my nose increases until I'm sure I can't hold back my tears.

Not now. *Come on.*

I swallow until my throat hurts, and drop the shirt. He's going to be okay, he is. I can't lose him now. I force myself to my feet and into the bathroom. My clothes come off without any clear acknowledgment of the act. I'm not thinking, not even really in the moment. My body is slowly going numb from the pain swirling in my chest.

Over the next half an hour, I wash, shave, clean and scrub any parts of my body that need it. Then I get out, dry and brush my hair, and then pull on the clothes Ash left on my bed – a pair of jeans and a turtle neck sweater. When I'm done, I make my way back downstairs.

That's when my phone rings.

The sound is surprising, and it takes me a moment to realize it's mine. I rush down stairs as fast as my sore leg will take me, but Ash has already answered it. She's saying something I can't hear, she nods, and then she hangs up. Turning to me, she whispers, "He's awake."

~*~*~*~

Driving to the hospital has never taken so long. The walk down the halls seems to go on and on; even at the fastest pace I can manage. By the time I reach Maddox's room, I'm shaking. I hesitate at the door, my hand hovering over the handle. I close my eyes when I feel the hand curling around my shoulder.

"It's okay," Ash whispers. "Go on."

I take a deep breath and push the door open. The first thing I see is Mack's back and a whole lot of nurses and a doctor. I take a shaky step in, my hand going out to rest on Mack's shoulder. He turns, staring down at me with a smile. I don't take long to focus on it; instead I let my eyes travel past him to the blue eyes set on me.

Something inside me breaks as I take in the face of the man I love. His eyes, God, so perfect, are bloodshot. His cheeks seem slightly sunken and his lips are paler than usual. He looks beaten, broken and sore. I shove past the nurses in my way, ignoring their protests. I reach Maddox and my hand curls around his. There is so much inside me, so much hurt and emotion, yet none of it comes out.

"Hey," he croaks.

"Hey," I whisper, my voice too shaky.

"Miss," the doctor says, "can you step back."

"No," I growl, so low it has *him* stepping back.

I turn back to Maddox, lowering my face and pressing my forehead to his. A gesture that means so much to us. It means more than a kiss. More than a hug. It's our love. His breath comes in short bursts against my cheek, and I breathe him in. Even in the hospital, I can still smell a slight amount of him coming through.

"I'm so sorry," I whisper.

"No," he croaks. "Fuckin'...*no.*"

His big hand lifts, curling around my cheek and he holds my forehead to his. His arm shakes and I know how hard it is for him to keep his hand up, but he does. My big, beautiful, strong man.

"I understand you're relieved," the doctor begins. "But we need to check him. Please, miss."

I pull back slightly and Maddox nods, weak and short. I press a kiss to his cracking lips, feeling that familiar burn in my nose. I step back, my entire body breaking out in shakes that weren't there before.

It happens. There and then.

Everything I've held in, all the strength I've shown, it all crumbles. My entire body begins to shake and a heart-wrenching sob rips from my throat, causing everyone to turn and stare at me. Maddox's eyes fill with a pain I've never seen coming from him, and it only makes it worse. I back up towards the door.

God.

Why now.

"Sweetheart."

A soft voice. Mack's... *I think.*

"Come on, let's get you some fresh air."

I shake my head. "I c-c-c-can't leave him."

My voice comes out broken and pathetic. Tears are streaming down my face.

"Let's just-"

"I can't leave him!" I scream. "Don't you fucking dare take me away."

The doctor looks at me, stepping away from Maddox.

"How about we give them a minute," he suggests to the nurses. "His vitals are good. We'll return in an hour."

Before I know it, the room has cleared. Maddox is still watching me, his face breaking my heart even more. Mack looks to his brother, then back to me and says, "I'm going to get coffee."

Then he's gone.

And we're alone.

CHAPTER THIRTY-SIX

2014 - Santana

"Come here," Maddox says, his voice sounding like a growl even though I'm sure that's not possible.

"Y-y-y-you're hurt and-"

"Here, Santana."

"He s-s-s-stabbed you. T-t-t-t-twisted the knife and-"

"Baby," he whispers. "Here."

"Y-y-y-y-you had so much blood."

"Santana-"

"W-w-w-we had to pay a doctor just to get you home and-"

"Santana-"

My wall breaks and I sob, "I thought I'd lost you."

His eyes soften and he reaches out a hand. "Come to me, please baby."

I go to him, crawling into his bed and into his arms. He wraps them around me, wincing in pain. I try to move but his arms tighten, even weak he's so strong. His face is pressed against my head and I can hear him breathing me in. I sob and sob, shaking and croaking his name until my body is drained of tears. My trembling stops and I sink into him.

Nurses come in and out, Mack returns and leaves, and eventually my eyelids become heavy. Before I drop off to sleep, I whisper, "I love you Maddox. Never leave me again."

I don't hear his response.

~*~*~*~

2014 - Maddox

My entire body fuckin' hurts. My bones, my skin, my insides. It's all burning. My arm is numb, but there's no way I'm moving the tiny, fragile form wrapped around me. It could drop off, but there's no way she's leaving my arms. Seein' her break down, all those tears, the way she shook, it fuckin' killed me. Took everything inside me not to break along with her.

The memory of being stabbed has played over and over in my head. Pushin' it down is proving to be harder than I imagined.

"She asleep?"

I turn my head to see Mack standing at the door. He looks as fuckin' terrible as Santana does. His hair is a fuckin' rats nest and his eyes are dark.

"Yeah," I say, still starin' at him. "You okay, bro?"

He nods, walking in. There's emotion in his eyes, and that's not something Mack gives away often. We've always been close, right from the day he came into our family. I know what me gettin' stabbed and nearly killed would have done to him.

"There was a second there, just a fuckin' second..." he looks away. "When I thought I'd lost you."

I stare at him, a strange swelling rising in my throat that has my voice halting. Fuck. Emotion.

"Yeah," I rasp. "Well...you can't get rid of me that easily."

He laughs hoarsely. "Nah."

His eyes flick to Santana and he shakes his head. "You know, that girl held herself in a way you'd be fuckin' proud of. Not one tear, not one breakdown.

Even when your body was put next to her, she didn't lose her shit. She held on like a God damned trooper."

I squeeze the tiny body next to mine. "Yeah, well, she just lost it all then. I let her. Poor kid. She must be fuckin' beside herself."

"She thought she'd lost you, but she never stopped tryin' to fight for your every breath."

"No, don't imagine she would have."

"We left a fuckin' mess back there, boss. I don't know how much shit we're going to have come back at us for this."

There'll be shit. A lot of it. We'll sort it, we always do.

"Don't worry about that now, we'll have a meetin' as soon as I'm out. Figure out our next move. Those Tinmen fuckers are goin' to pay for that set up."

He nods, his face tight. "Fuckin' yeah they are."

Santana shifts and I grit my teeth as her elbow brushes against my broken ribs.

"You want me to take her home?"

I shake my head. "She needs this, leave her."

"She's hurtin' you – she won't want that."

I give him a hard look. "I said leave her."

He nods. "Well, I'm goin' to go home and fuckin' sleep for ten days. Good to see you better."

He reaches out and I shake his hand. "Thanks. You did me fuckin' proud out there."

I watch his body flinch, but he doesn't say anything. He just flashes me the smile that never reaches his eyes, and leaves.

I tuck Santana into my side further, pain and all, and I sleep.

CHAPTER THIRTY-SEVEN

2014 - Santana

One Week Later

"Don't be such a baby," I say, waving the brush around.

Maddox gives me a glare so hard I would usually run with my tail between my legs, but he's an invalid right now. He's got nothing. His hair, however, looks like it's about to form into dreadlocks and unless he wants to let me shave it all off, he's going to have to let me brush it.

This isn't going down well.

"No fuckin' way are you brushin' my hair like I'm some sort of fuckin'...*woman.*"

I snort. "No one is watching, no one will know. You need to brush it and you can't lift your arm enough to do it...so it's me or the clippers."

He narrows his eyes, ice blue burning into me.

"Well..." I say, tapping my foot, waving the brush again.

"Shave it off."

I roll my eyes. "No way. Your hair is super hot."

"Don't wanna be super fuckin' hot. I wanna shave it the fuck off."

"Stop swearing, move so I can brush it."

"No," he grunts.

He's sitting up in the bed, still in his hospital attire, which he really *really* hates. It's the only thing that doesn't interfere with all the bandages, though. He's feeling better, but he has to be here for another few days before they'll let him go. As you can imagine, this hasn't gone down well. He's like a bull in a china shop, scaring everything that comes near him and breaking things on a daily basis.

Broody asshole.

I'm glad I've got him back.

"Come on, I won't tell."

"They'll fuckin' know when my hair looks like it belongs on a fuckin' cover of a magazine because you've brushed it so fuckin' much it's shinin'."

I huff. "Wrong, I'll just stop it forming into a rats nest."

"Cut it off."

"Maddox…"

"Do it."

"No."

"Yes."

I sigh and throw my hands up. "You stubborn fool. I'm not cutting your fucking hair off."

"Don't swear at me, woman."

A nurse enters the room, staring at both of us. "Ah, sorry," she says, her cheeks flushing when she catches sight of Maddox. She's new; I guess she hasn't experienced his royal hotness yet. "It's…ah…I mean…"

Oh for fucks sakes, she's stuttering.

"Can we help you?" I say, staring at her with a hard expression.

"The doctor has said Maddox can shower today, so ah, I'm here to help him. It's my…ah…job."

Help him?

Oh *hell* no.

"Help him?" I say, my voice a little squeaky.

"Yes, in the shower…"

"I don't think so," I growl.

Maddox is grinning, the son-of-a-bitch. I glare at him, which only makes those gorgeous dimples pop out on his cheeks.

"It's nothing personal, ma'am," she assures me. "It's just he'll need help."

"Listen to me, love. There's no way in hell you're going in the shower with my very gorgeous, very *naked* man. You're going to have to tell me what to do, because I promise you there'll be some serious crash tackling if you even try to get his clothes off."

Her cheeks grow pink and Maddox laughs, loud and booming. It ends on a wince and I turn to him. "Serves you right."

He bares his teeth at me, like a hungry animal. *Oh boy.*

"Well, I guess…" the nurse begins. "I can tell you what to do."

"Damn right you can."

She nods and we help Maddox out of the bed. His big body isn't light, even when he's taking most of his weight. When in the bathroom, the nurse sits him down and explains to me what needs to get wet and what doesn't. I assure her it's fine, and she leaves. Then I turn to the big man sitting on the shower stool.

"Get your dress off."

He glares at me. The kind of glare that burns through you.

"It ain't a fuckin' dress, and I don't get a fuckin' choice in wearin' it."

"It is a dress," I say, stepping behind him and undoing the hospital gown. "And you look lovely."

I bite my cheek to stop my fit of laughter as he makes a feral hissing sound and barks, "It ain't a fuckin' dress, woman!"

I can't help it; I burst out laughing. He grunts as I turn the shower on, take it off the handle and make sure the water is only a trickle. The poor man hasn't had a decent shower, only some wiping down. I bet he's busting for one. I walk around the front of him and...*oh my God.*

"Maddox!" I cry, flushing and turning away.

The man has the king of all erections.

"I'm horny, we're in the shower..."

"You're wearing a dress!"

"Am not!" he barks.

I try to avoid his jutting cock as I crouch in front of him, gently running the water down his legs, soaping where I can. I move up to his thighs and when I reach his cock, he grins. "Gotta wash it..."

"I should have let the nurse do it," I grumble.

"Sure about that?" he says, curling his fist around himself.

"Asshole."

"Wash it, baby."

With a sigh, I place the drizzling showerhead over it and let the water slide down his impressive length. Then I take the soap and begin lathering him, from tip to base. He lets out a guttural moan and rasps, "Suck me, please honey."

God, when he says things like that in his silky voice...

"We're in a hospital," I breathe. "And you're hurt."

"My dick ain't hurt. Put your mouth on me..."

I stare down at him, God, I do want to suck him.

"Take your clothes off."

I jerk my head up. "What... *no*... why?"

"I decided I don't wanna be sucked, I want you to fuck me."

"No."

"Baby... *yes.*"

I glare at him, he grins at me.

"I'm not fucking you. Maddox, you're hurt."

"You can sit on me, ride me real slow."

"Maddox!"

"Come on, honey..."

His voice is smooth and silky.

I can't fuck him. It's too risky. If I slip and hurt him then I'll never forgive myself. I can, however, suck him. I don't give him the choice; I just lean forward and close my mouth over his cock. He groans, deep and throaty. He tries once or twice to pull me up but he's still in too much pain to do so.

"Fuck... this... ain't... gonna... take... long..."

His words are dragged out, and his breathing is ragged. I cup his balls, rolling them in my hand as I lower my mouth down to the point of gagging. My saliva comes up and coats his cock as I suck, taking him as deep as I can go. My tongue swirls his head and his moans increase to pained bellows.

I know it hurts him to tighten up, and it's why I didn't fuck him.

"God, fuck, yes," he bellows.

A hot spurt of cum hits the back of my throat, followed by another and another. His cock pulses in my mouth and his balls tighten. His moaning turns into deep panting and when I feel him begin to soften, I pull back, my pussy clenching with need. His eyes, God those blue eyes, are glittering with lust.

"Come here," he growls.

"No," I whisper, using the shower to wash the last of his cum away.

"Baby…come here."

"No."

"Get the fuck up here, drop your fuckin' pants and let me put my fingers deep into your snug cunt. It ain't an option."

Oh boy.

"Now, Santana."

"You're so bossy," I whisper, standing. "Even when you're wearing a dress."

He growls and hisses; "I'm goin' to make your ass red for those comments when I'm strong enough to spank you."

I grin at him.

"Now, drop your fuckin' jeans."

I don't hesitate, I drop them.

"Panties."

They go, too.

He stares at my naked flesh and his eyes grow warm and lusty. "Fuck, you have the sweetest cunt. Look at those little lips, ready, wet, waitin' for me."

My knees begin to shake. He reaches out, pulling me closer, one arm wrapped around my waist and the other sliding up between my legs.

"Spread, honey."

I do.

His finger slides up my slick folds and I whimper. His arm tightens around my waist, holding me as much as he can. I try to keep my feet from slipping, so he doesn't have to take anymore weight. His finger swirls around my clit and I cry out. It's so swollen it almost hurts.

"I've missed you," I whimper as he begins to massage the hard nub.

"Fuck, baby, me too."

He massages until I'm on the edge, then his finger goes up and inside me. He begins fucking me with them, while his thumb works my clit. Fuck, oh God. It's so fucking good. I drop my head back, my knees weak, and cry out his name.

"Lean forward," he orders, his voice low. "Let me suck those gorgeous nipples."

I do, and his mouth closes around one of my hard peaks. That's when I come. I come so hard I cry out, not caring who can hear. His fingers work slower, lazier, dragging out every shudder from my body. By the time I've finished shaking, he's got an erection again. Jesus. I want to climb over him so badly. *So badly.*

"God do I want to fuck you, Maddox."

He pulls me closer. "Fuckin' do it. I need it. Fuck me, honey."

"But I'll hurt you."

He shakes his head. "Come here."

He takes control, lifting my leg so it rests over his thigh. He moves the other so I'm straddling him, but only our legs are touching. He lifts me and grips his cock, pulling it between us. The thick head presses against my swollen opening and he pushes in, both of us crying out in pleasure.

"You're so tight, swollen and slick. Fuck. *Yes.*"

I lower myself over him, loving how it feels when he stretches me. I place my hands on the shower walls so I don't have to grip him, and I sink fully down. Oh God...yes. So fucking good. His cock fills me so beautifully, stretching my insides in the most amazing way.

"Maddox," I whimper. "Fuck..."

"Jesus...fuck me baby. Fuck me hard."

I rotate my hips, using my feet to slide my pussy up and down his thick, hard length. Up and down I go, fucking him, my slick passage taking him fully. His breathing turns ragged and he begins panting hard and fast. His fists are clenched, resting on my thighs, and his jaw is tight.

"Come," he demands. "Come on..."

I close my eyes, losing myself in the moment. I lost the showerhead along the way, but I can hear the soft hissing of the water. My hands are flat against the tiled wall and I slide up and down as gently as I can until I feel myself clenching tightly, hanging on the edge.

Maddox's finger finds my clit, and I come.

God do I come.

"Maddox, oh God, oh yes," I scream.

"Fuck, yes," he pants.

I keep rocking, milking my own orgasm, when he finds his for a second time. He roars and his cock pulses, jetting inside me yet again. When I come down, my body feels amazing. I gently slip off him, and let myself kneel back on the floor. I drop my head onto his thigh and steady my breathing.

"Best fuckin' shower ever," he rasps.

I laugh softly.

Then I pick up the shower and clean him up.

~*~*~*~

2014 - Santana

"Jesus, what the fuck were you two doin' in there."

I hear Krypt's voice the minute we step out of the bathroom. My cheeks grow pink as I see that he's not alone. He's got Pippa, Ash, Indi and Mack with him. They're holding food, clothes and magazines. Oh boy. Maddox's arm is around my shoulder, but I feel his body shake with laughter.

"Don't laugh, princess," I growl at him.

He leans down and bites my ear. I squeal and let Mack help him off me. When he's back in bed, I shoot him a nasty glare. He just grins at me.

Prick.

274

"Ah," Ash begins. "I guess he's not completely broken."

"Shut up!" I say to her.

She's biting her lip, trying not to laugh. Poor Pippa looks like she's about to pass out – her cheeks are so red.

"Sorry, Pippi," I say.

She shakes her head. "Oh, no, it's fine."

God.

"How you doin', girl?" Maddox asks her.

She still doesn't know how to take Maddox, but she's getting there.

"Ah, I'm good. Thanks."

He smiles at her, and then turns to me. "Go and eat, I've got shit to talk about with Mack and Krypt."

I cross my arms. He winks at me.

"Fine, but if there's one discussion about that shower...you're dead."

He laughs.

I can't help it, I smile.

Then Ash, Pippa, Indi and I leave.

~*~*~*~

"Oh. My. God." I gasp.

Maddox is sitting in the bed, staring at me. Krypt is beside him, clippers in hand and Mack is grinning, clearly proud of himself.

"Told you I wasn't lettin' you brush it."

275

I stare at him, shocked. Maddox no longer has long hair…instead he's got short locks and fuck…*holy fuck*…he looks smokin' hot. His once long, thick hair is now a few inches in length and messy. The sexy kind of messy. Not only that, it brings out his face. His jaw looks more chiseled, his eyes more blue and his lips fuller.

"Everyone leave," I breathe.

Krypt turns to Maddox, then to me. "I think you're about to get raped."

Maddox's eyes flare and he growls, "Leave."

"Like now," I demand.

Ash laughs. "I think you better listen, she looks like she's about to rip his clothes off. You look hot, by the way," she says to Maddox.

Krypt glares at her.

"Oh stop it. No one is as hot as you. Come on."

He shakes his head, and he and Mack walk past me. Mack leans in as he goes past and whispers, "Take it easy on him, tiger."

Then they're all gone.

I don't hesitate; I walk forward, climbing onto the bed. I lean over Maddox and I kiss him. I kiss him so hard and so deep his breathing quickly turns ragged and feral little hisses leave his throat. He kisses me right back, just as hard and just as sweet. Mmmmmm. I pull back after a few minutes and whisper, "You're so fucking hot."

He laughs and curls his hand around the back of my neck. "If you look at me like that for the rest of my life, I'll die a happy fuckin' man."

"If you look like this for the rest of your life, there'll be no problem with me doing that."

He chuckles and pulls me into his side.

"It was the best fuckin' day of my life when I found you, Santana."

My heart thuds and I snuggle in closer. "For me, too."

"I'm gonna marry you when this shit is over, then I'm gonna put a baby inside you…"

"So romantic," I giggle.

He runs a finger down my arm. "I'm goin' to be fuckin' you real slow when I put a baby in you, that's romantic."

I flush. "Slow?"

"Real slow."

"Mmmmm."

"Tana?"

"Yeah?"

He pulls me closer. "Best fuckin' day…you hear me?"

"Yeah, handsome."

"Want to know what else you need to hear?"

I nod into his chest.

"I love you."

Shit. There goes my heart.

"Jesus," I whisper. "I love you, too."

"Then nothin' else fuckin' matters."

He's right about that. Nothing else does matter.

CHAPTER THIRTY-EIGHT

Two weeks later

"You have to tell him," Ash says, pacing the bedroom.

"He'll flip," I panic, rocking on the bed. "We just spent a few days burying people he loves, it's not the right time."

"He'll understand," Pippa says, rubbing my back. "It'll help him...trust me."

"No," I croak. "He won't. He said after this shit is over...*after*...not before."

"He'll understand," she repeats.

"Your sister is right," Ash soothes. "Come on, you have to tell him."

"Can't...oh God..."

"He's at the club, why don't we take you over and you can talk to him?" Ash suggests.

"No way!"

"Santana," she warns. "I'm puttin' it down to you in a way I don't want to have to. You go and fucking tell him, or I will."

I jerk my head up. "Seriously?"

She crosses her arms. "Hell yes."

"I hate you."

"Oh you so don't."

Pippa giggles from behind me.

"It's not funny," I snap.

"It kind of is."

I can't help but soften at the sound of my sister's giggles. It's a sound I'm still relishing. She's been doing so well, and seeing her happy makes it all worthwhile. She spends two days a week with counselors, which really seems to help. The other few days she spends with me at home, just adjusting to her new life.

"Fine," I say, dropping my head into my hands. "But he's going to flip."

Ash helps me off the bed and I stare down at the positive pregnancy tests lying all over it.

Boy am I in trouble.

~*~*~*~

"Ohhhh Maddox!" Ash calls as soon as we enter the club.

"Stop it," I say, shoving her.

She turns and shoves me back. "You stop it. Brat."

"Bitch."

"Preggers."

I gape at her and she bursts out laughing.

"You'll pay for that," I growl.

"What are you going to do?"

I shove her again. She shoves me back. Both of us trying not to laugh. Pippa stares between us, shaking her head with her own ghost of a smile.

"Ladies?"

We both turn to see Maddox, Mack and Krypt standing at the bar.

Ash shoves me forward. "Santana has something to tell you, Maddox."

He turns to me, a piece of his new short hair dropping down over his forehead. Sheesh he's good looking. He's up and about now, though he's not really meant to be riding. He still sneaks one here and there. His eyes flicker to me and he tilts his head to the side, trying no doubt, to guess what I'm about to drop on him.

"You're going to pay for this," I snap at Ash as I edge closer to Maddox.

He's still watching me, his expression showing his confusion.

"Can we...ah...talk?"

He nods, taking my hand and turning, leading me down the hall to his office. When we're in, he closes the door and pulls me to the couch, where we sit. I don't look at him; instead I pull my hand from his and place them in my lap.

"Santana..."

I swallow. God. He's going to flip.

"Ah, so, ah..."

"Santana," he warns. "Speak."

"It's just...well..."

He takes my chin, forcing me to look at him. His eyes study my face and he leans in, brushing his lips across mine. I sink into him a little. It might be the last kiss I get for a few days when he finds out what I've so stupidly done.

"Come on, honey," he murmurs against my mouth. "Tell me."

I pull back, taking a deep breath. "Well, the thing is...I um...well...when we were away I didn't take my pill."

His body flinches and his eyes widen. Oh no. Here we go.

"And…" he says, his voice low.

"Well. Ah. Shit."

"Santana," he growls.

"I'm pregnant, Maddox."

Silence. Dead silence.

I look up, terrified. He's staring at me, his eyes fixed on my face. There's nothing in his expression. I can't tell if he's angry or happy or sad…

"You're…pregnant?"

"Yes," I squeak. "I found out yesterday and-"

He cuts me off with a holler that's so loud I leap backwards with a squeal. Then he stands, drops his shoulder into my belly and lifts me into the air. He's got one broken collarbone and a broken arm, but he uses his good shoulder and good arm to throw me over him. This isn't good. He'll make his injuries worse.

"Maddox!" I cry.

He literally charges out of the office and down the hall. I pound his back, knowing he shouldn't be carrying me like this, but he doesn't care. He reaches the bar and roars, "I'm gonna be a fuckin' dad!"

The men erupt in cheers and hoots, and I can't help but laugh. Maddox puts me down, pulling me into his arms and planting kisses on my face. Ash is squealing and jumping up and down, clapping her hands. Pippa is laughing, her face bright. Happy.

When I'm finally back on my feet, Maddox drops to his knees in front of me, circling my waist and pulling my belly to him. "We're gonna have a fuckin' baby!" he breathes, pressing his lips to the shirt covering my stomach. Tears well up in my eyes as I stare down at the big man kneeling before me.

"We're going to have a baby," I whisper.

"I fuckin' love you, Santana."

He pulls me close and drops his forehead to my belly. His sign of love. His sign of affection. I smile through my tears and wrap my arms around his head. Two years ago I was alone, thinking my sister was dead and that I'd never find my happily ever after. Now I've got her back and the man I love is cradling me as our child slowly grows inside my belly.

I'm going to have a family, one of my very own. I lost everything, yet slowly…really slowly…

I'm getting it all back.

EPILOGUE

2014 - Santana

A knock sounds at Mack's door, and I put the cookies I was baking down and wipe my hands on my apron. It's his birthday and Pippa, Ash and I have spent the morning baking for when he arrives home. I try to remove as much flour off my hands as I make my way to the door. I open it and see a woman standing on the front step, a baby in her arms.

"Can I help you?" I ask.

"Ah…" she looks at me, confused. "I'm looking for…Miakoda…"

"Mack?" I say, wondering who she is.

"Yes."

"He's not here right now, did you want me to call him?"

She stares down at the bundle in her arms, and then looks back up at me. "Please."

I nod and pull out my phone, dialing Mack's number.

"What's your name?" I ask.

"Tracy."

I give her a warm smile, wondering who she is. I've never heard Mack mention a Tracy before.

"Yeah."

"Mack, it's Santana. There's a lady here to see you…she says her name is Tracy."

Silence.

"What?"

"A woman…at your door. Her name is Tracy."

More silence.

"Fuck."

"Ah…"

"I'm comin'."

Then he hangs up. Interesting. I look back up at the woman and smile again. She looks terrible. She's got long, black hair that's dull and the darkest blue eyes I've ever seen. Her skin is pale and she's skinny…really skinny.

"He's on his way. Can I get you a drink?"

"No, I'll wait here."

I nod, but don't leave her side. I make small talk until the rumble of a Harley Davidson fills the quiet street. She turns and we both watch as Mack pulls up. He throws his leg over the bike and walks up the front path, but stops dead when he sees her and the baby in her arms.

Oh man.

"Tracy?" he says, his eyes still on the bundle in her arms.

"Miakoda…I'm sorry to have to do this, but…I had no choice."

"What are you doin' here?"

I should turn away, but I can't.

"This is what she wanted…I had to follow her wishes…"

She? She? Who is she?

Mack's face pales.

"Tracy…" he says. "Why are you here?"

"Ingrid died…there was an accident and…"

Mack looks like someone just punched him in the face. His entire body flinches and he takes a step back. This isn't good. I don't know who Ingrid is, but it's clear she meant something to him.

"What?" he rasps.

"Car accident. She died and…"

He shakes his head. "No," he rasps. "I saw her…only twelve months ago."

"I'm sorry, Mack."

"She fuckin' left me," he roars. "She left me twelve months ago, and I couldn't fuckin' find her…now here you are tellin' me she's dead?"

Oh no. This isn't good.

"She left because…she left because…" she looks down at the child and it clicks. Oh no. *Uh oh.* "She was pregnant."

Mack actually takes a few steps back, his hand pressing to his heart. "You're lying…"

Tracy shakes her head. "She was scared. She didn't think you would stick around…things were rocky between the two of you. She was going to tell you, after he was born she started looking for you, but…there was an accident and…"

"No!" Mack bellows.

I walk past Tracy, carefully approaching Mack.

"Don't fuckin' come near me!" he roars.

Oh shit.

286

"She did up a will…she made it clear what she wanted to happen to Diesel if something was to take her…"

Diesel. That's Maddox's middle name.

"What did you call him?" Mack breathes, panting.

"She called him Diesel after your brother. She knew how much you loved Maddox and…"

"No!" Mack roars again.

She turns the baby over, showing his face. God he couldn't be more than a few months old, the poor little thing. There's no missing it though, even at this young age. He's got a mop of dark hair, the brownest eyes I've ever seen, and his skin is a gorgeous light olive. That is a mini Mack…no doubt. God, he's beautiful.

I turn slowly to Mack and he's staring at the baby, panting so hard his body is shaking.

"That ain't my kid…"

"It is…and you need to take him, Miakoda. You're all he's got left. You know it was only Ingrid and I…we don't have anyone else who can take him."

"You take him," Mack says, his voice frantic.

"You know I can't…I have four kids and I'm struggling. I can't give him the life he needs. She wanted you to have him, please don't make me send your son out for adoption."

"No," Mack says, his hands on his head.

He backs up towards his bike.

"No."

"Mack," I say.

"NO!"

He turns and paces towards his bike, getting on. It roars to life and he disappears. Shit. I turn to Tracy, who has tears running down her cheeks. Dammit. I walk over, placing a hand on her shoulder. Ash and Pippa are at the door, watching the whole thing go down, silent.

"It's okay," I soothe. "I promise it'll be okay."

"I can't take him with me," she sobs. "He needs to be with his dad."

"He will be, I promise you that. Mack will come around – he will."

She turns to me, dark blue eyes scanning my face. "Are you his girlfriend?"

"No," I say quickly. "I'm Santana...I'm with Maddox."

She nods. "I've heard of you..."

"It'll be okay," I assure her, even though I'm not sure it will.

"I have to go and..." she stares down at Diesel. "I can't take him."

"I can take him," I offer.

"If Miakoda doesn't accept him... I can't just leave him if he won't accept him, and..."

"What choice have you got?" I say softly. "If you take him you're going to have to take him straight to an adoption center. You leave him here; we have the chance to bring Mack around. I promise you, Tracy, right here and now...I won't let anything happen to him."

She studies me, really studies me. "You'll take care of him?"

"He's my nephew, in a sense, so yes. I promise you no harm will come to him. If Mack refuses to accept him, I'll make sure he goes to the most loving home, but not before I do everything in my power to keep him with us."

"Santana," Ash says from behind me.

I turn and stare at her. "He's family, Ash. We're taking him."

Facing Tracy again, I say. "I promise you."

Tracy is crying heavily now, God the poor woman. I can't help it; I pull her in for a hug. "I'm so sorry for your loss."

"She was all I had left," she sobs. "The only family I had...now she's gone, and..."

"It's going to be okay."

"This baby was her life, I can't bear to see him left without a family, too."

"He won't be, I'll do everything I can to make sure of that."

And I will. There's no way I'll just let Mack run from this, and if he does then I'll find someone who will give this little baby the love he deserves. We're a family now, all of us, the entire club...this little man is a part of that.

Tracy, sobbing, lowers her face and kisses the baby. My heart breaks.

"Can I...can you please let me know what happens?"

"Of course," I whisper, my emotions getting the better of me.

"And...maybe I can visit...bring my kids to see him."

"Of course."

She nods, tears still running down her cheeks. "I would have taken him, but...I can barely feed my kids...it's not fair."

"I understand," I say, my voice shaky. "We'll let no harm come to him."

With a heart-wrenching sob, she extends her arms and hands the tiny bundle to me. My heart breaks and tears spill down my cheeks as I stare at the baby, who looks just like his daddy. He's so warm, he smells so beautiful. My own baby hormones erupt and I begin sobbing, too. Ash rushes down, taking the baby from my arms.

I reach out and hug Tracy, because I can't imagine how this feels for her. She holds onto me for a long while, and then lets go.

"Here's my number," she croaks, pulling out a tiny slip of paper. "Please…let me know he's okay."

"I promise."

She nods and with one last broken stare at the baby, she leaves. My shoulders slump as I watch her car disappear. I turn to the small bundle in Ash's arms.

"Shit's going to hit the fan."

She stares at the baby. "You're right about that."

~*~*~*~

"What the fuck were you thinkin'?" Maddox growls, pacing the living room.

I've got Diesel tucked tightly in my arms, sitting on the couch. We're still waiting for Mack to come back.

"It's his son, Maddox."

"And he's losin' his shit somewhere. It wasn't your choice to make."

"Seriously?" I cry. "You would rather I let her give him up for adoption? What the fuck is wrong with you?"

He stops, sighs, and turns to me. "Fuck…no…that's not what I want. But Mack is goin' to be in a bad way…he can't look after a kid."

"I can…"

"You've got our baby growin' inside you, you need to be there when he or she is born. You can't be this baby's mother…"

"No, but I can take care of him and help Mack until he figures something out. If this baby gets put up for adoption, it needs to be by him, Maddox."

"I know that," he mutters, staring at the ceiling.

"Until then, there are enough ladies in the club to make sure he is taken care of."

"Fuck."

"Yeah," I agree.

We hear the sound of a bike rumbling up the driveway, and I stare at Maddox. Here we go. A few moments later, the front door swings open and Mack enters. He looks at Maddox, then his eyes turn to me and he stiffens. "What the fuckin' hell have you got…that baby for?"

"He's your son, Mack. She couldn't take him."

"No," he barks. "You didn't get to make that choice."

"I did, and I would do it again. Go ahead and scream at me, this is your son, you fucking selfish asshole. His mother is dead. There's no way you're just letting him get passed off. You're a better man than that."

"I know his mother is dead," he bellows so loudly I flinch. "You think I don't fuckin' know!"

"Come on," Maddox says, taking Mack's shoulder. "We're gonna figure this shit out right now."

"I can't have that baby," he almost pleads, sounding desperate.

"We're gonna sort it out," Maddox says again.

"Fuckin' can't…"

God, my heart breaks for Mack.

It breaks for the baby.

It breaks for his mother.

I don't know how we're going to fix this problem…

THE END

Don't worry! Mack is getting his own story, and it'll be released in October so you don't have long to wait! Here's the first chapter! Enjoy.

ANGUISH – Releasing October 2014.

CHAPTER ONE

"You can't be serious, Jaylah!"

I turn and scowl at my best friend, Josie.

"It's a job, it gets me away from the house. If I'm away from the house, I'm not so easily tracked," I point out, popping a piece of carrot into my mouth and chewing loudly. Josie glares at me.

"You're not a nanny!"

I snort, choking on a piece of carrot and throwing myself into a coughing fit. When I'm done, I straighten, patting my chest and rasping, "How hard can it be? Changing nappies, feeding…it's a piece of cake."

"It's a child…" she gapes. "You know…not a dog!"

I wave a hand. "It's live in, it's good pay, and it's only a baby."

"Babies poop, and cry, and spew…"

"So do dogs," I point out.

"Jesus, Jay…there's got to be something else."

I take a step closer. "I have Gregor after my ass. He doesn't play nice. I need somewhere he can't find me. He won't find me there; it's two hours away. I can pay him off and then it'll all be over. It's a thousand dollars a week including food and a room! All to look after one baby…"

Josie sighs and shakes her head. "I can see there's no talking you out of this. At least go and make sure it's what you want before saying yes…"

I smile. "Good news…I'm going right now to meet the child and his father."

"Oh God," Josie groans.

"It'll be fine," I wave my hand, grabbing my keys with the other. "You'll see."

~*~*~*~

It's not fine.

Oh no. It's far from fine.

I'm standing in front of, what is quite possibly, the most dazzling man I've ever seen in my life. He's Native American, of that I'm sure. He's got these chocolate eyes and dark hair that, I won't lie, makes me want to punch him. It's that beautiful. Long and thick, flowing around his shoulders. He's tall and muscled, wearing a leather vest over a dark, tight tee.

Oh boy. Oh boy. Oh boy.

"Ah….are you, um, Mack?"

He looks me up and down, slowly. "Yeah."

293

God. His voice. Like melted honey, mixed with cream…oh man.

"Oh, good. I'm Jaylah…I'm here for the, ah, nanny position."

His eyebrow quirks. *"You're a nanny?"*

My spine straightens and I put my hands on my hips. "Excuse me, buddy, but I'll have you know I'm the best damned nanny there is."

He stares at me, expressionless. He's a hard man; you can see it in his eyes and the firm expression that seems set in his face.

"What did you expect?" I go on. "Mrs. Doubtfire?"

His lip twitches, but he doesn't smile.

"You available all day, every day?"

I tilt my head to the side. "I don't get a day off?"

"No."

"You want me to babysit…every day?"

He stares at me, like that's already obvious.

"What are you, like some fancy businessman or something?"

I already know that's a joke before it leaves my lips, but I say it anyway. He gives me a 'seriously' look, and I realize it really was a stupid question.

"Okay, well, clearly you're not a businessman, but what could possibly keep you so busy you need me to look after your kid seven days a week?"

"None of your fuckin' business," he snaps.

"Keep your shirt on," I huff. "I was only asking."

"You either want the job," he says, his voice low and deep. "Or you don't."

"I do," I point out. "But I have a life, you know…friends and stuff…"

294

"You can visit them, with the baby."

"Seriously?"

He does that staring thing again.

"Only one thousand dollars a week? To basically be the child's…mother?"

"One and a half if you start now."

"One and half thousand?" I breathe.

"No, one and a half fuckin' dollars."

Oh, a smartass. Nice.

"And I live…here?"

He nods sharply.

"And…you live here?"

He looks like he wants to slap my stupidity right out of me.

"Okay, I'll do it."

He nods. "Come in."

"Wait, aren't you going to ask me some nanny questions. Like, what are you going to do if my child runs onto the road and gets hit by a car?"

He gives me a strange expression. "He's a baby. Come in."

"What about if he chokes?"

"Baby…" he grinds out. "Drinks fuckin' milk."

"Climbs through a window?" I call out, following him inside.

He grunts.

"Plays with your hairdryer?"

He stops, turns, and gives me a mortified expression.

"What?" I say, shrugging. "You have nice hair…it's only an assumption."

Okay now he looks like he wants to punch me, or throttle me…

"I mean seriously…you're not going to ask me anything?"

He growls. "You a murderer?"

"What? No."

"Rapist?"

I gape. "Ew. No."

"You cook?"

"Ah, yes."

"You capable of heating a bottle?"

"Yes."

"Gettin' up when he cries?"

I nod.

"Then you're hired. Now move."

Bossy.

We step into a really nice, really modern place. The cool floor is pleasant against my feet as I follow him into the lounge room. I skid to a halt when I see all the people on the lounge. There are a few really pretty girls, but the rest are males. Big, burly males that look like they've dropped out of heaven and been rolled in leather. They're *gorgeous*.

They're also…oh no.

Oh no no no.

Mack nods to one of the girls and she stands, walking over to me, a baby wrapped up in her arms. She stretches it out to me with a smile. God she's pretty, like a mini Pocahontas or something. Her eyes sparkle with humor at my expression. I reach out, take the baby and hold it close. I've never held a baby…shit…where's his head?

"I'm Santana," she smiles, warmly. "Welcome."

I turn back to the group, who are all staring at me and I'm about sure I'm going to pass out.

I know who they are. I've seen the news.

Motorcycle club. The biggest in the city.

Jokers' Wrath.

Oh God. I'm a nanny for a biker.

This could be interesting.

*****

YOU WILL SEE MORE OF JAYLAH AND MACK'S STORY SOON!

Plus – you will see more of Krypt and Ash, Santana and Maddox and all the other guys in the club!

Don't miss it!

CPSIA information can be obtained at www.ICGtesting.com
Printed in the USA
LVOW12s2018121114

413338LV00007B/1091/P